Praise for the novels of Cathie Linz

Bad Girls Don't

"A humorous tale . . . The secondary characters are comical and outrageous . . . You won't want to miss *Bad Girls Don't*." —*Romance Reviews Today*

"Cathie Linz gives her beautifully matched protagonists lots of sexy chemistry and some delightfully snappy dialogue, and the quirky cast of secondary characters gives *Bad Girls Don't* its irresistible charm." —*Chicago Tribune*

"Linz, known for her fast-paced, snappy romantic comedies, once again sparkles in this heartwarming, funny tale. And her secondary characters . . . make an already excellent story exceptional." —*Booklist* (starred review)

"Linz's characterizations are absolutely wonderful. I fell in love with the protagonists from the first page of this book . . . We've watched Ms. Linz's writing develop and grow over the years. It has always been a pleasure to read her books, but I must say that this one is a fantastic novel!" —*Rendezvous*

"Totally delightful." —*Fresh Fiction*

continued . . .

Good Girls Do

"Humor and warmth . . . Readers are going to love this!"
—Susan Elizabeth Phillips

"Cathie Linz is the author that readers of romantic comedy have been waiting for. She knows how to do it—characters with depth, sharp dialogue, and a compelling story. The result is a charming, offbeat world, one you'll hate to leave."
—Jayne Ann Krentz

"Sometimes even good girls need to take a walk on the wild side. Linz deftly seasons her writing with her usual delectable wit, and the book's quirky cast of endearing secondary characters adds another measure of humor to this sweetly sexy, fabulously fun contemporary romance."
—*Booklist* (starred review)

"Sexy, sassy, and graced with exceptional dialogue, this fast-paced story is both hilarious and heartwarming, featuring wonderfully wacky secondary characters and well-developed protagonists you will come to love . . . A winner that will leave readers smiling long after they have turned the final page."
—*Library Journal*

"Lively and fun, and you won't be able to put it down."
—*Fresh Fiction*

"A fun contemporary romance . . . Fans of *You Can't Take It with You* who like romantic romps will enjoy this funny family tale."
—*The Best Reviews*

Big Girls Don't Cry

. . . .

Cathie Linz

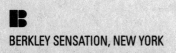

BERKLEY SENSATION, NEW YORK

THE BERKLEY PUBLISHING GROUP
Published by the Penguin Group
Penguin Group (USA) Inc.
375 Hudson Street, New York, New York 10014, USA
Penguin Group (Canada), 90 Eglinton Avenue East, Suite 700, Toronto, Ontario M4P 2Y3, Canada
(a division of Pearson Penguin Canada Inc.)
Penguin Books Ltd., 80 Strand, London WC2R 0RL, England
Penguin Group Ireland, 25 St. Stephen's Green, Dublin 2, Ireland (a division of Penguin Books Ltd.)
Penguin Group (Australia), 250 Camberwell Road, Camberwell, Victoria 3124, Australia
(a division of Pearson Australia Group Pty. Ltd.)
Penguin Books India Pvt. Ltd., 11 Community Centre, Panchsheel Park, New Delhi—110 017, India
Penguin Group (NZ), 67 Apollo Drive, Rosedale, North Shore 0632, New Zealand
(a division of Pearson New Zealand Ltd.)
Penguin Books (South Africa) (Pty.) Ltd., 24 Sturdee Avenue, Rosebank, Johannesburg 2196,
South Africa

Penguin Books Ltd., Registered Offices: 80 Strand, London WC2R 0RL, England

BIG GIRLS DON'T CRY

A Berkley Sensation Book / published by arrangement with the author

PRINTING HISTORY
Berkley Sensation mass-market edition / October 2007

Copyright © 2007 by Cathie L. Baumgardner.
Cover art by Aleta Rafton.
Cover design by George Long.
Interior text design by Stacy Irwin.

ISBN: 978-0-425-21831-0

BERKLEY® SENSATION
Berkley Sensation Books are published by The Berkley Publishing Group,
a division of Penguin Group (USA) Inc.,
375 Hudson Street, New York, New York 10014.
BERKLEY SENSATION and the "B" design are trademarks of Penguin Group (USA) Inc.

PRINTED IN THE UNITED STATES OF AMERICA

10 9 8 7 6 5 4 3 2 1

Chapter One

· · · · · · · · · · · ·

Broke and skinny beat out broke and chunky every time. Leena Riley was convinced of it. She should know. She was a size-sixteen, plus-size model in a swizzle stick, size-zero world.

How ironic that now she was down on her luck, she was forced to return to her down-on-its-luck hometown of Rock Creek, Pennsylvania. Leena hadn't been back since she'd left for the big city of Chicago at eighteen, and she honestly hadn't missed the place one bit.

Things had changed . . . a little. The Tivoli Theater was open again. The nail salon and comic-book store were new additions. And there was a new vet in town. Looking for a receptionist. Leena pulled the HELP WANTED sign out of the window as she strolled into the animal clinic.

She needed this job. It was this or work the graveyard

shift at Gas4Less. Rock Creek wasn't exactly a hotbed of financial opportunities.

But the vet's office appeared to be deteriorating into total mayhem. Leena ducked as a parrot dive-bombed her while a beagle howled in the corner accompanied by a yowling cat in a carrier. Another cat, the biggest one Leena had ever seen, hissed from atop a metal file cabinet as a pair of wiry terriers yelped at the pissed-off megafeline from down below.

The situation called for drastic measures. No problemo. Her sister Sue Ellen was the Queen of Drastic Measures so Leena instantly knew what had to be done. Putting two fingers in her mouth, Leena let out an ear-piercing whistle that made cabs on Chicago's Mag Mile squeal to a stop beside her.

The room instantly fell silent. Realizing that would last only a second or two, Leena spoke quickly. Her dad had done a stint in the Marine Corps and had never lost his drill-sergeant voice. She mimicked him as she barked out orders. "Okay, terriers and owners outside. Beagle and owner in there." She pointed to an empty exam room. "Parrot, come here." She held out her hand and—miracle of miracles—the bird obediently flew onto it with a flurry of feathers. "Cats, as you were."

A tattoo-covered older biker dude in a leather vest and jeans moved forward. "Thanks for catching that old buzzard!"

"This your parrot?" Leena asked.

"It's a friend's. Mrs. Trimble asked me to bring the stubborn buzzard to see the doc here for a checkup. She'd have my ass if he flew out the door or something."

"Why isn't he in a cage?"

The senior citizen biker dude shifted awkwardly from

one booted foot to the other while guiltily pointing to the cage. "I, uh . . . have a hard time seeing creatures jailed."

Leena calmly opened the cage door and carefully set the parrot inside. "Keep the cover over the cage if you have trouble looking at him."

"You're good with animals."

"I've worked with a few in my time." One grabby photographer at a lingerie photo shoot several months ago certainly came to mind.

The senior biker held out his beefy hand. "The name's Jerry."

"Leena Riley." Yeah, right. Leena. Another joke since she hadn't been *lean* a day in her life. In school they'd mocked her by chanting that she should have been named Lotsa Riley.

Of course, it hadn't helped that she'd grown up in the poorest mobile home in the Regency Trailer Park. Sure, it was supposed to be ritzier than the Broken Creek Trailer Park, but that really wasn't saying much.

The two trailer parks had a rivalry going similar to the rivalry between Rock Creek and Serenity Falls. Leena had read somewhere that Serenity Falls had recently been listed as one of the best small towns in America. Which made Rock Creek the ugly stepsister yet again.

Not that her own older sister Sue Ellen saw things that way. Of course, Sue Ellen saw things no one else did, like the face of Jesus in the fur of a llama.

Leena loved her older sister, but she didn't understand her. Few people did. Which was why Sue Ellen earned the nickname Our Lady of the Outlandish.

Baby sister Emma was the one with the brains and fancy job title in the family. Leena was the one with the big dreams, very few of which had actually come true.

Not that she'd told her sisters that. No, her reports to them had been filled with plenty of optimism and major exaggerations.

Which made her homecoming all the more humiliating.

Leena was still reeling from the bigger-they-are-the-harder-they-fall jokes that had been thrown her way when her modeling agency had fired her. The Image Plus Modeling Agency in Chicago was no Wilhelmina.

"And you're no Kate Dillon," her agent Irene had shot back at her before showing her the door.

Okay, so Kate was one of the leading plus-size models. And okay, so Leena's assignments weren't photo shoots for *French Vogue* or even Lane Bryant. That didn't mean she was a total failure.

What about that layout for the Sears spring-sales flyer last year? That had gone well, once the photographer and makeup artist had recovered from hurling after eating bad sushi they'd had catered in.

Before she could think of her other professional accomplishments, Leena was almost knocked down by a nun on the run who flew into the waiting room and rushed up to a family hidden from view by a large ficus.

Leena heard someone say, "Is he dead?"

Great. Her first day on the job and someone had to bite the dust on her watch. Not a good omen. Should she call 911?

"You called me here to give last rites," the nun, whom Leena now recognized as Sister Mary, said.

"Yes," a little girl replied.

"To a hamster?"

"Not just any hamster," the little girl explained. "To Harry the Hamster."

"I can't give last rites to a hamster," Sister Mary said. "What's going on out here?"

Leena stared at the hunk in the white lab coat who'd just drawled that question. She knew this guy. She recognized the wicked twinkle in his blue eyes. Cole Flannigan.

She thought he'd be bartending in some tropical hot spot by now, his Hawaiian shirt hanging open to reveal his muscular chest. At least his chest had been muscular the last time she'd seen it. Of course that had been almost a decade ago.

Still, he didn't look like he'd gained a beer belly yet. In fact, his worn jeans made him look lean and extremely bedable. By a lean and equally bedable babe. Not by her, broke and chunky Leena Riley.

Had her career really taken off the way she'd told her sisters it had, why then things would have been different. Then she'd have had the confidence to stroll right up to Cole and kiss him silly, had she wanted to.

Her lack of confidence had to do with her empty bank account, not her body image.

Well, okay, maybe it did have something to do with her body image. After all, she wasn't a saint . . . or a nun.

"You want to know what's going on here?" Sister Mary repeated. "I was just telling your patients that I can't give last rites to a hamster."

"What about a special prayer?" the little girl asked.

"I told you that Harry is just fine," Cole reminded the family. "You didn't have to call in Sister Mary."

"Well, since I'm here, I might as well say a prayer." Sister Mary bent down and spoke quietly to the little girl and Harry the Hamster. So quietly that Leena couldn't hear what she said, but it made the kid feel better, judging by the shy smile she gave the nun.

"Your next patient is in exam room one," Leena efficiently announced.

"Really?" Cole pinned her with a stare. "And you are?"

"Your new receptionist."

Cole raised an eyebrow. "You're applying for the job?"

"No, you're *hiring* me," Leena stated confidently.

"Why is that?"

"Because you need me," Leena told him. "I'm here to rescue you from utter chaos."

"Sounds good to me," Sister Mary declared. "It's not like you've had people knocking down your door demanding to work here, Cole."

"No, she's the first," Cole agreed. He studied Leena for a moment. "Have we met before?"

Leena hesitated, unsure how to answer that question. She'd beaten him up once when she was in the sixth grade and he'd hung out with a bunch of younger kids who'd called her fat. Now probably wasn't the best time to admit that fact, however.

Too late. "Wait a second." Cole snapped his fingers. "Aren't you Sue Ellen's sister Leena?"

Right. Like that's how she wanted to be known for the rest of her life. As Sue Ellen's sister.

That was one of the reasons she'd left. Because she was sick and tired of always being referred to as Sue Ellen's sister. Or Sue Ellen's fat sister. Or Sue Ellen's chubb-o sister. "I'm Leena Riley."

"I thought you were in Chicago doing modeling or something like that."

He made it sound as if she were doing pole dancing on Rush Street. "That's right. I was."

"And now you want the job as my receptionist? Why?"

"Do you really care?" Leena retorted as another bunch of patients and animals entered the already overcrowded waiting room and the phone started to ring. Chaos was threatening to return.

"No. You're hired. For the day. We'll talk about the future after that."

Oh yeah. How the mighty had fallen. All the way from cover model on the Sears spring layout to small-town vet receptionist. Not exactly a lateral career move by any stretch of the imagination.

But it would do in a crunch. And she was definitely in a crunch.

Leena Riley, rising star, reverting back to Leena the Loser.

No, she refused to think like that. She couldn't afford to go down that road. It led nowhere.

Of course, some might think that Rock Creek qualified as nowhere.

But at least she had a job. For today. And that's all she could handle for the moment. Today. Tomorrow would have to take a number.

After getting their names, Leena pulled the files on the patients waiting in the waiting room and then went outside to check on the two terriers and owners she'd banished out there. Luckily the spring weather was warm enough that they weren't shivering in their boots, had they been wearing any. Leena was wearing a lovely pair of Italian leather Prada boots she'd gotten at a sample sale.

They looked good at a photo shoot and went great with her jeans and crisp white wrap shirt, but were perhaps not the best choice for a vet's office. Not when one of the banished terriers decided to squat and pee on Leena's leather-encased right foot.

"Oh, I'm so sorry," the owner, a harried-looking woman in her forties, declared. "Oscar gets a nervous bladder whenever we come to the vet."

The other terrier started gnawing on Leena's left boot.

Suddenly the job at the graveyard shift of Gas4Less was looking a lot more appealing . . .

• • •

Cole finished with his last patient, a Siamese male named Si who needed his shots updated, and headed out toward the empty waiting room.

He was surprised to find Leena still there. He'd have thought she'd have taken off screaming when the Great Dane with anxiety issues had come in two hours ago. Or the depressed boa constrictor.

Instead, there she was. Standing behind the U-shaped desk of the receptionist area, looking totally out of place. But looking good. Her dark blond hair brushed her shoulders in what was no doubt an expensive cut. Her fingertips displayed a perfect manicure.

She'd always had a bossy streak, which was no doubt how she'd gotten that Great Dane to behave. It hadn't made him behave when they'd been kids. He was ashamed to recall how he'd made fun of her weight and how she'd flattened him with a lucky sucker punch. He'd been two years younger than she—a cocky fourth-grader.

"You still pack a mean right hook?" Cole asked as he handed her the file on his last patient.

"If necessary, yes." She stared him down, which gave him a good look at her gorgeous blue eyes. "I hope my actions that day taught you a valuable lesson."

"Which was?"

"That if you say something cruel, it will come back to bite you in the ass."

"I suppose I should be thankful you didn't do that and only punched me."

"Yes, you should. I was suspended from school for a week because of you."

"And yet here you are, begging me for a job."

"Wrong. Here I am, saving you from trouble yet again."

"That's why you came back to Rock Creek from Chicago? To save me?"

"Do you need saving?"

"Do you?" Cole countered.

Leena shrugged. "I gave up looking for a knight in shining armor to save me ages ago. These days, I save myself."

"And you also save overworked vets."

"That's right."

"Even though you have no experience working in a vet's office."

"I have experience booking appointments." As a model she'd usually been on the other end of the booking arrangements, dealing with bookers to arrange for photo shoots. But how hard could this side of things be? Her organizational skills were very good. Everyone said so.

Even in kindergarten she'd organized the other kids' cubbies. And in their mobile home, at age eight Leena had rearranged the entire contents of the kitchen cabinets for greater efficiency.

By the time Leena was a teenager, she'd perfected time management so that she knew exactly how long to study for a test to get a B or a C.

Emma was the A student in the family, so Leena hadn't wasted her time on academic matters. Instead, after reading an article in a magazine about plus-size models, she'd focused on learning everything she could about the modeling industry. She'd gone to model shows and model talent searches at shopping malls all over the state.

And when she'd graduated from Rock Creek High, she'd packed her bags and headed to Chicago with her portfolio under her arm—consisting of several headshots and one full-length shot.

She could still remember her excitement at driving her used Toyota down Chicago's famous Lake Shore Drive, seeing all those tall buildings lining Lake Michigan. Someday, she'd promised herself, she'd live in one of those pricey condos along the Gold Coast.

Instead she'd ended up sharing a small apartment with two other girls on the outskirts of the Ukrainian Village area of Chicago.

"So you have experience booking appointments." Cole's voice brought her back to the present, refocusing her wandering attention on him. The man was hard to ignore. His light brown hair had a bit of a wave to it and was totally rumpled, giving him that I-just-got-out-of-bed look that worked very well for him. She wondered if he slept in the nude.

She probably should be paying attention to his questions instead of imagining him starkers. She'd known him when they'd been kids. Surely that should make her immune to his charming ways, right? Come on, she'd beat the guy up once.

So why were her hormones humming like queen bees zipping around a hive?

She should know better than to judge a person by their looks.

But then Cole's charm went beyond his looks. It was also generated by the way he talked, that sexy drawl he'd mastered when his voice had deepened during adolescence.

"Hello?" He waved his big hands in front of her face. "Anyone home in there?"

"Sorry." Leena blinked. "I was, uh . . . thinking about, uh . . . something else."

"Your Prada boots?"

"How did you know they were Prada?"

"One of my patients told me. The terrier owner."

"Ah, Oscar, the terrier with the nervous bladder."

"You've got a good memory."

"I never forget a bitch named Oscar who ruined my Pradas."

"They named her Oscar before they realized the dog was a she not a he. And then they refused to rename her."

"Which is probably why the dog has a nervous bladder. Gender identification issues."

His laughter caught her by surprise.

"A sense of humor is a requirement for this job," he said.

"So have I passed the audition?"

"I still can't figure out why you'd want to work for me when you're a model. Something happen in Chicago?"

Leena shrugged. "Lots of things happen in Chicago."

"And you don't plan on telling me about them? You don't think, as your prospective employer, that I've got a right to know?"

Leena was prevented from answering by the dramatic arrival of her sister Sue Ellen, who burst onto the scene as she always did, with maximum effect.

"It's true! You're really here! You've come back home!" Sue Ellen engulfed her in a mighty python hold that squeezed the air out of Leena's lungs. "Why didn't you tell me you were coming? We could have set up a special welcome celebration. A parade or something. And what on earth are you doing over here at the vet's office? Did you get a pet while you were in Chicago? Is it one of those designer dogs? Don't tell me, let me guess. Is it a schnoodle? A labradoodle? A yorkipoo? Is it sick? Is that why you're here?"

"I don't have a dog."

"Some exotic pet then? A lynx maybe?"

"I don't have any pets."

Sue Ellen frowned and released her. "Then why are you in the vet's office? Unless you came to see him?" She jabbed her thumb in Cole's direction. "I thought you didn't like him. Didn't you beat him up once?"

Leena tried not to squirm. "That was a long time ago."

"And you came here to apologize?" Sue Ellen beamed proudly. "Isn't that just like you. Even though you're a big star now, you still remember the little people you beat up along the way."

"Hey, watch who you're calling little," Cole protested.

"Well, of course you're taller now, Cole," Sue Ellen said. "Leena probably couldn't take you down with just one punch like she did then."

"It was a sucker punch," Cole growled.

Sue Ellen patted his arm. "Yeah, that's what Luke claimed that time Julia hit him before they were married."

"Who are they?" Leena asked, trying to follow her sister's line of thought, which was never an easy task.

"My friend Skye's sister and brother-in-law. I can't wait to introduce them all to my famous sister," Sue Ellen said, before admitting, "I never bragged about you before because Skye and her family are a little weird about makeup and stuff. But now that you're here, they can see for themselves how great you are." Sue Ellen paused to take a much needed breath. "But I still don't know what you're doing in the vet's office."

"She's here about a job," Cole replied.

Sue Ellen frowned. "What kind of job could a super-model do for you? She knows Iman, you know."

Which wasn't a lie . . . exactly. Leena knew *of* Iman. Who didn't? The famous supermodel was married to rock star David Bowie. She possessed a tall, graceful elegance that Leena could never even aspire to.

But Leena had aspired to the world of plus-size modeling and thought she'd made her mark.

"Then maybe Iman should give her a job," Cole retorted.

"Don't be silly." Sue Ellen smacked Cole's arm. "My sister doesn't need a job. She's one of the most successful models in Chicago. Tell him, Leena."

Leena sighed and wished she could sink through the

floor. But years of posing in front of a camera had given her the ability to mask her inner emotions. "I'm having a temporary reversal of fortune," she said, "which requires my returning home for a short period of time."

"How short?" Cole demanded suspiciously. "I don't want to hire you as my receptionist only to have you take off a few days later."

"What do you mean reversal of fortune?" Sue Ellen demanded. "Do you have a gambling problem?"

"No, of course not." Leena answered her sister's question first because it was the easiest. "I don't gamble."

"You taking off to Chicago was a gamble."

Okay, so Sue Ellen had her there. Apparently her question wasn't as easy as Leena first thought. Which left Cole's question. "I wouldn't leave without giving two weeks' notice."

"So you'd work two days and then give two weeks' notice?" he countered.

"I anticipate being here through the summer." Saying the words aloud made Leena feel ill. But the bottom line was that unfortunately, it would take her that long to get her act together financially to climb out of debt enough to start over.

She'd used her organizational skills to come up with a time line that charted out the least amount of time she'd have to spend in Rock Creek. And given the salary this position was offering, proudly displayed on that HELP WANTED sign she'd seen, it would take her a couple of months to regain control of her life.

The job paid well for Rock Creek, which surprised her at first. Apparently she wasn't the only one a little desperate. The vet seemed to have trouble getting the position filled. Not that she planned on asking why no one in town wanted to work for him.

Not yet.

"So are you accepting my offer to help you?" she asked Cole.

"How are you going to help him?" Sue Ellen demanded.

"By working as my receptionist," Cole replied.

"No way! Stop right there. No way is my sister working in a crummy vet's office. Not that you're a crummy vet," Sue Ellen hastily assured Cole. "I didn't mean that. I just meant that your office is crummy. Not that it's dirty, although it smells like dog urine in here."

"That's from my boots." Leena looked down at her ruined footwear. "Oscar peed on one of them earlier. I tried to clean it off . . ."

Sue Ellen glared at Cole. "You allowed a dog to pee on my sister? Do you have any idea who you're dealing with here? She's *famous*! She is *not* someone to be peed upon!"

Cole shrugged, his mouth curved as if he were holding back a smile. If he laughed at her, Leena would have to punch him again. Instead he drawled, "I can't guarantee it won't happen again."

"Then she is not working here," Sue Ellen stated firmly. "Come on, Leena, let's go."

Leena recognized Sue Ellen's bossy-big-sister mode. Sue Ellen was seven years older than Leena and she took her job as the elder sibling very seriously.

But Leena had no intention of being bossed around. Not unless it was by someone who was signing her paycheck.

Cole, curse his twisted soul, just stood there, arms

crossed across his chest, a stupid grin on his face. She could read his mind. *Whatcha gonna do now, big girl?*

Okay, maybe the "big girl" bit at the end was her own interpretation, but the challenging look in his admittedly sexy blue eyes was definitely being broadcast to her loud and clear.

"I'll be back in the morning," she told him firmly before heading for the door.

"The office opens at nine," he called after her, "but staff should show up at eight thirty."

"No problem." Right. Talk about a huge lie. Leena had tons of problems. Boatloads of them. But at least she had a job. Now she just needed to find somewhere to stay.

"You're staying with me, right?" Sue Ellen said. "You know that Mom and Dad gave me their trailer. I haven't had a lot of time to redecorate it yet because I've been getting my real estate license. I'm sure I'm going to pass that test this next time around. Anyway, you can stay in your old bedroom."

Just kill me now. Leena reached through the open window of her blue Sebring, grabbed a paper bag from her front seat, and started breathing into it.

"What are you doing?" Sue Ellen demanded.

Leena just shook her head and held up her finger in the universal sign for *Wait a minute, I'll be right with you.* Right after she had a nervous breakdown.

"She's hyperventilating," Cole said as he joined them in the parking lot.

"You're a doctor, do something to help her!" Sue Ellen shoved him toward Leena, almost knocking her down in the process.

The second Cole put his hands on her waist to steady

her, Leena instantly wished she was thinner. Or richer. Or both.

She lowered her hands, and the paper bag, to remove his fingers from her body before he measured her further.

The rustling crush of the bag mimicked her rustling heartbeat.

His hands left her waist, but only to move to her shoulders in order to pull her even closer.

"What are you do—mmmbbb!"

His lips covered hers, muffling the rest of her words and answering her question. He was kissing her. Gently, softly, seductively, but this was a kiss all right. No mistaking that.

He didn't try to tongue-down right there in the middle of the parking lot, in front of her sister. No, he was just tempting her, exploring infinite possibilities before releasing her.

Just breathe, Leena told herself, inhaling a ragged gulp of air.

Grinning, Cole gently lifted the paper bag back to her mouth.

Leena batted it away and glared at him. If the man was amusing himself at her expense, he'd live to regret it, regardless of how awesome a kisser he was.

"Do you always kiss your employees?" Leena demanded.

Cole's grin widened. "You're not officially an employee until you fill out the paperwork tomorrow."

"You were kissing my sister?" Sue Ellen stared at him in disbelief.

"Just practicing a little mouth-to-mouth resuscitation, ma'am."

"Well, go practice it on someone else." Leena lifted

her chin to give him her best haughty queen-of-the-universe look. "I don't need you rescuing me."

"Yeah, so you said earlier. You've come to rescue *me*, right? You know, I think I could get used to that idea." One final devastatingly sexy grin and then he was gone, sauntering around the corner of the building and out of sight—but not out of Leena's mind.

Which left her with the sinking feeling she'd just jumped out of the frying pan smack dab into the fire.

Chapter Two

. . . .

"So what do you think?" Sue Ellen bounced with excitement as she pointed, a la Vanna White, at a wall in the mobile home's living room.

Leena stared in horror at the row of velvet Elvises hanging above a plastic-covered orange plaid couch.

"It still looks a little tacky, I know," Sue Ellen added.

Leena sighed with relief. "You think? I mean, come on. Velvet Elvises?" She laughed. "Talk about tacky."

Sue Ellen glared at her. "I was talking about the couch. It's too orange. I haven't had time to get new furniture yet."

"Wait a second . . . Isn't that Mom and Dad's couch?" Leena recognized it now. Clearly she'd managed to wipe it from her memory banks along with the mustard-colored shag carpeting coating the living room floor.

"I haven't redone things in here, other than add the

artwork." Sue Ellen again pointed to the Elvis gallery. "I can't believe you thought they were tacky." She shook her head. "Just goes to show what you know. You might be a famous model, but I'm the one with the interior design talents."

"Since when?"

"Since I took a course over the Internet. I even have a certificate. See?" She reached over to pull a frame off the wall. "And I've almost got my realtor's license. So not only can I find you a new home, but I can decorate it for you too. You know, a second home here in Rock Creek would be a great investment for you."

Leena didn't even have a first home, let alone a second one. She just wasn't sure how to break that news to her sister yet.

Okay, so Leena had exaggerated her success a bit. That didn't make her a criminal and it didn't mean she deserved all the bad breaks coming her way lately.

Yes, it was true that Leena had claimed she was really, *really* successful when she wasn't. But there had always been a slim slice of truth in each pie of exaggeration she'd served up to her sister. She'd just put a good spin on her situation.

Even now Leena just couldn't confess her career was in the tank and that her agent had just let her go. Instead Leena had described her situation as a temporary reversal of fortune. That was her story and she needed to stick to it.

"So tell me what you've been doing in Chicago?" Sue Ellen eagerly asked. "Hanging out with all the famous people? Have you met Oprah?"

"No, but we're members of the same health club." Or had been until Leena couldn't afford the fees any longer.

"What about guys?"

"What about them?"

"Are you seeing somebody special?"

Leena had thought Johnny Sullivan was special, but he turned out to be anything but. She thought he might have been Mr. Right—until she heard him talking to his buddies at a cocktail party after he'd had a few too many drinks.

He'd claimed afterward he wasn't really serious about the other model he was bedding and that he hadn't meant to say Leena had thunder thighs. Leena wasn't buying either seriously lame excuse.

Believing *in vino veritas*, she'd immediately dumped him. Kicked him to the curb. Successful lawyer or not, the man was a dirtbag who'd hurt her. Cheated on her. Humiliated her.

"I know that face. Come on," Sue Ellen coaxed her. "You can talk to me. I'm great at giving relationship advice. Just ask my friend Skye. I helped her and the town's sheriff Nathan Thornton get together. They're a very happy couple now. So sit down and talk to me." Sue Ellen plunked down onto the couch and tried patting the seat beside her. But her hand stuck to the plastic covering, making a squishy sort of noise Leena remembered from her childhood summers, when her thighs would stick to the plastic.

She didn't want to remember those days. She didn't want to talk about her recent breakup with Johnny. So she did what she'd often done as a kid. She distracted Sue Ellen by moving the spotlight from herself onto her sister. "What about you? Are you seeing someone?"

"Why? What have you heard?" Sue Ellen's expression

was defensive. "I can't believe someone already told you about the naked fireman."

"They didn't, but that sounds like an interesting story."

"I was seeing this guy for a while. A fireman. He posed for one of those sexy calendars, you know, to raise funds. He was good at that. Raising things. Very well endowed, if you know what I mean. In the end, it turned out he was just a player, so I broke it off."

Maybe Leena and her sister had more in common than she thought. "Other than the naked calendar deal, that pretty much wraps up what happened in my last relationship too. He was a player."

Sue Ellen wiggled her eyebrows. "A well-endowed player?"

"Not well enough to put up with his games. Like you, I got tired of being played."

"We deserve better. Or so Skye keeps telling me."

"Who is this Skye person?"

"She's one of my closest friends. She moved here a little over a year ago. You'll meet her soon. I'll have to throw a welcome-home party for you."

Leena could only imagine the kind of party Sue Ellen would come up with. Probably have a dancing Elvis theme or something. Time to change the subject again.

Sue Ellen took care of that before Leena could speak. "What about Mom and Dad? Did you tell them you were coming home for a visit?"

"No."

"They'd probably be jealous that you didn't go see them instead of me. Not that they don't have plenty to keep them busy down at Lighthouse Keys in Florida. You should see the mobile homes down there! They are huge. You'd never know they weren't regular houses.

And the community center is gorgeous. Mom has volunteered to be the librarian there, you know. Plus she's in charge of the special activities all year. They're having a fifties-style record-hop party this month."

"Yeah, well, Mom has always been a people person. That's one of the reasons she did so well as a hairstylist."

"The place where she used to work, Sherlock Combs, closed a few years ago. Like so many businesses in town."

Leena had noticed that Rock Creek wasn't exactly a boomtown. "What about Dad? How's he doing?"

"Stubborn Irishman that he is, he likes stirring things up."

Leena nodded. He'd been a pro at stirring things up those early years of her childhood, when he'd had a drinking problem. He'd been sober for nearly twenty years now, but Leena still had painful memories from that time permanently embedded on her mind's hard drive. Memories of yelling and screaming, of dishes being smashed, of the taste of fear in her mouth as she huddled in the corner of her bedroom with her younger sister, Emma.

Sue Ellen had been a teenager during those days and hadn't been home much, spending a lot of time at friends' houses. She'd never spoken to Leena about their dad's drinking. Neither had their mother. Da Nile wasn't just a river—it was a coping tool for Leena's older sister and mother. Total denial.

Her family excelled at avoidance. They were total pros. Leena had learned from the best.

She hadn't seen her parents much since they'd moved down to Florida a few years ago. Since then they'd been busy with their new life. Oh, she'd talked to them on the phone every couple of weeks. Her dad always said the same four lines.

How's it going? Everything okay? Good. Here's your mom.

Her mom's conversation always revolved around all their Florida friends, people Leena didn't know.

"Hey," Sue Ellen said. "Remember that time Mom and I came to visit you in Chicago?"

"Which time?" There had been several, each one worse than the one before.

"The last time."

"Right." Leena could never forget that last visit, no matter how hard she tried. Their mom had insisted on accompanying Leena on a photo shoot to see what it was like. She'd promised Leena that no one would even know she was there.

Yeah, right. That's why her mom had ended up arguing with the hairstylist about Leena's hair. Leena's face turned red at the mere memory. What a disaster. Leena and her mom had been kicked off the shoot.

Leena hadn't invited her family back to Chicago after that debacle, and she hadn't come back to Rock Creek either. She'd always vowed that she wouldn't return until she was on the cover of a national magazine. She'd come close once, but the cover deal had fallen through.

Instead Leena had stayed away, perfecting the avoidance and denial she'd learned at an early age. Her schedule kept her very busy so she didn't have to lie when she said she didn't have time to get together for Christmas or birthdays. She always sent presents. And e-mails. E-mail was Leena's favorite means of communication with her family. She loved them; she just couldn't cope with them.

Yet here she was, depending on her older sister for help.

A knock on the door interrupted Leena's thoughts.

"Who is it?" Sue Ellen shouted out.

"Me, Donny."

She got up and opened the door.

"Hey, Sue Ellen, I'm just returning that toaster you lent me. I didn't want you thinking I'd stolen it or something." The comment came from a tall, skinny guy wearing a gray Smiley's Septic Service uniform. He had dark hair and nice eyes. And he kept those eyes firmly focused on Sue Ellen.

"Donny, this is my famous-model sister, Leena."

"Hi." Leena greeted him but he barely noticed her. She had the feeling she could have been standing there stark naked and he wouldn't have blinked an eye.

He chatted a few more minutes before leaving. The second he did, Leena said, "Someone's got a crush on you."

"Really? Who?"

"Are you blind? That guy who was just here a second ago."

"Donny?" Sue Ellen shook her head. "No way."

"Way. The poor man couldn't keep his eyes off you." Leena grinned. "Sue Ellen and Donny, sitting in a tree. K-I-S-S-I-N-G." After being tortured by her older sister with that chant as an embarrassed twelve-year-old kid, it felt good to repay the favor.

"He's just a friend. I'm seeing someone else," Sue Ellen said.

"Who?"

"Russ Spears. He's the high school football coach. He also teaches there. He's a manly man."

"And Donny isn't?"

"What, you don't think I'm smart enough to have a teacher interested in me?" Sue Ellen raised her voice.

"Do you think that the only guy who'd want to get involved with me dumps shit for a living?"

"Whoa." Leena blinked in surprise. "Where did that come from?"

"I may not be famous like you, but I'm not stupid."

"I never said you were."

"Fine. Let's talk about something else. What price range were you thinking of?"

"Huh?"

"For your second home here in Rock Creek."

"I just got a job at the vet's office. I'm not exactly rolling in money here. Besides, this is a totally temporary situation. I'm only going to be in Rock Creek for a few months."

"Do you want to stay in your old bedroom? You can if you want. I've sort of turned it into an office now, but I could fix that . . ."

Leena swallowed her rising panic.

"Wait." Sue Ellen tapped one of her elaborately painted acrylic nails against her chin. "I might have another idea. Did I tell you I'm the manager here at the Regency Mobile Home Park? We've got a model double-wide that is sitting empty. Maybe you could rent that."

"How much would that be?" Leena asked, amused by the term *mobile home park*. What had happened to *trailer park*?

"The park owner was just telling me he wanted to do something to improve the sales side of the business. If you agreed to model in front of it for a print ad layout, I'll bet I could get a good deal for you."

Leena could see the write-up now: *Double-wide*

Leena loves her double-wide mobile home. Lots of extra room for those wide hips and tummy.

But what choice did she have? It wasn't like she had a ton of options here.

Okay, *ton* may have been a bad word choice given her present mood.

"Let me just make a few phone calls. Meanwhile, make yourself at home. What am I saying? Of course you'll make yourself at home. This *is* your home. You grew up here." Sue Ellen headed down the hall toward the back of the mobile home, tossing one final comment over her shoulder. "Make yourself comfy."

To really make herself comfy, Leena would have to leave town. There was nothing at all comfy about her return to Rock Creek.

Leena automatically got up and headed for the fridge in search of comfort food. Sue Ellen didn't disappoint. There was a box of supermarket brownies, a carton of Cool Whip, and a Sara Lee pound cake. She was about to reach for the cake when out of the corner of her eye she saw the two family-size packages of Cool Ranch Doritos on the counter.

Doritos. And not just any flavor. *Cool Ranch* Doritos. Leena's Achilles' heel.

That would be a start.

Ten minutes later, Leena felt sick after chowing down half the huge bag of chips. Only back in the trailer park for an hour and already she was reverting to bad habits.

She knew better.

Sue Ellen bounced into the room. "Good news. You can have the double-wide, which is furnished by the way, in exchange for you doing an ad for it. It's just a few steps away from here, so you'll still be nearby. Want me to show you now?"

"Sure." Leena guiltily dropped the Doritos bag and stood. Already her jeans felt tighter.

Sue Ellen headed outside, merrily traipsing along the path leading from her trailer toward the front of the mobile home park. "I'm the manager here now, did I tell you that? Oh, yeah, I did. Anyway, we're cracking down on people who don't maintain their spots. That's why we've got such nice little gardens now. And look at Mrs. Petrocelli's collection of cement geese. Don't they have the cutest little outfits? She changes them depending on the season. Their Santa outfits are my favorites. Mr. and Mrs. Goose Claus."

Leena tried not to hyperventilate again.

"I think I got my love for lawn art from Mom," Sue Ellen said. "You never really appreciated the art form, did you?"

"No."

"I got my love for Elvis from Mom too. Something else you missed out on. Not that I'm rabid about Elvis or anything. I like other singers. Like Taylor Hicks. And Carrie Underwood. I am a little rabid about *American Idol*. Ah, here we are. This is the model home." Sue Ellen pulled a fuzzy pink Beanie Baby key chain out of her pocket and unlocked the door. "It may need airing out a little bit. The last renter was a smoker."

It wasn't as bad as Leena had expected or dreaded. Everything was beige, but that was manageable. A few throw pillows on the couch would work wonders. She had that kind of stuff someplace in her car, maybe. She'd tossed things in so fast she wasn't really sure what she had with her and what she'd put into a storage unit back in Chicago.

Which reminded her, she sure hoped that her apartment neighbor Shayla Matera remembered to feed the stray cat by the Dumpster in the back of their building. Leena had left two huge bags of Cat Chow for the cat. She couldn't afford to pay Shayla for the favor, so she'd given her tons of new makeup samples she'd been given as incentives. She hoped Shayla kept her promise about the cat.

Leena planned on keeping her promise to herself to return to Chicago when the summer was over.

For the first time since arriving back at the Regency Mobile Home Park, Leena felt a glimmer of optimism. She could do this. She could get her act together, get some money together, and get back on her success track.

Ninety minutes later she'd completed a thorough cleaning of the mobile home, unpacked her car, and put everything away. A pair of Nate Berkus pillows adorned the couch, her brushed stainless frothy cappuccino machine sat on the kitchen counter, and all the closets were filled to capacity with her clothes, shoes, and bags. The queen-size bed was covered with her five-hundred-thread-count sheets.

Leena had things under control. She'd conquered chaos. Her surroundings smelled like Clinique Happy now instead of cigarette smoke. The windows were open, allowing a gentle night breeze to filter through with a promise of new beginnings.

Leena's optimism lasted until the next morning when the digital travel alarm clock went off and there was no hot water for a shower.

She arrived at the vet's office ten minutes late.

Cole was waiting for her. He tapped his watch as she walked in the door. "You're late."

"I was out of hot water."

"Well, you're *in* hot water right now."

"It's only ten minutes."

"It's the principle of the thing."

"Right. Is that coffee?" Leena grabbed the mug out of his hands. "I can't manage without caffeine." She took a gulp then made a face. "There's no sugar in this."

"I drink it black, princess."

She took one more cautious sip before shuddering and handing it back to him. "Where's the coffee-maker?"

"In the staff room. I thought I'd show you around this morning before the clients show up."

"You mean the animals?"

"And their pets, yes."

"Ha-ha. Are you always this funny first thing in the morning?"

"I guess you'll just have to wait and find out, won't you?"

"First, lead me to the coffeemaker."

"*You're* the coffeemaker. That will be part of your duties. I made the coffee this morning, but starting tomorrow it's your job." He led her down the hallway to a doorway on the right. As she trailed after him she couldn't help noticing that he had a great butt. "This is the staff room."

It held the usual stuff: table, chairs, microwave, fridge, caffeine . . .

Leena headed straight for the coffeepot, poured herself a cup, and added sugar and creamer. Cole's interest in her actions made her feel defensive. "What are you looking at? I suppose you don't think I should be using sugar? That I should be watching calories and starving myself down to some ridiculous weight that society finds appropriate?"

"Actually I was thinking about a surgery I've got scheduled later on today. On a Doberman."

"Oh." So much for her being the center of attention. A new thought occurred to her. "You've got someone else to help you with that stuff, right? I mean, surgery help isn't one of my duties, is it?"

"No, I've got two veterinary assistants for that. You know one of them already."

"I do?"

"Yeah, you went to school with her. Here she comes now . . ."

Leena looked over her shoulder at the woman who'd just entered the room. She had curly auburn hair and was shorter than Leena. No surprise there. At five foot ten, Leena was definitely on the tall side.

"Oh my God, is that you, Leena? It's me. Mindy."

"Mindy Oberhofen?"

"Actually it's Mindy Griffin now. I married T-Bone a year after we both graduated high school. He's a butcher, just like his dad. Only he's working over at the Giant Foods while his dad is at the local Peterman's Market. That caused some family friction in the beginning, I can tell you. His dad wanted him to work at the same store he did . . . Anyway they've worked out a truce about it now. Who knew butchers could be so competitive? But enough about me. Tell me what you're doing back here in Rock Creek. Are you here to visit Sue Ellen? How's big-city life in Chicago? You must have met lots of famous people in your job as a supermodel."

"I'm not a supermodel. I'm a plus-size model."

"I watch *Project Runway*," Mindy confessed. "I don't know why . . . It's not like I could wear anything they design or that I can relate to the people on the show." She looked down at her own pear-shaped body. "Everyone is so skinny."

"I am definitely not skinny," Leena said.

"For the record, I'm not into skinny," Cole said.

"Cole here likes *all* the girls," Mindy said. "He's an equal-opportunity flirt."

"Hey, don't go spreading rumors about me," Cole protested.

"She's not saying anything I didn't already know," Leena said. Cole was definitely a denim dude, one of those guys who looked great in jeans. She might have been caffeine deficient when she'd walked in this morning, but she'd noticed that much. She'd put him in Ralph Lauren instead of Armani. Not that his jeans were designer made. He was a Levi's man . . . with a nice tight butt.

Mindy set down her Humane Society of the United States canvas tote bag and reached for a matching mug with a puppy and kitten on it. "Leena, you still haven't said what you're doing here."

"Leena is our new receptionist." Cole seemed to take great pleasure in making the announcement.

"Yeah, right," Mindy scoffed.

"I'm telling you the truth," Cole said. "She's the new receptionist."

Mindy was stunned. "Why?"

Cole grinned. "She thinks I can't survive without her."

Mindy shook her head, clearly still unable to fathom this info. "But . . . she punched you."

"That was years ago. She's been remorseful ever since," Cole added.

"And so she gave up her fantastic job as a plus-size supermodel to come work as your receptionist to make amends? Sorry, but I'm not buying that."

"Why not?" Cole said.

"I came to stop him from charming the pants off all the women of Rock Creek," Leena said with a grin.

"Actually he's also busy rehabbing the monstrosity of a house where he lives," Mindy said.

"Hey, I am the boss here, remember?" Cole gave them both an irritated look. "Which means I'm in charge."

"We let him think that," Mindy whispered conspiratorially.

Leena laughed. "That's kind of you."

"I'm outta here," Cole announced. "I'm going to check on that black Lab with the broken leg. Mindy, will you give Leena a quick tour, fill her in on the basics?"

"Sure."

The minute he was gone, Leena asked, "So what kind of boss is he?"

"One who looks very sexy wearing a tool belt."

Leena blinked. "He wears that to work? What, he thinks he's going to need a hammer to operate on some poor puppy or something?"

"No, of course he doesn't wear the tool belt to work here. I just meant that I've seen him out back."

"What's he doing wearing a tool belt out back?"

"That's where his house is. Right behind the animal clinic here. It was part of the property, but the house hadn't been lived in for years. The old vet, a relative of Cole's, had moved to a newer house a few blocks away." Mindy set down her still-empty mug and gave Leena a shy hug. "I can't believe you're going to be working here now. You'll have to tell me all about your life in Chicago, but first I'd better fill you in on what the schedule is like. The receptionist answers the phone, schedules appointments, pulls patient files, handles the paperwork and billing, that sort of thing."

"Why aren't you the vet here? When we were in school, that's all you talked about . . . becoming a vet."

Mindy shrugged. "I wasn't smart enough."

"Says who?" Leena demanded.

"Says me."

"Well, you're wrong."

"That's nice of you to say, but—"

"It's the truth. You were always great at biology and that kind of stuff."

Mindy shifted uncomfortably. "Well, I'm very happy working here as a veterinary assistant. And I'm very lucky to have this job. There aren't a lot of HELP WANTED signs up in Rock Creek."

Leena had noticed that. Not that Rock Creek had ever been a hotbed of industrial expansion. At least not in her lifetime. At one point there had been a lunch-pail factory that had done a good business and provided a lot of jobs for locals, but that had closed decades ago. The town had pretty much gone downhill ever since.

When she'd left, Leena had decided that Rock Creek was for losers. Yet, here she was. Back again.

Loser, loser, loser. The chant went round and round in her head like a Chihuahua chasing its tail.

Leena tried to focus on the information Mindy was telling her, how to open files on the computer and change screens from patient records to billing to scheduling.

Leena had mastered the use of her BlackJack cell phone—an all-in-one smart device with Internet access, an MP3 player, and camera with video capability. She was a very fast learner, and this computer system was just a bigger BlackJack as far as she was concerned.

"Time to open up." Mindy unlocked the front door. "Looks like our first clients are already here."

"Don't you keep the dogs and cats separated?" Leena asked Mindy as a woman walked in with a Persian cat on a leash under one arm and a bulldog on a leash in her other hand.

"Not when they're owned by the same person," Mindy replied.

"Butch and Princess are best friends," the woman said.

"Butch, huh?" Leena smiled. "That's a cute name for a bulldog."

"That's my cat's name." The woman sounded highly offended. "The bulldog is Princess."

"Oh. My bad." Leena shook her head. "Sorry."

"You're new here, aren't you?"

The comment was said with suspicion. Residents of Rock Creek weren't real fond of outsiders. Since they didn't get many, it usually wasn't a problem.

"Yes, I'm new," Leena said, "but that doesn't mean I can't do a great job."

"You already messed up my pets' names."

Leena worked hard to make amends, even offering the woman some coffee, which she refused.

"Will there be a long wait?" the woman demanded.

"I don't think so. What's your name?"

"Mrs. Dabronovitch. Edie Dabronovitch."

"Can you spell that for me?"

"Of course I can spell it."

Leena waited expectantly. When the woman said nothing, Leena began without her. "D-o . . ."

"It's D-*a*-bronovitch. Who are you?"

"I'm Leena Riley, the new receptionist here."

"You're not related to Sue Ellen Riley, are you?"

"Yes, I am. She's my sister."

"You must be the supposedly smart sister then, not the model."

"Why do you say that?"

"Well, look at you. You don't look like a model any more than Mindy here does. Models are thin. Neither one of you is."

The woman had just insulted her. And Mindy. Leena knew it. Mindy knew it. Even Butch and Princess had to know it.

Leena wasn't about to let Mrs. Edie Dabronovitch get away with it.

Call her mean, but Leena saw red when someone got nasty and went out of their way to make her feel bad about herself. Leena already had tons of self-doubt. Especially in her current circumstances. She sure didn't need anyone else adding to the pile.

Plus the überskinny woman had just insulted Mindy, who'd never hurt a fly or say anything in her own defense. That called for definite action.

Mindy nervously cleared her throat. "Uh, Edie, why don't you and Princess and Butch come on back into an examining room with me."

"Don't you need her file?" Leena asked.

"I'll come back for it."

Mindy was clearly concerned that Leena might haul off and smack Edie Dabrono-bitch right then and there.

As if Leena would do such a thing. She was an adult

now. She didn't have to beat up someone the way she had as a kid. Now she had words to use in her own defense. And Mindy's.

"What's the hurry? Edie and I were just getting to know one another," Leena said. "I didn't realize she was an expert on the modeling world."

Edie didn't appear to appreciate Leena's sarcasm. "It doesn't take an expert to see—"

"Yeah?" Leena challenged her, a deliberately dangerous edge to her voice. "To see what?"

"That Americans have a huge problem with obesity." Edie looked at Mindy and then back at Leena before looking down at her own size-zero self and smiling so smugly it was all Leena could do not to leap over the counter and strangle her with Princess's leash. "I used to be overweight myself." Edie patted her flat stomach. "And I have a daughter who struggles daily with her weight." She pointed to a girl who stood half hidden behind the large ficus in the corner. The poor kid blushed and hung her head.

The thing was, the girl wasn't overweight. Granted she was no size zero, but she seemed to be average for someone with a large-boned, athletic build. Leena knew, because she too had a similar build that came from her mom's side of the family. That and her height. At five foot ten, Leena was no petite little thing and never would be.

Neither was this girl.

"She looks fine to me," Leena said.

"Hannah is great at softball and basketball even though she's only a freshman," Mindy added. "My niece is on her team."

"I don't look like my mom," Hannah half whispered.

"You're not supposed to," Leena said.

Edie protested. "I hardly think you're qualified—"

"I agree that you hardly *think*, or you wouldn't have said any of the things you have here today. That's okay. *Your* bad. I forgive you."

"I . . . I . . ." Edie sputtered.

Mindy quickly herded Edie and her entourage down the hall into an examining room. As Edie's daughter passed by, she paused to look at Leena and mouth the words *thank you* before scurrying after her mother.

Leena's blood was still boiling when the outside door to the waiting room burst open and a very pregnant woman staggered inside. She made it to the reception desk before gasping and staring down. "Oh, no! My water just broke!"

Chapter Three

. . . .

I am not cleaning that up! was Leena's first panicked thought, quickly followed by *I don't know nothin' 'bout birthin' babies!* a la *Gone With the Wind.*

The pregnant woman leaned across the counter and grabbed Leena by the front of her favorite DKNY shirt. "Do *not* let Angel give me a natural childbirth."

"Right." Leena had no idea what Manic Mom-to-Be was talking about, but at that point she wasn't about to ask questions.

"Call 911!" the woman gasped.

"You've got it. Uh, you need to let me go first or I can't reach the phone."

The instant Leena was released she grabbed for the phone and dialed emergency services.

"We've got some crazy pregnant woman here at the vet's office. She's having a baby!" she told the dispatcher.

"Is she conscious?"

"Yes."

"Is she breathing?"

"Yes, she's doing that panting stuff that pregnant women do on TV."

"Ask her how far apart her contractions are."

Leena took one look at the contorted expression on the pregnant woman's face. "She, uh, doesn't feel like talking right now. The EMTs can ask her that question when they get here. Just send an ambulance now. Her water broke."

"We've got a unit on the way."

Leena hung up. "They're on the way."

"What's going on out here?" Cole demanded. "Julia?" He looked at the woman about to give birth at any second. So now she had a name.

Julia grabbed Cole by the front of his white lab coat with even greater vehemence than she'd grabbed Leena moments earlier. "I am *not* having this baby in a vet's office!"

"Of course you're not. Breathe." He looked around. "Did anyone call her husband?"

By anyone, he must mean me, Leena thought to herself. "I didn't even know who she was until two seconds ago, so how could I call her husband?" Leena said defensively. "She ordered me to call 911, so I did."

"Do *not* let Angel make me give a natural birth." Julia paused to pant for a few seconds. "I want drugs!" She jerked Cole closer. "Do you have drugs?"

"The ambulance should be here any second," Leena said from behind the safety of the reception counter. No way was she getting close enough for Julia to take her down. She'd never seen a woman in labor before. Not a pretty sight. Made her want to rethink the subject of having kids of her own someday . . .

"Where is she?" A woman with curly hair and a swirly Indian cotton dress burst into the waiting room. "Don't worry. Angel is here. Your mother is here, Julia. Everything will be fine. Just breathe and picture yourself in a happy place. Remember that childbirth is the most natural thing on earth, a wonderful and magical time for a woman," Angel said with a New Age smile.

It sure didn't look very magical or wonderful to Leena. And from the I-want-to-hit-someone expression on Julia's face, she didn't seem to agree with that statement either.

"The ambulance is almost here." Leena could finally hear the sirens coming.

"We don't need them—" Angel began.

"Yes, I do!" Julia snarled. "They have drugs."

Leena's attention shifted to Cole, who was trying to charm his way out of Julia's clutches. He flashed the pregnant woman a sexier-than-hell smile. "Come on, honey, you're doing great."

Honey? The man was flirting with a woman in labor? Did he have no shame?

"I need you all to move aside, folks," an EMT ordered the rowdy group as he came through the front door.

"Are you sure you don't want to have a natural childbirth at home, Julia?" Angel asked her daughter. "It's still not too late . . ."

Julia's only response was a heartfelt growl. Seconds later the EMTs had Julia on the gurney and were whisking her outside to the waiting ambulance.

Angel trailed after them, leaving Cole, Leena, and Mindy in the waiting room.

Leena spoke first. "Well, that was enough to give a girl second thoughts about having kids."

"The miracle of birth is a powerful thing," Cole said.

"It sure is," Mindy agreed. "I'll just clean things up here."

Leena felt guilty, but her stomach had definitely taken a turn toward queasy. "Am I supposed to help?"

"No. Trust me, after dog diarrhea and kitty pee, this is nothing."

"Is this place always so wild?" Leena had to ask.

Mindy nodded. "Very often, although we don't usually have women about to give birth in the waiting room. We have had a litter of golden retrievers and several litters of kittens delivered here, but no human babies."

Minutes later, Mindy had everything restored to normal, or as normal as this place appeared to get.

"That was so exciting," the owner of a poodle said once clients were allowed to reenter the building. She and her dog both had white curly hair adorned with little pink bows. "I wonder if the baby will be a boy or girl."

Leena wondered what she'd gotten into here. Signing up to work as the vet's receptionist hadn't seemed like that big a deal yesterday. Now she was very tempted to reach for another paper bag to hyperventilate into.

"You look a little pale, dear. You're not going to faint, are you? Rock Creek only has one ambulance and it's busy at the moment. Cole, your assistant looks like she's going to pass out."

"I'm the receptionist, not the vet assistant," Leena immediately replied. "Mindy is the veterinary assistant. I'm just . . ." Crazy? She saw a flutter of wings out of the corner of her eye and then felt the landing. "I'm . . . I . . . I've got . . . a bird on my head."

"I'm so sorry," said a middle-aged man with thinning hair as he hurried over. "Tweetypie, you get back here."

"Birds are not allowed out of their cages." Leena pointed to the sign she'd put up that very morning.

"I was just trying to calm Tweetypie down after all the excitement of the evacuation and all. She's a precocious parakeet."

Leena felt something wet on her neck. Parakeet poop. Yuck! She grabbed hold of Tweetypie and handed the bird off to its owner.

So it had come to this. From successful model to bird potty house. Leena was now the equivalent of the paper at the bottom of a birdcage. It was too much.

"Are you going to quit?" Cole looked at her as if he'd already written her off as a failure.

"Don't make me punch you again," Leena growled.

"Here, dear." Poodle Lady gave her a wet wipe, but before Leena could use it, Sue Ellen burst into the waiting room. Didn't anyone enter this place like a normal person? Were there any normal people even left in this town? If so, Leena had yet to meet one.

"I heard Julia was having her baby in here!" Sue Ellen looked at Leena. "Why didn't you call me?"

"Because I was dialing 911."

"You should have called me."

"Why? You're not a midwife."

"I could have been, had I not chosen to become a realtor instead."

"You faint at the first sight of blood."

"So do you," Sue Ellen replied. "What do you have on your neck?"

"Parakeet poop."

"Eeew! Wipe it off! You have to be gorgeous for a photo shoot this afternoon. Don't give me that blank look. I told you last night. In exchange for staying in the model mobile home, you agreed to do a print ad for Regency Mobile Home Sales Incorporated."

"Today?"

"There's no time like the present."

That was for sure. Leena had never had a time like she'd had today. And the day wasn't even half over with yet.

"But I'm working today."

"Cole will let you off early, won't you, Cole?" Sue Ellen batted her baby blues at him.

"No, honey, I won't."

There he went, calling women *honey*. It was insulting. It was demeaning. Sadly Leena also found it kind of appealing, flowing over her like melted dark chocolate when he said it in that husky voice and punctuated it with his decadent smile.

Good thing Leena was immune.

Totally immune.

Denim Dude didn't get to her one tiny bit.

The zany shiver she felt inside was a result of her traumatic day, not the product of Cole's seducing ways or cute butt.

Only further exposure to the man would prove her point. "I'm staying here," Leena told her sister. "You'll have to reschedule the photo shoot."

"I didn't realize I'd be competing for your time with photographers," Cole said after Sue Ellen left in a huff.

"It's a one-time deal," Leena said.

"I've heard that before."

"You've probably said it yourself to some poor girl who thought you'd settle down with her." *Oops.* "Uh, forget I said that."

"No way. I'm intrigued by your obsession with my relationships concerning the opposite sex."

"I am not obsessed."

"Just opinionated."

"Blame it on the parakeet poop." Leena grabbed more tissues to wipe her neck. She needed a shower . . . bad.

"I doubt that's the reason you're opinionated."

"Stop saying that."

"And bossy too."

"Okay, I'll admit to having some bossy tendencies," Leena said, "but no way I'm opinionated."

"Edie told me you were rude to her."

"The woman should be horsewhipped. Not that whipping horses is a good thing in any way, shape, or form. So let me rephrase that. The woman should take a long walk off a short pier." An old phrase her mom used, but Leena couldn't come up with anything original at the moment.

"Any particular reason why you have a grudge against Edie?"

"She told her daughter she was fat!"

Cole was perplexed. "So? That's not a crime."

"Being fat or telling your kid they're fat?"

"Either one. Look, I've got patients waiting. Just do me a favor and try not to be rude to any more clients."

"Sure thing, Boss Man."

"I *am* the Boss Man and don't you forget it."

Forgetting him wouldn't come easy, but then nothing worthwhile did.

● ● ●

"Interesting day, huh?" noted Sheriff Nathan Thornton, Cole's best friend, as the two men sat in Nick's Tavern after work that evening.

Cole nodded. "Yeah, I hear the White Sox won today. That must make you happy."

"It does." Nathan paused to take a sip of his Heineken. "But I was referring to the matter of Julia almost having her baby in your waiting room."

"Yeah, that was interesting too."

"I saw you've got a new receptionist. Who is she?"

"I would have thought you'd already know, seeing as how you're the sheriff and all."

"That good-ol'-boy drawl ain't gonna work on me," Nathan said. "And yes, I do know who she is. I heard she's the woman who punched you."

"Hey!" Cole took offense, despite knowing that was his buddy's intent. "I was only a kid."

"So fill me in on this woman. I heard she was some kind of model in Chicago? If so, then what the hell is she doing in your office?"

"She's working as my receptionist."

"Yeah, that's a logical career move."

"She wasn't real specific about why she was back home again. I did hear she's rented a mobile home near her sister. I heard it was some kind of barter deal."

"What's that supposed to mean?" Nathan asked suspiciously.

"Not whatever you're thinking, obviously."

"And how do you know what I'm thinking?"

"I can read you like a book," Cole said.

"Oh yeah?"

"Yeah."

"So what am I thinking now?"

"That you're pissed. And that you want to challenge me to another arm-wrestling match, but you know you'd lose."

"In your dreams. Man rule number four: Never pick a fight you can't win. But let's get back to Leena. What did you mean by a barter deal?"

"I heard that she's going to do some kind of ad for the owner of the mobile home park."

"When I was a kid it was called a trailer park."

"No longer politically correct." Cole took another sip of his Bud straight from the bottle. "Anyway, Sue Ellen flew into the clinic today and muttered something about an ad or photo shoot. What do you know about the owner of the trailer park?"

"He's been out of town for many years and has recently returned. Some clown named Bart Chumley."

"So he's an idiot, huh?"

"No, I mean he really is a former circus clown. Traveled with Barnum & Bailey for nearly thirty years, or so I hear. I haven't actually met the guy yet."

"I would have thought a clown like you would want to bond with your own kind."

Nathan tossed a handful of peanut shells at Cole. "Very funny. So why'd you give this Leena a job?"

"Do you see anyone else lining up to be my receptionist?"

"Your reputation precedes you."

"What reputation?"

"As a *lady's* man." Nathan clearly took great pleasure

in drawing out the word, making it sound like *laaay-deee's*.

"Yeah, right. You sound like a skit from *Saturday Night Live*. Frankly, I'm amazed Skye hasn't tossed you out yet."

"She's been tempted a time or two."

"So what stopped her? Not your charming personality. That's my strength, not yours," Cole added with mocking modesty.

"I said that's your *reputation*. I never said it was true. That's why I never asked for your advice about Skye."

"Like you'd listen even if I had given it to you."

Nathan shrugged. "Hey, it might have happened."

"Yeah, right. And a meteor might land on Rock Creek."

"A meteor might help clean up parts of this town." Nathan looked around the bar, which had seen better days. "As long as it doesn't land on the Tivoli Theater. Skye just got the latest renovations done on the place. So, getting back to this Leena woman. You never answered my question. What's the deal with you two?"

"There is no deal. I already told you. I hired her as my receptionist. Why are you so interested all of a sudden?"

Nathan shrugged. "You hassled me about my love life, so I figured it was only fair for me to return the favor."

"It's no favor."

"Yeah, I know. I just like putting that pissed-off look on your face." Nathan paused to reach for his vibrating cell phone and check the number flashing on the screen. "It's Luke," he said to Cole before turning his attention to the caller. "Hey, I hear your wife almost had your baby in Cole's waiting room. Wrong doctor, buddy. You don't want a vet delivering your firstborn."

Cole listened to Nathan's side of the conversation, but part of his brain remained focused on Leena. What was her story? Kissing her that first day was meant to be a joke, but the joke was on him.

Kissing women was nothing new for Cole. He was damn good at it, or so he'd been told on more than one occasion.

But Leena had been different. Which made him want to kiss her again to figure out *why* she was different.

"Julia had a girl," Nathan told Cole. "Named her Jayne Ann after some romance author Julia likes to read."

Julia worked at the Serenity Falls Library. "Those librarians sure are a wild bunch."

"Luke seems to think so. He sounded pretty damn proud of himself. Baby and mom are doing good."

"Glad to hear it."

"So if you won't talk about Leena, how about the renovations on your house? How are those going?"

"Why? Are you volunteering to help?" Cole asked. "Because I've got an extra tool belt if you need one."

"No, I don't need one."

"Come on. I'll supply the cold beer."

Nathan shook his head regretfully. "Sorry. Skye already has a list of stuff for me to do."

"Is she still trying to feng shui the sheriff's office?"

"No, she's pretty much given up on that for now."

"You think you're ever going to move from that apartment over the theater into a real house with a real yard?"

"If we do, it will be a real house that isn't falling down the way yours is."

"It was part of the property when I bought the practice for a good price from my dad's cousin."

"The house was unoccupied for about a decade. That should have given you a clue."

"It's a fixer-upper."

"Or fixer-downer, depending on your perspective."

"Nothing gets me down," Cole said.

"Right. You're a tough guy through and through."

"Absolutely."

"Who'd never take in a stray dog or cat. How many misfits do you have under your roof now?"

"None of your business."

"So, tough guy, is Leena another misfit you've taken under your wing?"

"Anyone ever tell you that you're full of shit?"

"Frequently. Doesn't mean I don't speak the truth."

"Shut up and drink your Heineken," Cole said.

"Spoken like a true Bud man."

"You've got that right." But Cole refused to believe that Nathan had gotten anything else right. Leena was no misfit. She was all woman—with sexy curves and plenty of smart-mouth attitude. She was also his employee, and he'd do well to remember that fact instead of remembering their too-brief kiss that had left him wanting more.

Chapter Four

. . . .

Leena walked into Angelo's Pizza wishing she'd refused Sue Ellen's invitation to dinner. Actually, she *had* refused, but Sue Ellen had insisted.

And they claim I'm the bossy one, Leena thought. *Hah!*

After the day she'd had, Leena wanted nothing more than a little peace and quiet. Neither of those two objectives were Sue Ellen's strong suit. They didn't seem to be Sue Ellen's friend Skye Wright's specialty either.

Leena wasn't particularly eager to meet the bad-girl sister of the woman who'd almost given birth in the vet office earlier that day. Apparently Skye had moved to Rock Creek just over a year ago, yet Sue Ellen acted as though they'd been BFF—best friends forever—since birth.

But then Sue Ellen never did things halfway.

Leena had taken a cold shower the instant she'd driven back to her rented model home. The hot water still wasn't working, but she needed to remove all memory of the parakeet poop.

The jeans she wore cost more than she'd make in a week working at the vet's office. And the trendy empire-cut top hadn't seemed an extravagance when she'd bought it a few months ago. Now Leena wished she had the cash.

And she wished she could turn around and leave Angelo's. But it was already too late.

"There you are!" Sue Ellen jumped up and hugged Leena as if she hadn't seen her in decades. "We've been waiting for you. We already ordered our pizza."

Leena gasped in Sue Ellen's python hold. "I . . . can't . . . breathe! Let . . . go!"

"Sorry." Sue Ellen stood back and looked at Leena with guilty regret. "I keep doing that to people. Leena, this is my friend Skye."

Leena felt the waves of suspicion emanating from the redheaded woman wearing a wildly colorful tie-dyed T-shirt.

"You must be very proud of your sister," Skye said.

"Oh, I am." Sue Ellen beamed.

"I meant Leena must be proud of *you*, Sue Ellen."

"Huh?" Sue Ellen blinked in confusion.

Leena would have done the same but didn't want to appear as if she didn't know what Skye was talking about. She hated feeling dumb, and for some reason Skye was making her feel that way right now.

"I meant that Leena must be proud of how well you're doing here in Rock Creek," Skye said.

"Well, my success doesn't compare to Leena's," Sue Ellen said.

"Was Leena ever Miss Chow?" Skye countered.

"It was Miss Chow-Chow," Sue Ellen corrected her. "And no, she wasn't."

"How about Miss Scrabble?"

"It was Scramble, and again, no."

"I rest my point."

"Which was what, exactly?" Leena demanded, not one to back down from a fight, especially after the day she'd had.

"That your sister is someone special," Skye said.

"I know that," Leena said defensively.

"Do you?"

Skye seemed to see too much, forcing Leena to look away and mutter, "Maybe it would be better if I didn't join you for dinner after all."

"Don't say that," Sue Ellen wailed. "Sit down. Look, our pizza is ready. Sit, Leena."

Leena might work in a vet's office, but she wasn't a pet that obeyed commands like *sit* and *behave*. But the pizza smelled divine. And her stomach was growling. So she sat. Reluctantly.

"What did I miss?" a young dark-haired woman dressed in goth attire and covered with tattoos demanded as she slid into an empty chair at their table. A pair of skeleton earrings jangled in her ears. "Anything good? Anything bad? Anything juicy?"

"This is our friend Lulu, who won't let me give her a makeover," Sue Ellen said. "Maybe she'll let you do it, Leena."

"Don't count on it," Lulu said before scarfing down a slice of pizza.

Leena was feeling increasingly uncomfortable. "What did my sister tell you two about me?"

"Not much," Skye said. "Just that you live in Chicago and that you're bossy."

Leena turned to her sister. "That's all you said?"

Sue Ellen surprised her by countering, "Do you tell *your* friends a lot about me?"

"Not exactly," Leena had to admit, squirming a bit in her chair.

"Well, I'm an only child," Lulu announced dramatically before reaching for another slice of pizza. "Do you know how many only children commit suicide?"

"Stop with the suicide stuff. You're going to give my sister the wrong impression," Sue Ellen said.

Lulu just laughed. "She got the wrong impression the second I sat down. It was written all over her face."

"That wouldn't happen if you'd let me redo your makeup," Sue Ellen said.

Lulu glared. "I thought you wanted to be a realtor now. That you'd left your Mary Kay Cosmetics dreams behind."

"I have. My sister is a model," Sue Ellen said proudly. "A famous one."

"Famous, huh?" Lulu wasn't impressed. "I've never seen her before."

"Like you're an expert on the fashion industry," Sue Ellen retorted. "And Skye, I know you're funny about things like animal testing on beauty products."

"There's nothing funny about it," Skye said.

"That's why I didn't tell you guys a lot about her before. I wanted you to meet Leena first."

"She doesn't talk much, does she?" Skye gave Leena a mocking look.

"You three were doing so well without my input, I didn't see the point," Leena said. "To paraphrase Lulu, you'd already made up your mind about me the second I arrived."

"I don't judge people by their looks." Skye sounded highly insulted.

"Neither do I," Leena shot back.

"Oh, come on," Lulu scoffed. "You looked at me and thought 'weirdo.'"

"Sure I did," Leena readily admitted. "Which is exactly what you wanted me to think."

Lulu blinked. "Huh?"

"Your fashion is your statement. You don't like being told what to do. You want to be noticed. You don't color between the lines. I like the T-shirt by the way." Leena pointed to the PROCRASTINATE NOW message. "But you and Skye both wanted me to feel uncomfortable here tonight. I can't help wondering why."

"I bet you could figure it out if you really tried," Skye said.

Leena sighed. "What is it with you people?"

"And what people might that be?" Skye growled.

"People who like Rock Creek," Leena said.

"Doesn't sound like you're a fan of your hometown."

"I'm not," Leena admitted.

"If you hate it so much, why'd you come back?" Skye asked.

Leena was asking herself the same question. Maybe she should have gone to visit her parents down in Florida instead of coming here. Hard to tell which would make her feel like more of a loser: parking herself on senior citizen's row or having parakeets park themselves on her head.

Florida, however, was looking better by the second. Especially with Sue Ellen's friends giving her a hard time.

At least Sue Ellen *had* friends, even if they were strange. Unlike Leena, who was feeling very isolated at the moment. No merry band of gal pals to hang out with her.

Sudden tears filled her eyes.

"Look. You made her cry," Lulu told Skye.

"You're supposed to be my friends, and you made my sister cry!" Sue Ellen's voice rose with every word. So did Sue Ellen, who was now standing and glaring at her friends.

"I'm not crying." Leena desperately yanked her sister back into a chair. "I've got allergies."

"Since when?" Sue Ellen asked suspiciously.

"Since coming to Rock Creek," Leena muttered.

Skye leaned forward to stare at Leena. "You remind me of my sister Julia."

"That's not necessarily a good thing," Sue Ellen warned Leena.

"That's not true. Julia and I have made up," Skye said. "We're no longer feuding like we used to. I've told you that."

"Uh-huh." Sue Ellen didn't appear convinced.

"And your sister may be bossy, but you're no slouch in the bossy department yourself, Sue Ellen," Skye said.

"Thank you." Leena lifted her glass and toasted Skye, who grinned at her.

"I am not bossy!" Sue Ellen shouted.

Skye, Lulu, and Leena all rolled their eyes. And in that moment, a bond of sorts was formed. Maybe Sue Ellen's friends weren't so bad after all . . .

An hour later, they were on their second pizza and giggling over some story Lulu had just told them when they were interrupted by a man's voice.

"Sue Ellen, I didn't expect to see you here tonight."

"Russ." Sue Ellen fluttered her eyelashes.

Skye and Lulu performed another eye roll.

"This is Coach Russ Spears," Sue Ellen announced.

"I know," Skye said. "I taught his football team yoga, remember?"

"That lettuce position really works," Russ said.

Skye sighed. "It's lotus position, Coach."

But he wasn't listening. "And who's this?" He stared at Leena.

Sue Ellen made the introduction. "This is my sister Leena."

Russ frowned. "You never told me you had a sister. It's nice to meet you," he said, turning toward Leena and shaking her hand with enough force to make her wince. "Would it be okay if I stole Sue Ellen away for a few moments?"

"Sure, take her," Lulu said.

"How long has she been dating the coach?" Leena asked her sister's friends once Sue Ellen was gone.

Lulu's eyes widened. "She's dating the coach?"

"Never mind," Leena hurriedly said. "Forget I said anything. My bad." She'd had several today.

"Tell us everything you know about your sister," Lulu demanded. "Starting with the coach."

Skye spoke first. "If you paid more attention to things outside of Cosmic Comics, Lulu, then you'd know that Sue Ellen and the coach have been seeing each other for a couple weeks now." Turning her attention to Leena, she said, "Let's talk about you."

"I don't use cosmetics from companies that do testing on animals," Leena quickly assured her. "And I don't wear fur."

"I'm glad to hear that. I want to know what we said to make you cry earlier."

Leena looked away. "I told you, I've got allergies."

"Right."

"I don't cry in front of people."

"Maybe you should."

Leena blinked. "What?"

"Maybe you should let your emotions out sometimes instead of keeping them all bottled up."

"Skye's family is into that kind of touchy-feely stuff," Lulu told Leena. "Except for their grandmother Violet. She rocks."

"I met Julia and your mother Angel at the clinic today," Leena said. "Well, we weren't formally introduced or anything, given the situation."

"Cole's a good guy," Skye abruptly said.

Leena wondered where that comment came from. She was having a hard time keeping up with Skye's free-flowing topics of conversation. They were all over the map. That must be one of the reasons she got along so well with Sue Ellen, who had a similar communication style. "I heard Cole is very popular with the female population in town."

"We're very protective of him."

"He seems perfectly capable of looking after himself."

"He is."

"Then there's no problem." What a lie. Leena had more problems than she could count. Including her too-sexy boss. But she also had a plan and a time line on her BlackJack. She simply had to follow it and she'd be back on the road to success. Never underestimate the power of a woman with a plan . . .

Of course, she'd had a plan back in Chicago too, and that had blown up in her face.

Maybe she should have stayed in Chicago and gotten a job as a barista at the local Starbucks, but the thought of someone she knew seeing her handing out skinny espresso macchiato solos had sent her into a blind panic.

Far better to hide out in Rock Creek until she was back on her feet.

It was just that Leena had gone from up-and-coming to down-and-out so fast she still found it hard to accept.

Okay, so she wasn't a young ingénue, not some fresh-faced sixteen-year-old. And yes, twenty-eight was considered old in the modeling business. But dammit, she wasn't ready to quit yet.

So she'd stick to her plan. And remember that Julie Andrews quote: "Perseverance is failing nineteen times and succeeding the twentieth."

· · ·

Sue Ellen wondered why the coach wanted to speak to her privately. He'd told her to call him Russ, which she did in public, but privately she thought of him as "the coach." Or the manly man. A manly man respected by the entire community.

Finally Sue Ellen had a chance at something she'd never attained. Respectability. Not that she'd ever admit that desire to her friends.

Sue Ellen was no dummy. She realized what some people thought of her. What *most* people thought of her. That she was outlandish. Strange. But they didn't know her. Not even Skye. Not really.

Sue Ellen knew that Skye didn't care what anyone else

thought of her. Sometimes Sue Ellen wished she could be more like that. Because caring could hurt big-time.

No, Skye and Lulu wouldn't understand. Neither would Leena.

But that didn't matter because Sue Ellen knew what she wanted and she wanted it so much that it made her downright nervous. She'd never been this nervous. Not since her divorce ages ago. She'd been stupid to marry Earl as a teenager, but at least she'd been smart enough to dump him.

She never thought about the divorce or Earl these days. So why now? What was up with that? Sue Ellen wiped her damp palms on the knees of her daisy-printed cropped pants, pausing to admire the tiny yellow daisies painted on her acrylic nails.

She could do this. She could snag the coach. She *would* snag the coach.

"Did you hear what I just said?" Russ asked.

"Sure I did." Sue Ellen hated admitting otherwise.

"And what's your answer?"

She stalled. "What do you want my answer to be?"

"Yes."

"Well then my answer is yes."

"Great. So you can have four dozen cupcakes baked by tomorrow morning and ready to bring to the high school bake sale by 7 a.m., right?"

Bake? That required an oven, didn't it? Sue Ellen stored her scrapbooking materials in the oven. She hadn't turned it on since moving in. Even so, she said, "Sure. No problem."

"Thanks, Susie. I appreciate it."

She didn't have the heart to tell him that she hated the nickname Susie. Instead she smiled as he kissed her cheek right there in front of everyone at Angelo's Pizza. Which was only about eight people, but still . . .

Smiling dreamily, she watched him walk out before turning back to her friends and sister.

• • •

"Four dozen cupcakes?" Leena had wondered why Sue Ellen had followed her home instead of letting her retreat to her own space. "Are you crazy? You don't bake."

"This oven is empty." Sue Ellen slammed it shut.

"Yeah, so?"

"So we can bake in it."

"There's no *we* here. There's only *you*. You can go home and bake in your own oven."

"I can't. I've got stuff stored in there."

"Then take it out."

Sue Ellen shook her head. "No time. We need to get started."

"No. I need to go to bed. I've had a long day and I've got another one tomorrow."

"So do I. I have to have these cupcakes done by to-morrow morning." Sue Ellen reached into her huge purse, pulled out a laptop computer, and turned it on.

"What are you doing?"

"Oh, I forgot. This place isn't wired for DSL Internet connections."

"Why do you want to get on the Internet?"

"They have recipes there. I've seen them. Even copied and pasted them. Never used any, but I might someday." She frantically hit several keys. "But I don't have any for cupcakes in my recipe file here. I don't know where to start."

"By going to Gas4Less Mini-Mart and buying cupcakes."

"They only have doughnuts. I already called them on my cell to ask."

"Why do you need four dozen cupcakes by tomorrow?"

"Because Russ needs them for the bake sale."

"Then let him make them."

"I can't. I promised him I'd do it."

"That was dumb."

"Like you've never done a dumb thing in your life."

"I've done plenty." Coming home to Rock Creek was beginning to look like dumb mistake numero uno.

"Do you know how to make cupcakes?" Sue Ellen asked her.

"No, but there's probably a recipe on a cake-mix box."

"Great." Sue Ellen started opening kitchen cabinets.

"What are you looking for?"

"Cake-mix boxes."

"I don't travel with cake mix. You have to go buy some."

"Come with me."

"Why?"

"For moral support."

"Since when do you need moral support to buy cake mix?"

"Since right now." Sue Ellen manacled Leena's wrist and yanked her out to the car. The giant pink car. A castoff of some Mary Kay salesperson, no doubt.

"I can tell that you don't like the pink Batmobile any more than you liked my Elvises," Sue Ellen said as she peeled out of the trailer park. "But that doesn't matter.

What matters is that I don't let Russ down. He's counting on me. He needs to know that I'm dependable. Reliable. I recycle, you know."

"Which is relevant because . . . ?"

"Because it proves I'm a responsible person."

Leena was concerned at how much her sister cared
about Russ's opinion. She was also concerned at how
fast her sister was driving. They made it to the mini-
mart in record time.

"Cake mix. Remember we're looking for cake mix."
Sue Ellen sounded like a drill sergeant barking out orders.
"Don't get distracted by the Doritos or the Twinkies.
Twinkies aren't cupcakes. Tastykake chocolate cup-
cakes *are* cupcakes, but they don't have any. Let's fan
out. I'll take this side of the store, you take the other.
Run, run, run!"

Leena didn't have the energy to run, but she walked
at a brisk pace past plastic-wrapped packages of bread,
cans of ravioli, and boxes of frozen burritos.

Oooh, they had the low-fat Ben and Jerry's Cherry
Garcia frozen yogurt. Good find. She opened the freezer
door and almost smacked Cole in the face with it.

"Sorry." She quickly closed the door. "Did I hurt
you?"

"Were you trying to?"

"Of course not! What kind of question is that?"

"You had a rough day at the office today. I wouldn't
blame you if you came out of the situation with a little
unresolved anger."

"At the parakeet maybe. Not at you."

"I'm glad to hear that."

She tore her wandering gaze from the solitary carton
of Cherry Garcia frozen yogurt still inside the freezer

and focused on Cole. He was wearing a white T-shirt beneath a light blue shirt and jeans. He had a sexy stubble thing going on. It worked well for him. Gave him a more dangerous bedroom look and made her forget about the Cherry Garcia. Until he opened the freezer door and reached for it.

She put her hand on his arm. "Mine."

"Only in town a few days and you're staking your claim on me already?"

"I meant the Cherry Garcia. It's mine. I was reaching for it when you interrupted me."

He held the carton in his hand. "Possession is nine-tenths of the law."

His reference to law reminded her of lawyer Johnny and how all men were dirtbags beneath the outward charm.

"How much do you want this Cherry Garcia?" He held it just out of her reach.

"Not enough to do whatever you have in mind."

"How do you know what I have in mind?"

"I can read you like a book, Pet Boy."

"Is that so, Princess?" He shifted so that her back was up against the glass front of the closed freezer door beside them. "Then what am I thinking right now?"

She glared at Cole. Or meant to. Instead she was unexpectedly sidetracked by his eyes. Maybe it was the blinking florescent overhead lighting in the back aisle of the mini-mart. Maybe it was the intensity of his gaze. Or maybe it was his proximity. But there was something new in his eyes. She could handle the wicked twinkle in his baby blues, but this was hot and seductive.

Her breath caught. Her knees wobbled. Her entire

body buzzed like that defective florescent light humming overhead.

"Come on." His voice was low and more potent than the thickest hot fudge. She could feel it vibrating through her when he spoke. "Come on."

Leena was very close to coming, right there in the frozen-food section of the mini-mart, Cole's body pressed tightly against hers.

"What am I thinking?"

Thinking? Who could think at a moment like this?

"Do you want me?"

Oh yeah. Big-time. She shifted her legs against his denim-clad thighs. Very, very big-time.

"Want me to . . . tell you?" His warm lips hovered just above hers. "What I'm thinking?"

She licked her lips, her tongue almost touching his mouth. She was melting. Not in a wicked-witch-of-the-west kind of way, but in a swirling-ice-cream-in-the-summer-sun kind of way. Totally melting.

"What are you two doing back here?"

Leena was so far gone that it took her a second or two to register her sister's voice. Not that Sue Ellen was speaking quietly. Her sister had only two levels: loud and louder.

The question was delivered in her louder voice.

Leena didn't even realize she'd raised her hands and placed them on the middle of Cole's chest until she lowered them and banged her elbow on the door handle to the freezer.

Swearing under her breath, she was released from the spell. Okay, the fact that Cole stepped away from her probably helped her free-fall return to reality.

Not one to overlook an opportunity, Leena grabbed the carton of Cherry Garcia from his hand. "Here's what I'm thinking," she said. "That this frozen yogurt is mine."

"Did you find the cake mix?" Sue Ellen demanded.

Leena shook her head.

"Come on. We're moving out." Sue Ellen had returned to drill-sergeant mode. "We've got to hit the Wal-Mart up by the interstate. The clerk told me they've got plenty of Tastykake chocolate cupcakes there. Easier than cake mix. No ovens involved."

"I've got to pay for this first." She held up her Cherry Garcia, holding on tight just in case Cole tried any sudden trick moves to swipe it from her.

"Well, hurry up." Sue Ellen impatiently tapped her foot, which was clad in a nice pair of knockoff Jimmy Choos now that Leena took a look. Normally she noticed things like another woman's footwear. But things hadn't been normal in her world for several days now.

That had to be why Leena had that momentary wild reaction to Cole. Even now, she was still somewhat under the influence, thinking he looked entirely too sexy for her peace of mind.

She worked for the guy. Sex and bosses never mixed well. Sex *with* bosses was a definite no-no and a rule she'd never broken. Never been tempted to. Until now . . .

Chapter Five

. . . .

"**What's** taking you so long?" Sue Ellen's question was accompanied by a pounding on Leena's bathroom door. "We're losing light outside."

They'd survived the cupcake incident and had now moved on to Sunday and the modeling incident. Leena wasn't sure she'd survive this one. She called through the door, "What kind of costume is this supposed to be?"

"You're supposed to be a Regency miss. You know, like in those movies. Bride of Prejudice.

"Do you mean *Pride and Prejudice*?"

"Whatever."

Leena stared at her reflection in the full-length mirror nailed to the back of the bathroom door. The dress was . . . She lacked words.

"What's wrong?" Sue Ellen pounded again, making

the mirror wobble. "Do you need help with the costume? Is it too small?"

Leena yanked open the bathroom door. "What do you think?"

"Wow." Sue Ellen was clearly impressed. "Did you get new boobs?"

"No, I just can't get them to stay in this dress." Leena tugged the bodice up.

"You look great. Sex sells," Sue Ellen said. "Come on. The photographer is legally blind in one eye so he won't notice if one of your boobs slips out. Just pull the dress up again. I'll let you know if too much is showing. We need to get the ad in the local papers, so the photo can't be too revealing. I'm sure you've done ads showing more than this. What about Victoria's Secret?"

"What about them?"

"They show more flesh than you're showing now."

"So?"

"So you must have modeled for them."

"They don't exactly cater to women my size."

"Yeah, what's with that? Why do they have tons of bras in those little sizes for women who could easily go without a bra?"

"Because they want to coax them into wearing one. Most of us don't have the luxury of having a choice."

"You haven't commented on *my* boobs yet." Sue Ellen thrust out her chest proudly. "Notice anything different?"

Leena shook her head, her gaze remaining focused on her own chest to check the status quo.

"I had a boob job done. Don't tell anyone."

"Who am I going to tell?"

"Gravity was starting to get me down. Not Gravity,

Skye's cat. I mean that invisible scientific thing that pulls everything to the ground, including breasts." She quickly shoved Leena out the door ahead of her. "Ah, Bart." She waved at an older man with a bald head waiting near the photographer. "Here she is. My sister, the model. Leena this is Bart Chumley, the owner of the mobile home park."

"I'm glad to meet you, Leena." Bart stuck out his hand.

Leena kept her own hands crossed and pressed against her breasts. "Excuse me if I don't shake your hand."

Bart frowned. "Is there a problem?"

"No, no problem," Sue Ellen hurriedly stated. "Everything is fine."

"Then why is your sister hugging herself like that?"

"She's a little chilly. She's keeping warm until you begin shooting. Are you ready? Is everything set up? Where do you want her to stand?"

"Let me just check," Bart said before turning to the photographer.

While the two consulted, Leena heard a wolf whistle.

Turning, she found Cole standing nearby. It was bad enough that the man had tried to seduce her out of her carton of Cherry Garcia at the mini-mart, but this was too much.

Infuriated, she marched over to confront him.

"What are you looking at? These? They're just breasts." Leena lifted them together so Cole could get a better view, almost popping her nipples from the confines of the low-cut bodice. "I'm sure you've seen more than your fair share. I happen to be working here and I don't appreciate your sexist wolf whistle."

"I wasn't whistling at you."

"Really?" She looked around, her body language indicating she didn't believe a word he said. "Then who were you whistling at?"

"That bitch over there."

"Hey!" Leena protested.

"Don't go ballistic on me. I was referring to Mrs. Petrocelli's Pekinese. She broke her leg. Mrs. Petrocelli, not her dog Misty, who just slipped outside, which is why I whistled for her. Misty isn't eating so I said I'd come look at her. I didn't come to look at your breasts. I didn't know they'd be on display this way. But now that you've pointed them out to me, I have to say that while it's true I have seen breasts before, yours are . . . very fine. Excellent cleavage."

Leena was accustomed to men looking at her. But not like this. None of them had ever had this kind of powerful effect on her. Cole was touching her with his eyes. Not in a creepy kind of way, but in a very seductive erotic way. Like he had in the back of the mini-mart.

Suddenly Leena couldn't breathe. She felt as if she'd swallowed an Altoid.

Wait—she *had* just swallowed her Altoid!

She didn't dare cough, for fear he'd pound her on the back and her breasts would launch themselves at him, fleeing the confines of her *Jane Austen Does Dallas* dress.

"Are you okay?" Cole asked, perhaps noticing how her face was turning red. She'd soon be turning blue from lack of oxygen if she didn't get some air . . . Thankfully the Altoid finally went down and cleared her air passages.

Stay calm and just breathe, she told herself while

nodding in reply to Cole's question. Of course she was okay.

Well, maybe okay was a stretch. If her life were truly okay she'd be back in Chicago working, not standing here in the Regency Mobile Home Park with a photographer who normally did wedding photos and could pass as Pee-wee Herman's twin brother. And Leena certainly wouldn't be standing here flaunting her cleavage at Cole.

Of course he wasn't whistling at her. What had she been thinking? The world did not revolve around her, as her former agent told her before dumping her.

She felt like the butt of a dumb-blonde joke. In fact, her entire life lately had turned into some dumb-blonde joke. But Leena wasn't laughing.

"Here." Sue Ellen joined them and shoved something into Leena's hands.

"What's this?"

"Double-edged tape. Actresses and singers use it all the time to keep their dresses in place. That should avoid a Nipplegate situation. Lulu told me they had one at the high school a while back. Something to do with a cheerleader. Hey, Cole." Sue Ellen smiled at him. "What are you doing here?"

"Your sister accused me of ogling her breasts," he replied.

Sue Ellen nodded proudly. "They are impressive, aren't they?"

"Hey!" Leena felt her face getting hot. "Next thing, you'll be asking Cole to help me tape them in place."

"Anything I can do to be of assistance." Cole's grin was one-hundred-proof wicked.

"Hold on a sec, I have to take this call." Sounding like

a showbiz mogul, Sue Ellen turned her back on them to answer her pink Motorola Razr phone.

"Don't even think about it," Leena warned Cole as he reached out for the tape. She tightened her grip on it.

"So now you're telling me what I can and can't think? Anyone ever tell you that you're bossy?"

"I prefer to think of it as being sure of myself."

"Right."

"Some men feel threatened by that."

"Not me."

"Right." She deliberately repeated his word choice, right down to the mocking tone. "You're probably used to women instantly obeying your every command. Just like Misty here." Leena pointed to the Pekinese, who was now perched at his feet, gazing up at him adoringly.

"Absolutely," Cole agreed. "And they usually drool too."

The man was too much!

"Yeah," Cole said reflectively. "There's nothing like doggy drool first thing in the morning."

"Don't try to tell me that you only hang out with canine females. I'm sure you've got more than enough human female companionship."

"Can one ever really have more than enough?" Cole countered. "I don't think so."

"No, you wouldn't, would you? You'd think the more the merrier."

"Now you're making it sound like I'm hosting orgies with multiple partners. I feel the need to remind you that my aunt is a nun."

"She must be so proud," Leena mocked.

Far from being insulted, Cole's expression softened with affection before he bent down to rub Misty's ears.

"Yeah, she *is* proud of me. Go figure. So is my other aunt, Nancy. She owns Crumpler's Auto Parts. Both of them will probably drop by to see you soon."

This got Leena's immediate attention. "What? See me? Why?"

"Because they like to look after my best interests."

"Which involves me how?"

"You said it yourself. You've come to town to save me. It's only natural that they'd want to meet the woman who would make such a bold claim."

"Yeah, well, I was only kidding . . ."

"Never kid a nun. They don't take kindly to it."

"I find that hard to believe."

"Not believing . . ." Cole shook his head. "Something else I wouldn't brag about to a nun."

"You're just trying to make me nervous."

"Is it working?"

It was, but no way was Leena confessing that to him, or to his aunt the nun.

"You don't have to answer that," he said.

"I don't intend to," she assured him.

"One more thing . . ."

"I have no interest in anything else you have to say," Leena loftily informed him.

"Are you sure? I really think this is something that would be of great interest to you."

"I am so *totally* not interested that I can't even begin to tell you."

"Okay." He shrugged. "So you're not interested in the fact that I can see through your dress? I thought you might want to know, but hey, it's your call."

"What?!" Leena immediately looked down.

"Your dress," Cole repeated. "I can see through it."

"Where?"

"Pretty much from the waist down."

She lifted her head to fix him with a narrow-eyed glare. "You're just trying to freak me out."

"I'm telling the truth."

"Oh yeah? Then what color is my underwear?"

Only after Cole focused his attention on that intimate part of her anatomy did Leena belatedly realize that this line of questioning wasn't prudent.

"Never mind," she quickly said.

"Pink. Your underwear is pink."

"A lucky guess."

He squinted a bit, highlighting the crinkly laugh lines at the outer corners of his eyes. "Pink with polka dots."

Damn. She knew she should have changed lingerie. One of the premier rules of fashion was to make sure your lingerie enhanced your outfit—not sabotaged it.

Pink polka-dotted underwear didn't go with this wild outfit. She should have worn something nude.

That seemed to be the word of the day.

Appropriate lingerie didn't solve the dilemma of her apparently semitransparent dress. Sure the material was kind of sheer, but when she'd looked at herself in the bathroom mirror it had seemed okay, aside from the how-low-can-you-go bodice.

So what had happened? Had she inadvertently pulled a Princess Diana by standing with the sun behind her like a giant spotlight?

She looked over her shoulder. Sure enough, that was the problem.

Leena quickly changed positions so the sun was at her side instead of behind her.

"Is that better?" she asked before remembering who she was speaking to.

"Depends on your point of view," Cole replied.

"Is this point of view as revealing as the previous one?"

"If you're asking me if I can still see through your dress, then the answer is no."

She heaved a sigh of relief.

"But now you're on the verge of going topless."

Leena frantically looked down.

Cole laughed. "Just kidding."

"Idiot!" Infuriated, she smacked his arm . . . hard.

"Ouch!"

Misty the Pekinese barked protectively, leaping up and down at their feet before taking a mouthful of Leena's dress in her teeth and yanking hard.

Rrrrip.

The next thing Leena knew, her ankle-length Regency dress had turned into a micromini.

"Nice legs," Cole noted.

Leena and the dog both growled in reply.

"That's a cute look," Sue Ellen told her sister as she rejoined them.

Leena growled again. She hated her cottage-cheese thighs. Okay, maybe *hate* was a little intense. They weren't her strong point, was the way her agent had put it in their better days. Her agent's and hers. Not her thighs' better days. Her thighs hadn't had any better days.

The thing that really burned her butt was skinny size-zero models saying they hated their fat thighs. That was just so wrong on so many levels.

On a good day, dressed in the right pair of shorts, Leena could actually feel okay about her thighs. But not today. Not with Cole commenting on her polka-dotted underwear and then her legs. She felt he was mocking her, laughing at her behind her back just as he had when they'd been kids.

She'd already socked him once today. She refused to stoop to his level and hit him again, as much as she was tempted. Besides, the yappy guard dog at his feet might yank off a hunk of her flesh next time.

"I hate to break up your little tête-à-tête," Sue Ellen said, "but we've got to get this photo shoot going."

"I am not having my photograph taken in this outfit," Leena said between clenched teeth.

"I just told you, you look great. Doesn't she look great?" Sue Ellen asked Cole.

Cole nodded. "Really great."

"He looked through my dress." Leena realized how silly her words were the moment she said them.

Sue Ellen frowned. "What are you talking about? He's not Superman with X-ray vision."

"I was standing with my back to the sun and it made my dress transparent . . . Never mind. I told you this dress was a mistake the minute I put it on, but would you listen to me? Noooo. And you," Leena turned her anger toward Cole, "standing there and making fun of me."

"I assure you, I wasn't making fun of you," Cole replied.

"Great legs," she mimicked.

"Thanks," he said wryly, "but mine look better in shorts."

"See, that's what I'm talking about."

He raised one dark eyebrow. "My legs?"

"Your attitude."

"I'm not the one with an attitude. You are."

Sue Ellen clapped her hands. "Children, we're running out of time here. You'll have to continue your bickering later."

"I told you, I'm not being photographed in this dress."

The distant rumbling of thunder reflected the increasing tension in the air. A storm was rapidly approaching.

Sue Ellen cast a worried look at the sky and then at her sister. "But you have to be photographed in that dress. And fast."

"No way!"

Leena stormed off to her trailer. She wanted to place her hands on her butt to make sure her barely there dress covered as much of it as possible, but she refused to show any vulnerability.

Not that showing cellulite was much better.

She climbed the steps to the front door and yanked it open as another much louder clap of thunder made her jump. Only when she was inside did she realize that Cole had followed her. A tide of anger rose inside her, taking energy from everything that had gone wrong in her life lately.

"What are you doing in here? I've had enough of your insulting brand of humor for one day."

Cole was clearly clueless; otherwise, he would have gone running for his life. Instead he stood there and gave her that you're-acting-hormonal look that men sometimes gave women. "If you'd just calm down and listen to me a minute—"

"Why? So you can lie and tell me you weren't making fun of me?"

"I wasn't."

Leena decided to call his bluff. She didn't believe he was attracted to her. There was only one way to prove it.

"Fine." She crooked her finger and beckoned him closer.

He moved cautiously, sensing perhaps that she was up to something.

Her kiss caught him by surprise. She saw his eyes widen a second before her lips met his.

She'd turned the tables on him, and she fully expected him to back up or reject her. She didn't expect him to return the kiss . . . and deepen it.

This wasn't supposed to be happening. This wasn't what she'd planned. The man was a prime-time kisser. A master. He took it slow, as if savoring the very taste of her.

She parted her lips for him. How could she not when he was doing that yummy move with his tongue along the crease of her mouth? Cole didn't rush her in order to stake his claim. But his groan told her he was enjoying this sensual oral exploration as much as she was.

It was almost a religious experience. Like Moses, he'd parted the Red Sea, in this case her red lips. Now he was at the pearly gates, sliding his tongue past her pearly white teeth into the dark dampness of her mouth.

Did the fact that his aunt was a nun have something to do with her weird visuals? Who cared?

He pulled her closer until she was plastered against him, her lush breasts pressed against his muscular chest, his hands sliding down her back to cup her generous bottom.

Blind passion took over all her senses. Mouth to mouth, body to body. His hands speared through her hair, tilting her head to increase the intimacy of their hot kiss. Her hands slid beneath his T-shirt to climb his spine. His skin was so warm beneath her fingertips.

The embrace was quickly spiraling out of control when a brilliant bolt of lightning immediately followed by a deafening clap of thunder made them jump apart.

A second later Sue Ellen and a shivering Misty tore into the trailer.

"It's raining cats and dogs out there. Or dogs and dogs. Here." Sue Ellen thrust the little dog into Cole's arms. "You take her."

Leena lifted trembling fingers to her mouth. Unable to stand there and pretend that nothing had happened, she beat a hasty retreat to the bathroom, where she closed the door and locked it.

But there was no escaping the fact that her pass at Cole hadn't made him retreat, blowing her theory that he was just making fun of her right out of the water. Which left her more confused than ever.

• • •

Sister Mary came knocking on Leena's door later that evening, with a covered dish in hand. "Welcome to Rock Creek."

"I'm not a newcomer," Leena felt compelled to say. She didn't want to be accepting food under false pretences. Especially from a nun. "I grew up here."

"Yes, I know. But you've been gone a long time. You do eat, don't you? You're not one of those anorexic or bulimic models, are you?"

"Do I look like I don't eat?"

"You look normal, but looks can be deceiving."

"I'm not skinny by any stretch of the imagination."

"Does that bother you?"

"She hasn't invited you inside yet? That's not a good sign, is it?" These two comments came from a woman who'd just joined Sister Mary.

"You must be Sister Mary's sister," Leena greeted her.

"Do you like it when people introduce you as Sue Ellen's sister?"

"Well, uh, no," Leena admitted.

"I don't like being referred to merely as someone's sister either. Or as Cole's aunt. I'm Nancy Crumpler."

"I'm sorry."

"Sorry that I'm Cole's aunt? Why's that?"

"No, I meant I'm sorry that I referred to you as Sister Mary's sister. And sorry I haven't invited you both inside sooner." The earlier rainstorm had passed but the air had a chilly edge to it. "Please come in. Would you like some coffee or something?"

"By something are you referring to an alcoholic beverage of some kind?" Nancy asked, then added, "What?" when nudged by Sister Mary. "You don't think we should find out if she has a drinking problem?"

"You seem surprised by our appearance here this evening," Sister Mary said. "Didn't Cole tell you we'd be stopping by?"

"I thought he was kidding."

"And why is that?"

"Well, he, uh, he seems like the kind of guy who likes to kid around," Leena said weakly.

Nancy fixed her with an eagle glare. Not that Leena had ever seen an eagle glare, but if she had, she was sure it would've looked just like Nancy's steely-eyed stare. "And by that you mean . . . ?"

"He told me that both his aunts are very proud of him."

"And why shouldn't we be?"

"No reason." Leena set the covered plate on the dining table. "Would you like some coffee or lemonade?"

"We'd like some answers. What?" Nancy sounded increasingly crabby as Sister Mary nudged her again. "I'm simply speaking the truth. You should be happy about that."

"You don't have to be so blunt about it," Sister Mary reprimanded.

"I don't see her offering any information."

"You haven't given her much of a chance. So, Leena, tell us about yourself. We know you grew up here and . . ." The nun prompted her.

"I'm not a Catholic," Leena blurted out.

"No surprise there," Nancy said. "Tell us something we don't know."

"I make really good mocha madness brownies."

"From scratch or from a mix?" Nancy asked.

"From scratch."

Nancy nodded approvingly. "That's good. What else?"

"I've never made cupcakes."

"I meant something else about yourself besides your baking abilities."

Leena felt as if she were in the midst of the Spanish Inquisition. "Are you two always this . . ."

"Direct? I am," Nancy said. "My sister tends to be a little more . . ."

"Empathetic," Sister Mary suggested.

Nancy turned to face her. "So empathetic that you were giving last rites to a hamster."

"The hamster wasn't dead. I merely prayed for its continued recovery."

"Tell her how many times you've done that."

"Prayed for someone's recovery? More times than I can count."

"I meant prayed for one of Cole's animal patients," Nancy said.

"Why do you care?" Sister Mary said.

"Because it's silly to pray for an animal."

"You think it's silly to pray at all."

"So?"

Leena cleared her throat. "Uh, did you want me to leave you two alone to speak privately?"

Nancy frowned at her. "Why would we want that?"

"Because you seemed to be speaking about private matters."

"Nah, everyone in town knows how we feel. They'll know all about you before long too. That's why we want to know first. Because you're working for Cole now and we always check out his employees. So tell us, why'd you leave Rock Creek and why did you come back?"

Easy questions first, that was always Leena's motto. "I left right after high school to go to Chicago to work as a plus-size model."

"Yeah, I heard that." Nancy frowned. "You don't seem that big to me."

"I'm a size sixteen in a size-zero world."

"There are worse things," Sister Mary pointed out.

Nancy shook her head. "What a nun thing to say."

"I am a nun."

"Yeah, well you're here as an aunt, so try to check your habit at the door."

"We don't actually wear habits . . . Never mind. Go on, Leena. You were saying?"

"Well, I worked successfully for a number of years in Chicago."

"And then? What went wrong?" Nancy demanded. "Something clearly went wrong or you wouldn't have come back here."

"Maybe she missed her hometown and her family."

"Oh, puh-lease." Nancy rolled her eyes. "We're talking about Rock Creek and Sue Ellen here."

"Don't insult my sister!" Leena was quickly losing patience.

"Uh-oh. She has a temper," Nancy told Sister Mary.

The nun nodded. "She's loyal to her sister. That's a good thing."

"And she's getting aggravated by your attitude," Leena added. "Here. Maybe you should take this back." She handed the covered dish back to them.

"She's got gumption. She'll need that to deal with Cole. No, you keep that." Nancy returned the dish to the table.

"It's not Angel's squash cookies, is it?" Leena asked suspiciously.

Sister Mary shook her head. "Of course not. We wouldn't do that to someone."

"How did you hear about Angel's cookies?" Nancy asked.

"Sue Ellen told me."

"Angel's cookies have become pretty infamous."

"There's nothing pretty about them," Nancy noted. "But back to your reasons for returning to Rock Creek."

"And your reasons for wanting to know are?"

"We're concerned about our nephew."

"Because you heard that I punched him as a kid? I won't do that again."

"Will you rip out his heart and stomp on it?"

Leena blinked. "Huh?"

"Just answer the question."

"To use your phrase, Nancy, puh-lease. Do I look like the kind of woman capable of doing that?"

"I think she's referring to the fact that she's a size sixteen," Nancy told her sister.

"Cole could have any woman he wants," Leena said. "And he probably has. Did you interrogate all of them?"

Nancy nodded. "We've tried."

"Why aren't you worried about Cole breaking my heart?"

"He doesn't do that. He remains friends with all his former girlfriends, strangely enough."

"Probably because he's not really committed to them in the first place," Leena noted.

Sister Mary and Nancy looked at her with newfound respect. "A size sixteen and smart. We like you."

"Gee, thanks." Leena's voice was mocking.

"No, I'm serious. We like you. You'll be good for Cole."

"I certainly intend to be a good employee."

Sister Mary frowned. "That could complicate things."

"What? Me being a good employee?"

"No, you working for him. Sexual harassment and all."

"You think I'm going to sexually harass Cole?"

"You wouldn't be the first woman to try. But no, I didn't mean that. And before you ask, no, I didn't mean he'd sexually harass you either."

"He's never had to before," Nancy said.

"He's had affairs with his employees before?" Leena asked.

"No. That's why I said that you could complicate things."

"Getting involved with your boss is never a good thing," Leena said.

"Has it happened to you before?" Sister Mary asked.

"No, and I'm not about to let it happen now. I've got enough problems in my life at the moment. I certainly don't need more."

"Unfortunately life doesn't always go according to plan," Sister Mary said.

"No shit." Leena clapped her hands over her mouth in horror. The words had slipped out before she could stop them.

"I couldn't have said it better myself." Nancy's grin was huge. "For once my sister and I agree on something. You *will* be good for Cole."

But would he be good for Leena? That wasn't something she was willing to bet her heart on.

Chapter Six

. . . .

"I'm going to kill someone!" Leena yelled at Sue Ellen several days later.

Since it was barely seven in the morning, Sue Ellen wasn't really awake, but she did sit up in bed and stare at her sister as if she were an escapee from a horror flick.

Then Sue Ellen yawned and flopped back down.

"Did you hear me?" Leena demanded.

Sue Ellen groaned and put the pillow over her head.

Leena marched over and yanked it away before waving the local newspaper at her. "Did you see this?"

"I don't have my contacts in."

"It's a picture of me. In the ad for the Regency Mobile Home Park."

"Really? Wow, that was fast."

"Fast? I'll tell you what's fast. The lawsuit I'm gonna file against these people."

"You signed a waiver."

"I what?"

"You signed a waiver. Saying they could use the photos."

"But I didn't say they could use *this* photo. I didn't even know they took this."

"You don't have approval over the shots."

"*They* deserve to be shot for using this picture. I'm half naked."

"What does the ad say?"

"Don't get ripped off." Leena read the huge-font tagline. "Buy your mobile home from Regency Mobile Home Sales."

The photo showed Leena waving her hands and looking down at her torn dress.

Or she could have been looking down at her cheesy thighs. The look of dismay on her face would cover either possibility.

"I can't believe they did this," Leena growled.

"I can't either." Sitting up, Sue Ellen took the paper and squinted at it. "They did a really good job."

"Of screwing me over and making me look like a fool. Yes, they did. A really good job."

"You don't look like a fool."

"How can you tell? You don't have your contacts in. Besides, you always see things that aren't there and you don't see things that are."

"Okay, so I said I saw the face of Jesus in the fur of that llama. That was a year and a half ago. Old history. Getting back to your photo . . ." Sue Ellen perched a pair of hot pink reading glasses on the bridge of her nose. "This doesn't look bad."

"Easy for you to say." Leena yanked the paper away. "I think it's awful. *Titanic* proportion awful."

"The face that sank a thousand ships?"

"It's supposed to be the face that *launched* a thousand ships. And that was Helen of Troy, not the *Titanic*."

"Whatever."

"I'm doomed."

"I had no idea you could be this dramatic so early in the morning. You never used to be like this."

"Appearing half naked in the *Serenity News* will do that to a person."

"The ad is actually scheduled to run in all the area newspapers," Sue Ellen said. "Not just this one."

The phone rang before Leena could reply.

"Get that." Sue Ellen plopped back into bed.

Leena grabbed the phone off the bedside table, almost hitting Sue Ellen in the head with it.

"Is this Sue Ellen?" the caller demanded.

"No, it's her sister Leena. Just a second, I'll put Sue Ellen on . . ."

"Wait! It's you I want to speak to. I just saw your photo in the newspaper this morning."

"That wasn't my idea—"

"And I was calling to find out when I'll be getting my royalties."

"Your what?"

"Money. My dog Misty was in that photo. She's a pretty girl, isn't she? But she doesn't model for free, you know. I'd think the least a big model like you could do would be to give her a year's worth of dog food. And not the cheap stuff either."

"Lady, I don't have enough money to pay for my own food let alone a dog's."

"You should have thought of that before you lured my darling baby girl into your decadent photo shoot."

"Your darling baby girl ripped my dress off!"

"Was it one of those tear-off dresses? I hear they have those in Vegas."

"No, it was not a tear-off dress. And if you have a problem with the photo, then I suggest you get in touch with Bart Chumley." That was certainly what Leena planned on doing.

• • •

Sue Ellen tossed and turned but was unable to fall back asleep. She hated when that happened. Or when she had that recurring dream where she stubbed her toe and woke up with a jerk.

When she'd been married to Earl, she'd woken up with a jerk every morning. Her life was much better now. So why was she feeling so unsettled? Maybe because her sister had gone all model diva on her, screaming that she was going to kill someone.

Sue Ellen had stayed up late last night watching one of those slasher movies on cable. Not something she normally did, but lately normal was just a setting on the washing machine, not a characteristic of her life.

Okay, maybe normal hadn't been part of her life since . . . she was four? Maybe growing up with a father who drank led to such an unpredictable life that there was no point in aiming for normal. Or maybe she just thought that unpredictable *was* normal.

Was that why she liked Skye and Lulu so much? Because they weren't normal either? Skye sometimes referred to them all as a band of misfits, but Sue Ellen had never taken that seriously until this moment.

She didn't like the feeling of being a misfit. Her friends seemed to relish the role, but not her. Sue Ellen wanted something else. She wanted the security and respect that Russ Spears represented. Yep, that's what she wanted. That and chocolate.

Yanking on a pair of shorts and a T-shirt, Sue Ellen padded out to the kitchen, where she grabbed a brownie before remembering she hadn't brought in the mail from yesterday.

The pink flower on her flip-flops matched her T-shirt so she felt coordinated enough to step outside. She'd just bitten off another bite of brownie when she heard her name being called.

"Hey, Sue Ellen." Donny waved at her from his Smiley's Septic truck.

She weakly waved back and tried to hide the brownie behind her.

Don't stop, don't stop, she willed Donny. But being a guy, he totally ignored her telepathic message and got out of the pickup with a bouncy step that said this was a man accustomed to early mornings.

"Hey, Sue Ellen," he said again. "What are you doing up so early this morning?"

"Getting my mail."

He got to the box before she could and reached inside to pluck out her stack of bills and then hand them over to her. She put out her left hand to take them. Her right hand was still clutching the brownie and was partially hidden behind her.

"Well, uh, thanks," she said. "Gotta go now."

"Hold on."

She was. Holding on to the iced brownie so tightly that the frosting was starting to squish between her fingers. What a mess.

"What's your hurry?" Donny said.

"I have things to do."

"Can't they wait a minute or two?"

Sue Ellen eyed him suspiciously. "Is something wrong?"

"No. Can't a guy talk to a girl without something being wrong?"

A girl. For a moment he made her feel sixteen. Sue Ellen hadn't felt sixteen even when she *was* sixteen.

But Donny shouldn't be the one making her heart go *Sixteen Candles* fluttery. That was Russ's job.

Sue Ellen glanced down at the stack of mail, relieved to find that the top credit-card bill was Leena's and not her own. At least she wasn't the only one messed up.

Wait, Sue Ellen refused to be messed up anymore. She had a goal. Two goals. Her realtor's license and Russ. And a pair of pink kitten heels from Nordstrom.com. That made three goals. Wait, also redecorating the living room in her trailer. Okay, that made four goals. None of which involved Donny.

"I saw your sister's picture in the paper this morning," he said.

"She isn't happy with it. You'd think she would appreciate the fact that I finally got her shower fixed so she has hot water, but *nooo*. Instead she wakes me up by yelling at me." Deciding she didn't care what Donny thought, Sue Ellen brought the brownie into sight, lifted it to her mouth, and took a bite.

"You've got a smear of chocolate on your mouth."

Before she could protest, Donny reached out and rubbed his thumb over her bottom lip.

Whoa, where did those shivers come from? It was a warm sunny day. No reason for shivers. No how, no way. Not caused by Donny of all people.

He was a good guy. A nice guy. But he was *not* the guy for her. Not the one who was supposed to be rubbing chocolate from her mouth in the morning.

That was Russ's job. So where was the coach when she needed him?

* * *

"You're late. Again." Cole stared at Leena with disapproval, giving no hint of the man who'd kissed her on Sunday as if the end of the world were approaching. What a difference a few days made.

"Do not mess with me today," Leena growled. "I'm having a very bad day."

"Does that mean you saw the ad in today's paper?"

"Yes, Einstein, that's what it means. It also means I left twenty voice-mail messages for Bart Chumley and he still hasn't called me back."

"By the expression on your face, I'm guessing you weren't pleased with the ad."

"Right again."

Cole grinned. "I thought it was great."

"You would. You enjoy making a fool out of me. Or seeing others do that for you."

"So you've accused me before. It still isn't true."

Had she been in a more coherent frame of mind she'd have confronted him about the kiss right then and there. But she needed caffeine more than she needed anything else, so she passed Cole and headed straight for the coffeemaker. He'd apparently put on the first pot himself, so she decided not to go too hard on him—for now.

Then he made the mistake of following her and saying, "I'm not the settling-down type."

"No kidding." She inhaled the coffee fumes before drinking half the cup.

"Women seem to think that just because I'm a vet and I care about animals that I must be all warm and fuzzy."

Leena shook her head. "What idiots."

"Of course, I *am* warm and fuzzy—"

"Yeah, right." She paused, coffee mug halfway to her lips. "Oh, you were serious." She sipped her coffee. "Anyway, I do agree. No way are you the type to settle down."

"Why not?"

"I don't know. Probably some trauma in your childhood or something. Maybe the Peter Pan syndrome."

"I had a totally normal childhood, and I don't have any syndromes."

"Then why ask me why you don't want to settle down?"

"I was asking you why you thought I wasn't the type to do that."

"Because you just told me you aren't." Was the man a few cards short of a full deck this morning?

"Yeah, but you acted like you already knew that before I said it."

"Of course I did. It takes one to know one. I'm not ready to settle down either."

"Why not?"

"I didn't ask you why not," Leena pointed out.

"I'm asking you."

The man was like a dog with a bone. What was his problem? He was the one who brought up this stupid topic to begin with. Obviously this was his way of warning her off after their kiss the other night.

Fine. She got the message. He didn't have to hire a plane and skywrite it overhead. She got it already. Warning understood.

So what gave him the right to question her now? Did he think that she was sitting around panting for him? Not in this lifetime. "Why am I not ready to settle down? Because I've got places to go and things to do. And I certainly wouldn't settle for Rock Creek or anyone who liked living here."

"Because you're so much better than the rest of us, huh? Glad you set me straight on that." The flash of pure Irish Flannigan fury in Cole's eyes was there and then gone a moment later. So was he.

"Where's he off to in such a hurry?" Mindy asked.

"I have no idea."

"He seemed angry."

"You think?"

Mindy nodded before setting down her overstuffed tote bag. "I saw you in the paper this morning—"

"Please stop." Leena held up her hand like a traffic cop. "I already know how bad it is. You don't have to tell me."

"I'd never do such a thing."

"No, you wouldn't." Mindy was much too kind to ever say a harsh word about anyone other than herself. "Sorry. I didn't mean to bite your head off like that. It's just that I am not happy with the situation."

"Which situation?"

"My picture being in the paper."

"But I thought you'd be used to it by now. I mean, you've been a top model for several years now."

Leena didn't know how "top" she was, but in this photo she appeared almost topless. And then there was the matter of her thighs . . . "Yeah, well, I've never had a photo like that done before."

"And that's what is so great. You had the courage to show off your body even though it's not a size zero."

That hadn't been Leena's intent. She'd just been trying to pay the rent. But there wasn't time to correct Mindy's misconception.

To Leena's surprise, the waiting area was filled within five minutes of her unlocking the front door. Strange. She didn't remember seeing that many appointments on the schedule for this morning.

She definitely didn't remember Nancy Crumpler having an appointment. Maybe she thought that since Cole was her nephew, she didn't need an appointment. "Are you here to see Cole?" Leena asked.

"No," Nancy said. "I'm here to see you."

Oh no. More questions. "I really don't have time to talk right now. As you can see"—Leena waved a hand at the people around them—"it's a very busy day today."

"This won't take long. I just wanted to thank you."

"For what?"

"For that photo in the paper this morning. It's about time that someone showed people what a real woman should look like."

"That's why I'm here too," someone else spoke up.

"How many of you actually have appointments this morning?" Leena demanded suspiciously.

Only one person raised her hand.

"We think it's wonderful that you did this," Nancy said. "That you represent the fact that women come in all shapes and sizes."

Leena couldn't believe she was being congratulated for showing off her cheesy thighs.

"You're a model, yet you have a figure," Nancy continued. "And curves. And thighs. Don't get me wrong. I realize there is a problem with obesity in this country. I'm not saying that women should eat until they drop or that they shouldn't be concerned with their health. But *not* eating enough is also an unhealthy situation. Starving yourself." Nancy shook her head. "It's not right. Young girls and women look at the Hollywood actresses with their stick figures and they think that's the ideal. That they should look like that or they won't be popular or pretty. Then you come along and—"

"Look like a fat cow." This comment came from Edie Dabronovitch, who'd just entered the waiting room with her bulldog Princess.

Nancy turned to confront her, as did half a dozen other women.

"Hey"—Edie held up one skinny manicured hand—"don't hate me just because I'm pretty and skinny."

"That's not the reason we hate you," Nancy assured her. "We hate you because you're bitchy and mean."

Edie was outraged. "If your sister the nun could hear you now, she'd be appalled."

"No, she wouldn't. She'd agree with me."

"Ladies, is there a problem out here?" Cole asked as he strolled into the waiting room.

Edie placed her hand on his arm before confiding, "I

was just telling these people that men like you prefer a slim woman to someone who's fat."

"She just called Leena a fat cow," Nancy told Cole.

Edie lifted her chin. "I was just saying what everyone is thinking."

"Say it again and you'll regret it," Leena said in her most dangerous voice—the one she'd used as a kid when someone had insulted her, the one she'd used on a photographer in Chicago who'd come close to assaulting her, the one she used on anyone who crossed the line with her.

Edie backed up. "She's threatening me. You heard her, Cole. What are you going to do about it?"

"Yeah, Cole. What are you going to do about it?" Leena put her hands on her curvaceous hips and confronted him. Yes, she needed this job, but she'd rather work the midnight shift at Gas4Less than be insulted and humiliated any further.

"I'm going to have to ask you to apologize," Cole said.

Leena shook her head. "No way!"

"I wasn't talking to you. I was speaking to Edie."

"Apologize?" Edie was stunned.

Cole nodded.

"Me?"

Cole nodded again.

"For what?" Edie demanded. "Speaking the truth?"

"For being rude to one of my employees."

Edie narrowed her eyes. "Need I remind you that I'm a client here and that I can and will take my business elsewhere."

Cole shrugged. "That's your choice."

Edie's face turned beet red. "And I'll tell all my friends to take their pets elsewhere too," she threatened.

"Who are you kidding?" Nancy said. "You don't have any friends in this town."

"I have some in Serenity Falls."

"No, you don't," Nancy said. "They're tired of your negative attitude in Serenity Falls as well."

At first Leena thought the growl was coming from Edie's bulldog, but then she realized it came from Edie instead. Without saying another word, the woman turned and stormed out, dragging her poor dog behind her.

The minute Edie was gone, the entire waiting room burst into applause.

"Don't you worry about her threats, Cole," one of the women said. "I'll bring all three of my cats here to you."

"I don't even have pets, but I'm sure tempted to go out and get one or two just to support you," another said.

"If you don't have any pets, why are you in a vet's waiting room?" Cole asked.

"Because I wanted to thank Leena here for empowering us all with this picture."

"Really?" Cole studied Leena for her reaction. "She wasn't very happy about it when I told her I liked it."

"You weren't?" Nancy turned to face Leena. "Why not?"

"I, uh . . . I really have to get back to work. The phone's ringing." Leena quickly backtracked to the protection of the U-shaped reception counter. "Rock Creek Animal Clinic."

"This is Sheriff Nathan Thornton. I just got a report of a verbal assault at the animal clinic. Am I going to have to come over there?" he demanded.

She put him on hold. "For you on line one," Leena told Cole.

Chapter Seven

· · · · · · · · · · ·

Cole took the call in his office.

"Hey, old buddy, old friend." Nathan was obviously trying hard not to laugh over the phone line. "How's it going over there at the animal clinic?"

"Just peachy."

"You're sounding a little stressed. Having trouble with the new employee?"

"No."

"That's not what Edie says. I bumped into her on her way out of your clinic."

"Look, she insulted Leena. I asked Edie to apologize and she refused. End of story."

"She claims you verbally insulted her."

"Not true. That would be my Aunt Nancy who did that. And insults aren't illegal."

"So no one threatened Edie?"

"No. Although she threatened me."

"Want to file a countercomplaint against her?"

"Hell, no! And stop laughing. This isn't funny."

"Sure it is."

"You wouldn't think so if you were in my shoes," Cole grumbled.

"But I'm not in your shoes."

"What kind of friend are you?"

"The kind that laughs at you when you're down."

"Gee, thanks. I've got patients to see." Cole hung up. It didn't seem like he'd had a moment's peace since Leena had come to town. Not that he'd had much peace before that. At least Leena seemed to have gotten his appointments in order.

A few moments later, Cole walked into exam room one to find Algee Washington waiting for him. The big black guy had the build of a defensive lineman but the heart of a marshmallow. Algee had opened a branch of his comic-book store Cosmic Comics in Rock Creek last year and was a close friend of Skye's. Over recent months, he'd become friends with Nathan and Cole as well.

"Dang, doc." A diamond stud flashed in Algee's ear as he shook his head. "You got a gang of women waiting out there. Maybe a herd even."

"They're not waiting for me."

"No?"

"No. They're waiting to talk to Leena."

"Your new receptionist? The one that punched you?"

"Who told you about that?"

"I never reveal my sources," Algee said.

"That happened a long time ago. When we were kids."

"You realize that Julia punched Luke once," Algee said.

Cole didn't get the connection. "So?"

"I'm just saying that men in these parts have a record of falling for women who KO them."

"Leena didn't knock me out. She just knocked me down. And it was a sucker punch."

"Yeah, that's what Luke claimed too."

"Luke and I are not alike."

"Because he's a bad boy and you're a doc?"

"No, because he likes the Steelers and I'm an Eagles fan. So, why are you here today, Algee?"

"I, uh, got this cat." Algee undid his jacket to reveal a skinny gray tabby. "Found her in the alley behind my store a few days ago. I just wanted to make sure she's healthy and all. And get her fixed so she can't have kittens. Skye is rabid about that."

Cole examined the cat. "Uh, Algee—"

The outwardly tough guy's face reflected his concern. "Dang." He sighed. "Is she real sick?"

"No, not at all."

"Then she's already pregnant, right? That's what you're telling me."

"Wrong."

"Then what's the deal? Come on, doc, spit it out."

"I'm trying to. First tell me, what's the cat's name?"

"Til-D," Algee said. "Like J-Lo, only different. Because I think she's gonna have a fine caboose on her some day, right Til-D?" He rubbed the tabby's ears and the cat immediately starting purring louder than a car without a muffler.

"Brace yourself, buddy." Cole placed his hand on

Algee's massive lineman shoulders. "I've got a surprise for you."

"I thought you told me she's not sick or pregnant."

"Right."

"Then what's the problem?"

"She's not a *she* at all."

"What?"

"Til-D here is a male cat. And he's already been neutered."

"Are you sure?" Algee stared down at the tabby. "She doesn't look like a tough tomcat to me. She looks like a dainty girl."

"I'm sure."

"Well, dang."

"Is that a problem?" Cole asked. "The fact that the cat is a male?"

"I was just surprised, that's all. So Til-D is healthy?"

"Seems to be. He could use some good food."

"I got shrimp and steak."

"I meant cat food."

"Right. I got that too. She, I mean *he* likes to eat."

"Good."

"You're, uh, not gonna tell anyone about this, right?"

"That you have a cat?"

"That I thought *he* was a *she*. I'd never hear the end of it."

"Kinda like me being punched by Leena, huh?"

Algee got the connection immediately. He didn't need to be told twice. "I hear you, man. I won't say another word about it."

"I appreciate that. I won't say a word either. Listen, have you gone to see Luke and Julia's baby yet?"

"Yeah. There's no hassle in the castle over there. I've

never seen Luke so over the moon. I heard the kid was almost born in your waiting room."

Cole shook his head. "I knew Julia would never allow that to happen."

"The woman does like to be in control."

"Most women do."

"Like Leena out there? Does she like to be in control?"

"She's downright bossy," Cole said.

"I recently met a woman like that too. Tameka Williams. She teaches English at Rock Creek High."

"And she has a cat named Opi after her favorite nail polish."

"I thought she'd name her cat something fancy like Shakespeare or something. Tameka bosses me around, correcting my English, telling me I should think about what I'm gonna say before I open my mouth."

"Think you're up to handling a bossy woman?"

"I am. How about you?"

"Always," Cole said confidently.

"You care to put your money where your mouth is?"

"Always."

"Fifty bucks says I get Tameka to go out with me before you get Leena to go out with you."

"Leena works for me."

"Ah, good point. We need ground rules. No fair threatening to fire Leena if she doesn't go out with you. That would be taking unfair advantage."

"As if I'd take unfair advantage of any female employee."

"I meant it would be taking unfair advantage of me in the bet."

"Oh, right."

"So Leena's job is secure even if she says no."

"I already said I'd never threaten a woman to get her to agree to go out with me," Cole said. "There's no need."

"Yeah, but this is a bossy woman."

"She's still a woman."

"So we're clear on this bet?" Algee asked.

"Totally."

They shook hands.

"May the best man win," Algee said.

"That would be me."

"Hey, I rescue cats from alleys. Women are into that."

"I *heal* the cats people rescue," Cole said. "Women are even more into that."

Algee picked up Til-D and returned the tabby to rest against his chest beneath his leather jacket. "In that case, I better get moving."

• • •

"I'm impressed," Skye told Leena as she leaned against the receptionist counter in the animal clinic's waiting room. "Only in town a few days and already stirring things up. I may grow to like you after all."

"Gee, thanks," Leena drawled. "I'm honored."

"As you should be."

"I didn't come here to stir things up."

"No, you came because you ran out of other options. Been there, done that. Angel and I came here from the West Coast because we had nowhere else to go other than my sister Julia's place."

"I didn't come to mooch off my sister," Leena said defensively before realizing how that sounded. "I didn't mean that you were mooching off Julia."

Skye shrugged. "It wouldn't matter to me if that was what you meant."

Leena remembered Sue Ellen telling her that Skye didn't care what other people thought about her, and apparently that was true. "So what did you mean by saying I was stirring things up?"

"With that photo of yours in the paper. You do know that your sister did an ad in the paper a while back for a local vision center in Serenity Falls, right?"

"No, she didn't tell me."

"You two don't seem to talk much."

"As you pointed out, I've only been back in town a few days. We haven't had a lot of time to talk."

"Everyone is talking about your photo."

"Not my intention."

"Whatever. Anyway, I just came over to see if you'd like to join our belly-dancing class."

"Me? Why?"

"Because having a healthy body image is a good thing."

"By exercising, you mean."

"I mean image. What you think in your head."

"Well, in my head I think my thighs are too big. Not every day, but in that photo for sure."

"Is that what you've been telling people?"

"No."

"Good. Don't."

Leena bristled at being told what to do. "I will if I want to."

"Right. You're right. You're free to do what you want. So what's the deal with you and Cole?"

"Huh?"

"You and Cole."

"He's my boss. What's that got to do with my thighs?"

"I don't know. Why don't you tell me? I heard he was there during the photo shoot."

"Making fun of me."

"Really? That doesn't sound like Cole."

"You know him pretty well, do you?"

"If you're asking if I ever had sex with him, the answer is no."

Leena blushed. "That's not what I meant—"

"Sure it is. Which makes me wonder why you'd care who your boss had sex with . . . unless you wanted to have sex with him yourself."

Leena frantically looked around the currently empty waiting room. Where were patients and their owners when you needed them? All morning the place had been packed. Granted, it had been with women who'd come to tell her how much they appreciated her making a stand about full-figured women, women who had curves.

"I don't discuss my sex life," Leena said.

Skye grinned. "I do."

"So I've heard."

"Your sister does too."

"I'm not my sister."

"Yeah, I know how that goes. I'm not my sister either. Sorry. Anyway the offer to join our belly-dancing class still stands. Think about it. You already know several of the people in the class. Me, Nancy Crumpler, Lulu, your sister."

"I'll think about it."

"And if you want to know anything about Cole, feel free to ask me. I may not have slept with him, but he's Nathan's best friend and has been for years. I have ways of finding things out. By the way, Cole's not seeing anyone at the moment. He just broke up with someone a few months ago."

"I'm surprised he hasn't had several relationships since then."

"I'm taking a break," Cole said from behind her. "Do I want to know why you two are talking about my personal life?"

"No," Leena said. "You definitely do not want to know."

"I think I do."

"Trust me, you don't."

Cole gave her that raised-eyebrow look. "And why is that?"

"A lot of reasons. Look, you've got a customer. Er, client . . . I mean patient." Leena greeted the newcomer with a smile of intense gratitude and relief. "Hi there. Welcome to the Rock Creek Animal Clinic. How can I help you?"

"You can pay my client the royalty she's requested," the young man said.

Leena blinked. "What?"

"Mrs. Petrocelli, owner of the dog named Misty, who appeared in the photo without permission, wants her share of the profits."

"He bit my dress in half and almost bit me. Cole was a witness. Tell him, Cole. Tell him what happened."

Cole sighed. "What are you doing here, Butch? You're not a lawyer. You're a culinary arts student."

"That doesn't pay very well," Butch said.

"Leena, meet my cousin Butch."

"Weren't you a state wrestling champ in high school?" Leena asked.

"Yes, I was. So? You don't think wrestling champs should be interested in good food?"

He looked aggravated enough to put her in a head hold. "I didn't mean that," she quickly assured Butch.

"She says a lot of things she doesn't mean," Skye said. "Don't let it bother you."

"So what's the deal with Mrs. Petrocelli wanting money?" Cole asked.

"She spoke to me about it this morning," Leena said.

"Don't worry about it. I'll talk to her," Cole said. "Sometimes she gets strange ideas into her head."

Butch nodded. "Yeah, strange ideas like making that brussel-sprout-and-strawberry Jell-o mold for the Fourth of July town picnic."

"If you think she's weird then why are you working for her?" Cole demanded.

Butch shrugged sheepishly. "Money. She said she'd give me ten percent of whatever I could get for her."

"What you got for her is a stern reprimand."

"I don't need ten percent of that," Butch hurriedly said. "I'm outta here."

Cole sighed as he watched his cousin leave before turning to Leena and Skye. "Welcome to my crazy family."

"Take a number," Skye said. "My family is much crazier than yours."

Cole grinned. "True."

"Mine's no walk in the park either," Leena said. "Sue Ellen leans toward the drama-queen end of the spectrum."

"What about you?" Cole asked. "What end of the spectrum do you lean toward? The bossy end?"

"The organized end. Despite the craziness in here today, I managed to reorganize your accounts payable files to make them easier to work with."

"Thanks." Cole's smile made Leena's insides go all wobbly and wicked, reminding her of the touch of his mouth on hers.

"To quote your cousin, I'm outta here," Skye announced, pushing off from the reception desk's counter she'd been leaning against. "I just have one thing to say before I go. Get a room, you two."

• • •

"I saw your sister's picture in the paper today," Russ told Sue Ellen after school that afternoon when he met her at the Dairy Queen.

She nodded proudly. "Wasn't it great?"

Russ shrugged.

Sue Ellen was surprised as his response. "What? You didn't like it?"

Another shrug.

"Why not?" A suspicious thought moved at warp speed through her mind, as most of her thoughts did. "Did my sister ask you to talk to me?"

"I hardly know her. Why would she ask me to speak to you? About what?"

"The photo."

"It was a revealing photograph." Russ's disapproval was evident. "I realize you can't control your sister's actions, but it's a shame she had to go and do something like that."

"Like what?"

"Make a fool of herself that way."

"You thought she made a fool of herself?"

"Don't you?"

"I, uh . . ." Sue Ellen shoved away her Blizzard, unsure what to say next. "Leena wasn't real pleased with the photo."

"Wise woman," Russ said.

His comment stung. No one ever described Sue Ellen as wise. Their baby sister Emma had the brains in the family and not Leena, but still . . .

Why did Russ have to put it that way? He made her feel like a dumb blonde. Nothing new for her, true. But still.

Was that destined to be the heading on the scrapbook of her relationship with Russ? *But still.*

Her *still* waiting for him to say how he felt about her. Her *still* waiting for them to have sex. Her *still* waiting, period.

"I'm sorry you didn't like the photo," she said. She wanted to add that she thought it was a great concept, but chickened out at the last minute.

That's when it occurred to Sue Ellen that she rarely told Russ what she thought. Rarely as in *never*.

Why was that? Normally Sue Ellen told everyone on the planet what she thought. She was hardly the shy type.

Was she afraid Russ would disapprove of her thoughts?

Damn right!

Her friend Skye would shoot her if she knew that Sue Ellen was hiding her true self to please some guy.

But Russ wasn't just *some* guy. He was the football coach. And the team had won last season. Which made him a big guy around town.

He was also a college graduate and people looked up to him.

So what if Skye would disapprove of Sue Ellen's tactics. Skye already had a guy. Easy for her to editorialize from the sidelines.

Leena wouldn't approve either. Too bad. Her sister wasn't her keeper. Never had been, never would be. Which was just the way Sue Ellen liked it.

Instead of saying what she thought, Sue Ellen said, "You don't like people making fools of themselves, do you?"

"Who does?"

Sue Ellen's stomach sank through the floor clear down to China. Or whatever country was on the opposite side of the earth from Rock Creek. Geometry had never been her strong suit. Or was it geography? Either one.

The bottom line was that Russ didn't suffer fools gladly or lightly or whatever "ly" word that was. Problem was, Sue Ellen had had more than her fair share of foolishness.

"I know what you're thinking, Susie." Russ reached out to pat her hand. "I know you've made mistakes in your past. But you're beyond that now. You've turned over a new leaf."

She perked up. "I have?"

"Yes. You're on the verge of becoming a respectable realtor. A professional like me."

Her stomach stopped its abrupt nosedive. Russ thought she was a professional. Like him. That she was respectable. Like him.

That was a good thing.

Basking in the glow of his approval, Sue Ellen reached for her Blizzard once more.

● ● ●

"Did you hear that the *Pittsburgh Post-Gazette* is look-ing for the sexiest bachelors in PA?" Mindy asked Leena.

"Hmm?" She was trying to figure out how to retrieve the page for tomorrow's appointment schedule that had somehow disappeared off the computer screen.

"Sexiest bachelor in PA. The paper is running a con-test. Well, I don't know if it's a contest, really, since they don't have a prize or a winner. They are just listing the best bachelors in the state. You send in the guy's photo and tell the readers about him. I thought of doing that for Cole, but I think it would embarrass him."

That got Leena's attention. The words *embarrass Cole* were not ones she often heard. Nothing seemed to rattle the guy. Not kissing her. Not hearing her and Skye talk about him. Not being told they needed to get a room.

As if she'd have sex with her boss. That was tacky. And very risky for job security.

Not that she planned on keeping this gig for very long. Just the summer. Then she was out of here, heading back to Chicago. Or maybe New York this time.

Why couldn't Cole make things easy on her instead of kissing her and trying to steal her frozen yogurt? Af-ter all, she was still trying to recover from the humilia-tion Johnny had caused with his drunken thunder-thighs comment back in Chicago. She didn't need this kind of aggravation from a sexy charmer who looked good with stubble.

If Cole thought having her photo in the paper was such a positive experience, maybe he should feel for himself what it was like not to control a situation. Sure, she was a model and used to having her photo taken. And yeah, she hadn't liked every shot taken of her. But none had left her feeling as pathetic as this one had, despite the town's unexpected response to the picture. She still wished it hadn't been taken.

So let's just see how Cole would feel in the same situation, Leena thought. "Do you have a picture of him?" she asked Mindy.

"He had a professional photo taken for the clinic business cards and website."

"What, the guy couldn't use a cute photo of a little kitten or puppy instead?"

"You didn't let me finish. He did end up going with the kitten and puppy stuff on the business cards." Mindy held one up for her to see.

"Yeah, I forgot."

"Forgot? But you've been handing them out all day with future appointments marked on the back."

"It's been a busy day, okay? So Cole's photo is on the clinic website?"

Mindy nodded. "But he wouldn't like us doing anything with it unless we had his permission."

"Of course not." Leena had no intention of involving Mindy in her plot. Or asking Cole for permission. The whole point was to surprise him.

"So you won't do anything?"

Leena patted Mindy's hand. "You have nothing to worry about."

Mindy sighed. "T-Bone tells me that I worry too much. And he's right. I can't seem to help it."

"What do you worry about?"

"I worry about everything. If I'm being a good wife. What to make for dinner. If I can get the washing done tonight or if I have to wait until tomorrow night. I worry about all the stray animals out there that aren't being cared for. About the pets left in disaster areas and war zones. I worry that I'm not doing enough to make a difference. Did you know that Cole volunteered at the Best Friends Sanctuary in Utah a while back? He claimed he was going hiking in canyon country on vacation, but he spent most of his time helping out with the animals. He also headed down right after Hurricane Katrina to assist with the rescue effort down there. That's where he got his dog Elf. And his three-legged cat Tripod. Plus he kept two spooked black cats abandoned in a box left at our clinic's front door."

"The guy sounds like a saint," Leena muttered. She was beginning to feel guilty about her plans for him. Not that being listed as one of the state's sexiest bachelors was an insult or anything.

"You girls talking about me again?" Cole asked.

How did the man manage to sneak up from behind her so easily? Twice in one day.

"Leena seems obsessed with finding out everything about me," Cole said.

"Wrong." He made her sound like a groupie or something. "People keep telling me all about you."

"Why would they do that?"

"I have no idea."

"Did you tell them that you think anyone who stays in Rock Creek is a loser?" Cole said.

Mindy turned hurt puppy-dog eyes toward Leena. "Is that true?"

"No, of course not."

Cole refused to allow her to get away with the fib. "Yes it is. You told me this morning that you had no intention of settling for Rock Creek or for anyone who stayed here."

"I only said that because you kissed me."

Mindy's eyes bounced to Cole. "You kissed her?"

"In a moment of insanity, yes."

"Total insanity," Leena said. "It was nothing."

Cole nodded. "Absolutely nothing."

"I already said that."

He gave her a pseudoinnocent look. "I was just agreeing with you."

"Well, don't."

"She's been in a bad mood all day," Cole told Mindy. "I've tried to stay away from her—"

"By sneaking up on me?"

"But each time I walk by, she's talking about me. You can understand my confusion," Cole said. "She tells me I'm a loser and yet she can't stop talking about me."

Leena felt the anger shooting through her. Cole was mocking her again. The man was no saint. He was a demon. A lean, mean, sexy demon. A wolf in sheep's clothing. "It's six o'clock. I'm leaving for the day," she said.

Cole just grinned. "Bye. Have a nice night."

"I plan to." Leena also planned on getting that photo of him and e-mailing it the newspaper ASAP. Then she'd see who had the last laugh.

Chapter Eight

· · · · · · · · · · · ·

The next week was a busy one, with Cole handling more cases than usual. Spring was a busy time with annual checkups and vaccines. Thanks to Leena's impromptu supporters who'd witnessed him reprimanding Edie, he'd gotten a half dozen new clients. He liked being busy.

Which is why he was working on his house on his day off. He had three doors to sand and refinish. The Sunday morning sun was warm on his shoulders. May was starting out hotter than usual.

He'd worked up a sweat and was thinking of going inside for something cold to drink when Nathan showed up. "Hey, buddy. Seen today's paper?"

"Not yet. Why?" Cole asked suspiciously. "What are you looking so happy about?"

"Can't a man be glad it's a beautiful day?"

"Some men, maybe. Not you. What's up?"

"I should ask you the same thing. Any news you care to share?"

"I did my first pet-rat castration this week."

"I meant news about you."

"Look, whatever it is, just spit it out. I don't have all day to stand around and figure out your cryptic remarks. I've got sanding to do. Unless you're here to help?"

"No, I just dropped by to say congratulations."

"For what? The rat castration?"

"No, for being named one of the state's sexiest bachelors."

"Yeah, right. Very funny."

"I'm serious. It's right here in the Lifestyles section." Nathan whisked it out and showed it to Cole. "See?"

Cole grabbed it out of his hands. "I don't believe this."

"I find it hard to believe too, frankly. There must be plenty of guys sexier than you out there. What made you throw your hat into the ring?"

"I didn't. I don't know anything about this."

"Then someone else must have nominated you. Maybe one of your ex-girlfriends?"

"No, they wouldn't do that without asking me for permission first, and I sure as hell wouldn't give it."

"Why not? What's wrong with being one of PA's sexiest bachelors?"

They were interrupted by the sound of the phone ringing. Cole let the answering machine pick it up. He could hear it through the open kitchen window a few feet away. "It's Cole, leave a message." Beep.

"Hi, my name is Tiffany, and I saw your picture in the paper this morning and wondered if you wanted to go out. Give me a call. You can find my picture at myspace.com."

The unknown Tiffany rattled off her site address and her cell phone number.

That call was barely finished when the phone rang again. "Hi, my name is Bambi, and I work at the Sugar Shack as a dancer. Anyway, I saw your pic in the paper and thought we would make a great couple. Call me." Another phone number left.

"Looks like you're gonna be a busy man," Nathan noted with a grin.

"How can the paper put my name and picture in there without getting my permission?"

"Did you sign anything without reading it lately?"

"No, only time sheets and office stuff for Leena . . ." Cole paused. "*Leena!* She's behind this."

"So now you know who to thank."

"Or to blame."

"What do you have to complain about? Your phone is ringing off the hook."

"This is payback."

"Payback? For what?"

"Because I liked her photo in the local paper."

"That ad for the mobile home sales?"

Cole nodded. "She was not a happy camper about it."

"And you rubbed her nose in it?"

"I did no such thing. All I said was that she looked great."

"You dog."

"Exactly. The woman is totally irrational."

"Well, she *is* Sue Ellen's sister."

"Yeah, but that's no excuse. Leena is not a scatterbrain or eccentric. She's very good at organizational stuff. The office has never been so streamlined. But when she deals with me, she's totally off the map."

"You have that kind of effect on her, huh? Not able to sweep her off her feet? What is the world coming to?"

"I never said I couldn't sweep her off her feet if I tried." Cole recalled the bet he'd placed with Algee last week. He hadn't done anything about it since then. He'd been too busy. But now that Leena had launched the first attack, it was up to him to think about mounting a counteroffensive. The sooner, the better.

• • •

Cupcakes. Sue Ellen was obsessed with cupcakes. She'd been feeling like a failure ever since she'd made that wild ride out to Wal-Mart to get the Tastykake cupcakes. Russ hadn't said anything, but she'd seen the way he'd looked at her offering compared to the gorgeously iced homemade creations by the other contributors to the bake sale.

Russ was too much of a gentleman to say anything, but she knew what he must be thinking. Trailer-park trash.

Sue Ellen was determined to prove him wrong. She was driven to create the most divine cupcakes ever seen by mankind. Cupcakes that would make Martha Stewart step back in awe. She just had to stop burning them first. Or undercooking them so that the middles were still raw.

Maybe it was her oven. She needed a new one.

She'd just pulled out another batch of defective cupcakes when there was a knock at her door. It was Donny.

"Do you know how to fix ovens?" she demanded, hauling him inside and shoving him toward the appliance in question.

"What's wrong with it?"

"I don't know. It won't make cupcakes. It either burns them or leaves them raw."

"Are you testing them with a toothpick?"

"You test the oven with a toothpick?"

"No, the cupcakes. You stick a toothpick in and if it comes out dry then the cupcakes are ready."

"I never heard of that. Are you kidding me?"

"No. My mom likes to bake."

"Will she teach me?"

"I can teach you."

Sue Ellen had her doubts about that.

"What?" Donny said. "You don't think a guy can make good cupcakes? Stand aside, woman."

He was wearing a white T-shirt and khaki pants today instead of his Smiley's Septic uniform. It was one of the few times she'd seen him in regular clothes. She was a little surprised at how good he looked.

"I heard about your cupcake run to Wal-Mart last week." At her startled look, Donny added, "My mom works there. She said you weren't in her checkout lane, but she saw you."

"I didn't know she worked there."

"She's worked all her life. Being a single mom with three kids was a rough job. She won't let me help her. Stubborn like you."

"Me? I'm not stubborn."

Donny laughed as he spooned her cake batter into the paper-lined cups in the muffin pan.

"What's so funny? I'm not stubborn. Not compared to some people."

"If you say so."

She pointed to his handiwork. "You didn't fill them to the top."

"You're not supposed to overfill them."

"Where does it say that?"

Donny held up the cake box. "Right here. In the instructions."

Small print was starting to look a little blurry even with her contacts in. And she didn't like to wear glasses because Russ had commented on how he didn't like them. She still had connections at the vision center in Serenity Falls. Maybe she should get her eyes tested again.

"So now I just wait and stick a toothpick in it?" She opened the kitchen junk drawer looking for a package of toothpicks.

"I'll wait with you, just to make sure you get it right."

Sore spot. "Do you think I'm dumb? That I can't get anything right, even baking cupcakes?"

"No, I think you're awesome."

"Damn right I am." Sue Ellen placed her hands on her hips and glared at him. "And don't you forget it."

"You're unforgettable, Sue Ellen."

"Right," she scoffed, unimpressed by his words. "Because I see Jesus in the fur of a llama."

"No, because you have a joy for life that is contagious."

"Contagious? Like the flu, you mean?"

"No, like a happy virus."

"So I'm someone who makes people laugh. Like some kind of clown?"

"I'm not saying this right," Donny muttered.

"No, go on. Tell me more. Tell me how you think I'm the laughingstock of Rock Creek."

"Says who?" Donny growled. "I'll deck anyone who says one bad thing about you."

"Why?"

"Because." Donny looked down, his cheeks turning ruddy. "You know."

"Know what?"

"How I feel."

"About?"

"About you."

"Sure." Sue Ellen patted him on the shoulder, easy to do since he was the same height as she. "We're friends."

"We're more than friends."

"Okay then, we're *good* friends."

Donny sighed. "Well, that's a start."

"Do you really think you can teach me to make great cupcakes? Russ will be so proud of me then."

"He should be damn proud of you *now*."

Sue Ellen shook her head. "He's somebody important in this town. He's respected. And I'm going to be respected soon too. When I get my realtor's license and can bake cupcakes."

"Why do you care so much what he thinks?"

"Because he's the man in my life."

"Oh. I didn't realize the two of you were serious."

"Well, we are. Why does that surprise you? You don't think a man like him should be interested in a woman like me?"

"I think any man would be the luckiest guy on the planet to be with a woman like you."

"Aw thanks." She gave him a friendly jab with her elbow. "You're a good buddy."

"Yeah, that's me. A good buddy."

Sue Ellen wondered why he sounded a little bitter

about that, but then was distracted by the sound of the oven timer going off. She couldn't worry about Donny right now. She had cupcakes to perfect.

• • •

Leena couldn't stand the stress. The Sunday morning newspaper had come out listing Cole as one of the state's sexiest bachelors. It was early afternoon already. Surely he knew by now. Someone must have told him. The paper had been out for hours. So why hadn't he come pounding on her door, demanding retribution? Why hadn't he called her on it?

Unless he was too busy fending off calls from other women, now that he was famous. It wouldn't be the first time she'd had a guy dump her once he made it. The road to success left plenty of bruised bodies along the curb. Hers had been one of many.

Not that he could really dump her in a romantic man-woman kind of way, because she was merely an employee of his. An employee that he'd kissed.

He'd certainly been playing it cool all week. Strictly business. She suspected he was still ticked over her dissing comment about Rock Creek.

There was just no pleasing the man. He'd told her he wasn't the type to settle down—this after a few kisses. It's not as if they were a couple or anything.

Flirting came as naturally to Cole as breathing. She'd seen it often enough in the office.

Leena wished he could have seen her when she'd been at the top of her game in Chicago. Her confidence levels then had been off the charts. How quickly that had all changed.

She already knew the psychobabble, that confidence

comes from within and shouldn't be affected by outward events.

But the truth was that even then the confidence had been an act designed to propel her success—and to cover up the darker secrets locked deep within her: the little girl who'd hid in the corner when her father had gotten drunk, terrified that this time he'd do something terrible to them all.

It was a cliché. It was stupid.

Get over it. She'd ordered herself to do that time and time again. But it only drove the scared little girl deeper inside of her, instead of removing her.

Since her return to Rock Creek, Leena had started having nightmares about those traumatic days of her childhood. Being back in the trailer park certainly wasn't boosting her confidence level any.

She was sure of one thing, though. Cole would not be pleased when he found out she'd nominated him as sexiest bachelor.

Which meant she'd have to make the first move. She'd drop by his place with some excuse and see for herself what was going on.

On her way out, however, Leena was sidetracked by the sight of Bart Chumley sitting out on the covered deck of his double-wide trailer. He'd been avoiding her since the photo shoot, and now was her chance to stop and confront him.

"You're a hard man to reach, Mr. Chumley," Leena said as she approached his deck.

"I thought I told you to call me Bart."

"Well, that's the thing, Bart. I have been calling you for over a week now and you haven't answered any of the numerous voice-mail messages I've left for you."

Bart just shrugged. "I never did figure out how to retrieve those things. Doesn't pay to leave me a voice message."

"Now you tell me."

"If you wanted to talk to me, all you had to do was knock on my door."

"Yes, well, you may have heard that I'm not happy about the photo of me that appeared in the ad."

"Really?" Bart was clearly surprised. "I have to tell you it's been a huge success. Sales have doubled this week, and the number of calls has tripled. What's not to like about that?"

Where to begin? "I looked like an idiot."

"Who said that?"

"I say that."

"Well, you're wrong. Like I said, business is great thanks to you. Humor is a very successful marketing tool. I should know. I was a professional circus clown. Traveled with the greatest show on earth—Ringling Brothers and Barnum & Bailey. I'm retired now, but I had a good run. Anyway, I wanted to talk to you about the mobile home community here. Sue Ellen has been making some improvements, but I'd like to do even more. And you can take that suspicious look off your face. I'm not planning on turning the place into a three-ring circus."

"Then what are you planning?"

"I grew up here in Rock Creek. I could have retired anywhere, but I chose to retire here."

"Why?"

"I take it from your expression that you're not a fan of your hometown?"

"You've got that right. I'm only here for the extremely short term, then I'm heading back to Chicago."

"And the big time. You think you're too good for this town, don't you?"

"You have to admit that Rock Creek isn't exactly a boomtown. Not like Serenity Falls, which was named one of America's best small towns."

"My point exactly. Serenity Falls is right next door. What do they have that we don't?"

"A nice town. A park with a gazebo. Sidewalks without cracks."

"They don't have the Tivoli Theater. Have you been inside yet? It's been restored to its former glory. I don't see why the rest of the town can't do the same thing."

"I do. It's a little something called money."

"True. I heard that Skye won the lottery and put her winnings into restoring the theater. Counting on the lottery is not a good business plan, however. Even an old clown like me knows that. But there are things we can do."

"Well, I wish you luck with that." Leena began moving away. The photo shoot was water under the bridge. No turning back on that now. She just had to stay in Rock Creek long enough to restore her funds, then she was so outta here.

"You're involved with the things we can do."

"No, I'm not. Like I said, I'm only here short term."

"But you have big ideas."

She gave him a suspicious look. *Big* ideas. Was he using code to refer to her thighs?

"You have a very expressive face, do you know that?" he said.

"It helps in my modeling career."

"Helped in my career too," Bart noted fondly.

"There's something incredibly powerful about the ability to make people laugh. It's addictive, really."

"Making people laugh was never part of my career plan." Leena just wanted to make sure Bart was aware of that fact, in case he got any more bright ideas for an ad campaign involving her.

"That's a shame, but I can understand your position. Doesn't change the fact that you could help Rock Creek out."

"I don't see how." Or why she should even want to.

"What aggravates you so much about this town?"

"The fact that we're always the ugly stepsister in the fairy tale. That's true of the trailer park too."

"Mobile home community."

"Whatever. The people with houses in town look down on the people here at Regency, and we in turn look down at the people over in the Broken Creek Trailer Park. There's a pecking order in modeling too. Super-models look down on runway models, who look down on catalog models. And they all look down on plus-size models like me. There's a pecking order in life and Rock Creek is near the bottom."

"What would it take to move us up the ranks?"

"A lot of money. And before you ask, I don't have any or I wouldn't be here."

"I figured that much out for myself. This town has good bones. It just needs a makeover."

"Then contact one of those makeover shows."

"That's an idea. But in the meantime, what cosmetic improvements can we do around here?"

"Ban the cement-geese lawn art."

"Not a fan?"

"No. The gardens are nice and a good idea. Maybe have a contest to see who has the nicest garden here at Regency. People are competitive. That might get them moving. And if you're going with a Regency England theme then an English cottage garden would be a good idea. Maybe a community garden down by the creek. In town, you could suggest that the businesses on Barwell Street put out whiskey tubs of flowers on the sidewalks in front of their storefronts. And pull the weeds from the cracked sidewalks. And paint the peeling lampposts. Get the football team to help out as a community service project."

"All wonderful ideas. I knew you'd have plenty."

"My sister knows the football coach. She could probably ask him. You should talk to her about that."

"*You* should talk to her."

"Not my job."

"So you're not speaking to your own sister?"

"I am speaking to her, just not about this. The renovation of Rock Creek is your baby."

"It takes a community to restore a town."

"It would take a miracle to restore this town."

"Yet you had a series of wonderful ideas," Bart said. "You must have given it some thought, whether you realize it or not."

No way. Leena refused to believe that. She had enough on her agenda without taking on the huge project of improving Rock Creek. And the first item on her agenda was checking up on Cole.

Saying her good-byes to Bart, she headed off in her Sebring.

Leena stared at the slightly ramshackle Victorian

house behind the animal clinic. A sign on the front door ordered GO AROUND TO THE BACK, so she did. And knocked on the door. "Hello?"

She heard the sound of power tools inside but no reply. Another knock and the door swung open to reveal Cole, wearing jeans and a gray T-shirt with the sleeves rolled up, leaning over a door on a pair of sawhorses in the middle of the kitchen. He had his back to her, tool belt around his waist, hanging down his lean hips and drawing her attention to his butt.

Her mouth went dry as she found herself unable to look away from his body. Up and down her eyes kept traveling, devouring him as if he were a Krispy Kreme doughnut. No, too sweet. As if he were the finest dark chocolate. Hard chocolate. She licked her lips.

He wasn't just standing there motionless. No, he was moving—thrusting forward and retreating back before thrusting again.

He was hot. Very hot. And he was making her hot. Very hot.

Cole turned his head to look at her before turning off his sander and removing his safety glasses. "I was wondering how long it would take you to get here."

It took her a moment or two to refocus her brain cells from his body to his words. "Excuse me?"

"Is that your idea of an apology?"

"An apology? For what?"

"You know what for."

"Why don't you tell me?"

"Sexiest bachelor in Pennsylvania. Ring any bells for you?"

"Really? You were selected?"

"You didn't think I would be?"

"All I did was send in the paperwork."

"I knew it!" he said. "I knew you were behind this."

"What's the problem? Don't you like having your picture in the paper?"

"I'm not a model. You make a career of having your picture taken. I make a career out of saving animals' lives."

"Yet another way of your saying you're so much better than me."

"You're the one who thinks she's better than anyone else. The one who would never settle for Rock Creek or anyone who lives here."

"And you're the one who kissed me and then warned me off, telling me you're not a settling-down kind of guy. You know, instead of giving me a hard time, you really should be thanking me," she said.

"You think so?"

"Yes, I do think so."

"Far be it from me to disappoint you." Cole set down his power sander and started undoing his tool belt.

"What are you doing?" Her voice sounded raspy.

"I was sanding the kitchen door. I did the others outside, but this one is too big to fit through the back doorway."

"No, I meant your tool belt." She shifted nervously, keeping the exit within easy access yet unable to look away from his hands or the rest of his anatomy. "Why are you taking it off?" And what else did he plan on removing? A glimpse of tanned skin between his T-shirt and his jeans made her go all jelly-kneed.

"So that I can thank you."

"You, uh, you could have thanked me with it on."

"No, I couldn't." He moved closer, bracing his hands

on the butcher-block kitchen counter on either side of her, effectively pining her in place.

"What do you think you're doing?" She sounded all Marilyn Monroe breathless, like one of those ads for 1-900 phone-sex lines.

"Getting ready to thank you." He lowered his head to nibble the circumference of her mouth. "Are you ready to be thanked?"

She nervously licked her lips. Big mistake. The tip of her tongue touched his lips and she was a goner. He French-kissed her. Latin-licked her. Yummy.

She slid her hands through his hair, noticing for the first time that he was just the right height for her. They fit together so well. Felt so good she had to shift against him—denim against denim.

He slid his hands beneath her top and undid her bra. The man clearly knew his away around lingerie. Before she could ponder on that fact, he'd cupped her bare breast in the palm of his hand and brushed his thumb against her nipple.

She could feel the hardness of his arousal through the placket of his jeans. A moment later she found herself perched atop the counter, her thighs opened wide, her denim skirt scooched way up, allowing him to move even closer against her.

Cole braced one hand on the back of her head as he continued kissing her, and she kept kissing him right back. But that left his other hand free to travel to new territory. Up her bare thigh beneath her skirt to brush the damp silkiness of her underwear. The friction was nearly overwhelming. So was the edgy pleasure he was creating with his fingers, tempting her without following through.

Hooking her fingers into the waistband of his jeans, she tugged him closer and wrapped her legs around him, capturing him as he'd captured her. Her Naughty Monkey sandals slipped off, but she didn't care. Cole and the rush of pleasure he was giving her was all that mattered.

His index finger crept closer to the elastic edge of her panties. Knowing he was deliberately taunting her, she returned the favor by nibbling on his lower lip and rubbing her hand against his arousal. She got the top fastener on his Levi's undone but then had to stop to catch her breath as he finally reached the spot, the silken nub that was aching for him.

He'd just completed one sweet sweeping caress, leaving her quivering on the brink of an orgasm, when the back door banged open and Skye raced into the kitchen. "Come quick. Lucy is in labor!"

Chapter Nine

. . . .

Leena quickly unwrapped her legs from Cole's thighs and slid off the counter to stand shakily on her own two feet.

Who the hell was Lucy? A former girlfriend? What was it with the pregnant women in this town—first Julia and now Lucy?

"Is she a friend of yours, Cole?" Leena asked.

"Oh, get over yourself," Skye said. "Lucy is a llama."

Of course she was. Cole was a vet. But that had been the farthest thing from Leena's mind. Up until a moment ago she'd known only that she was in the arms of one of the state's sexiest bachelors, his talented fingers on her clitoris. Naturally she still wasn't thinking clearly.

"You two can make out later," Skye said. "We've got to get out to Angel's farm."

Leena panicked, remembering all too well Skye's

sister Julia going into labor in front of her. "I don't know anything about birthing llamas."

"That's why you're staying here," Skye said.

"At Cole's house?" Leena asked.

"Here in Rock Creek."

"Right. You're right. I wouldn't be any help at the farm. Not with a llama. Mindy can help you with that, right?"

"Mindy is out of town this weekend."

Leena gulped and made a tentative offer. "If you need . . . I mean, if you really need help, I could . . ."

"You can stay here in Rock Creek," Skye said.

Leena nodded so fast she got a crick in her neck. "Right."

Cole remained silent, gathering up a black vet bag and—much to Lenna's surprise—showing virtually no sign that he'd had his tongue in her mouth and his hands all over her a few moments ago. How did he do that? How did he recover so quickly? Still, a quick glance at the enlarged placket of his jeans told Leena that she wasn't the only one still throbbing with unsatisfied lust.

He and Skye were gone before Leena could say another word.

She'd leave too, as soon as she was sure her legs would support her long enough to walk to her car. She stood there, hanging on to the kitchen counter like a survivor of the *Titanic* clinging to the edges of a lifeboat.

What had just happened here? Okay, besides the obvious physical stuff—which had been damn awesome.

But what else was going on? What was she thinking, making out with her boss, on his kitchen counter, no less? Real classy.

"Mrrow?" Leena looked down to find a gray cat winding around her leg. A three-legged gray cat.

Did it need medical attention? She was familiar with cats, but not one with special needs. "Uh, the vet's not here right now. Can you come back later?"

The cat plopped onto its side. Leena quickly squatted down. "Are you okay? Can I get you something?"

"Mrrrroooow."

"Do you want your tummy rubbed?" Not wanting to spook the kitty, Leena slowly reached out. The cat's fur was surprisingly plush. And her purr was incredibly loud. "You like that, huh?"

"Tripod loves having her tummy rubbed," Sister Mary said as she walked into the kitchen. "Midnight and Buddy are the shy ones. And Elf the dog too."

If Sister Mary had come a few minutes earlier, she would have caught Leena and Cole making out like randy teenagers. Leena had been embarrassed at being caught by Skye, but that was definitely preferable to being caught by a nun. A nun who was Cole's aunt.

"What are you doing here with Tripod?" Sister Mary asked.

"Petting her."

"Where's Cole?"

"He had to go treat a llama in labor."

"Lucy?"

"Yes, I believe that was her name."

Sister Mary nodded. "And he left you here by yourself?"

"I did offer to help, but he and Skye didn't seem to need assistance."

"So how did Cole take his newfound fame?"

Leena gave her a confused look.

"Sexiest bachelor in Pennsylvania," Sister Mary prompted her. "There's a rumor going around town that you nominated him."

"I, uh . . ." Was it a sin to lie to a nun even if you weren't Catholic? Probably. Time to change the subject, *fast*. "I, uh . . . I've been meaning to return your casserole dish to you."

"You should stop by the thrift shop sometime."

"Right. I've been meaning to do that too." Pause, pause, pause. Awkward silence. "I, uh . . . Did you know that Bart Chumley, the guy who owns the Regency Mobile Home Park, is a retired clown?" Brilliant. What did that have to do with anything?

Sister Mary showed no signs of thinking Leena was acting in a bizarre way. Instead she nodded calmly. "Yes, actually I did know that. Since coming back to town, he's been visiting sick children at the hospital. They love seeing him in his clown costume and makeup. What have you done for the community since you came back to town? Aside from nominating my nephew for sexiest bachelor."

"I never said I did that."

"You never said you didn't."

The nun was good. Hard to slip anything past this sister. "Bart is interested in improving Rock Creek and making it more like Serenity Falls."

"Why would he want to do that?"

"Because Serenity Falls is listed as one of the best small towns in America."

"That town is ruled with an iron fist by a mayor obsessed with the height of the grass on people's lawns."

"Well, half the houses here don't even have any grass left in their front yards."

"So?"

"So you're saying Rock Creek doesn't have problems?"

"I'm saying they can't be solved with a few cosmetic improvements."

"Why not? A coat of lipstick, some eyeshadow, and a little mascara work wonders on a girl's confidence." Wait, did nuns wear lipstick? Or eyeshadow?

"Confidence comes from within."

"Not all the time. Sometimes you have to fake it."

"Is that what you do? Fake it?"

"Doesn't everyone?" Leena countered.

"No." Sister Mary's expression turned sad.

Or was it pity Leena saw there on her face? That possibility totally freaked her. Had it come to this? She was so bad off that a nun was pitying her?

"Well, I'd better get going," Leena said briskly. "I'll leave you to lock up or whatever."

As Leena hurried out, she reminded herself that she'd better keep her own inner emotions tightly locked up while back in town or the results could be disastrous, making her crumble like one of the dozen Pecan Sandies she'd eaten last night.

She and Cole had absolutely nothing in common.

Okay, they had lust in common. Sexual chemistry beyond anything she'd ever experienced. But that was it. They had different goals in life. Opposing goals. He wanted to stay in Rock Creek. She needed to leave. He was a charmer with commitment issues. She'd already had her heart stomped on a few months ago.

Sounded like a recipe for happily *never* after.

• • •

"Isn't she just the cutest thing you ever saw?" Angel asked, gazing at the little *cría*. The fuzzy baby llama was nursing.

"What about your new baby granddaughter?" Cole asked.

"Julia's baby is cute as well. Lucy, you did a great job," Angel cooed to the momma llama. "You too, Cole. Good job."

"Thanks. Lucy here did all the hard work."

"The woman usually does," Angel said.

"What are you going to name the *cría*?"

"Enya. Had she been a boy I would have named her Bob Dylan."

"Good thing she's a girl then."

"You don't like Dylan?"

"I'm a country fan myself. You know, like Rascal Flats."

"No, I don't know, but I don't judge others' taste in music," Angel said. "Or in other things. Despite hearing rumors that concern me."

"What are you talking about?"

"Leena. Your new receptionist. She has very stressed chakras. Her colors are powerful yet muddled. I know you're not that into chakras, but I had to tell you. This one could break your heart."

"Do I seem like the kind of guy who gets his heart broken?"

"You appear to have avoided that misfortune so far, but you can be lucky only so long."

"Luck has nothing to do with it."

"What do you mean? That you deliberately don't open yourself up to a relationship?"

Cole shifted uncomfortably. "Look, I know you like talking about this stuff, but I don't."

"It's not *stuff*. It's the most basic element in the world."

"I thought oxygen was the most basic element. Or was it hydrogen? Where is my chemistry trivia when I need it?"

Angel gave him a reproachful look. "I'm being serious here."

"I know you are. But trust me, there's no need to worry about me. You keep your energy focused on Lucy here and her baby and this new business of yours. It really does seem to be taking off. And the farm looks great."

"I'm so glad we moved here. Tyler and I are much more comfortable in this location, closer to Mother Earth."

"It's a nice place." Cole looked around at the surrounding hills, alight with so many shades of spring green he couldn't even count them all. Angel had bought the farm after her business, Angel Designs, had taken off. He didn't know the details, just that she was a New Age entrepreneur more accustomed to failures than success and that she used yarn from the woof of her llamas and others to create scarves and stuff. Not something he'd ever think someone could make big bucks on, but apparently if Nicole Kidman wore it, then everyone who was anyone wanted it. And they didn't care how much they paid for it.

That didn't make much sense to a Levi's guy like him. Now Leena . . . she was into that kind of stuff. He might not know the name of the designers who made her clothes, but he sure wanted her out of them fast. Only years of practice at separating himself from his emotions in order to do his job as a veterinarian kept him focused on the task at hand and not on Leena's lush body. But now that his work here was done . . .

"Nice here?" Angel belatedly said. "It's nirvana here." That's what she'd named her farm.

"Catchy name."

"Are you ever serious?"

"I'm serious about the animals I care for."

"And that's it?"

"It's enough."

"Is it?"

"Yeah. I haven't exactly led a hermit's existence, you know. I've had a number of relationships with members of the opposite sex. And while it's true they all ended, they ended well and most of the women still consider me their friend."

"While I'm glad that you haven't hurt anyone, I'm sad that you haven't found what you're looking for."

"The only thing I'm looking for at the moment are my keys. Ah, here they are." He gathered his bag and headed for his red Ford F-150 truck.

Angel followed him. "If you'd like, I could read the runes for you and let you know if this Leena is going to cause trouble for you."

Cole already knew she was going to cause trouble. The only question was, how much.

• • •

Leena was driving over to the mini-mart for Cool Ranch Doritos when she got the call from Sue Ellen.

"You have to come over here right away."

"Over where?" Leena asked,

"The Broken Creek Trailer Park."

"Why?"

"Just come. It's important." She rattled off an address and hung up.

Leena was tempted to ignore the call, but there was no telling what was going on. Maybe it actually was something important. She couldn't imagine how, but it could happen.

Broken Creek Trailer Park hadn't changed much in the past decade. No lawn art here. Instead, a pair of rusty lawn chairs sat beside a discarded washing machine. Torn window screens were lined with Christmas lights that had never been taken down. Broken-down beater cars on their last gasoline gasp sat beside several trailers.

The address Sue Ellen had given led her to a trailer that was tidier than most. When she knocked, Lulu answered the door. "Welcome to our domain. Come in."

Leena hesitated. Not because of the I SEE DUMB PEO- PLE T-shirt Lulu was wearing along with a black-studded dog collar and black cargo pants, but because of the fact that Sue Ellen was standing behind Lulu and grinning like a maniac. That grin was never a good sign.

"Get in here." Sue Ellen yanked her inside. "Don't worry, Jerry isn't home."

"Jerry?"

"Lulu's granddad. His nickname is Animal. He's covered in tats."

"Tats?"

"Tattoos."

"I know." Leena was still trying to gather her thoughts. "I think I met him my first day in town. He was bringing someone's parrot in to the animal clinic."

"He loves animals. That's why he got the nickname of Animal. That and the fact that he was pretty wild in his younger years," Lulu said proudly.

"What was so important that I had to come right over?" Leena asked.

"This." Sue Ellen went to the Formica kitchen table and picked something up.

"What is it?"

"The Remote-Control MegaMax."

Leena frowned. "It looks like a vibrator."

"No, it's much more than just a vibrator. It's your new best friend. Tell her, Lulu."

"It's wicked awesome."

"What's going on here?" Leena said.

Lulu snapped her gum before answering. "You've heard of Tupperware parties, right? Well this is a Sexware party. To introduce you to Sexware's wonderful line of adult sex toys."

Leena laughed. "You're kidding, right?"

"Look, I don't name the product," Lulu said.

Sue Ellen threw her arm around Lulu. "She's just starting out in this new business venture and I said we'd help her."

"Skye was with us earlier," Lulu added, "but she had to go because Lucy was in a labor."

"Yeah, so I heard."

"Cole wasn't answering his phone so she went over there . . ." Sue Ellen's eyes widened. "You were there. At Cole's? You were. Don't bother denying it. I can tell by the look on your face. Did Skye interrupt you two?"

"Anyone ever tell you that you have an overactive imagination?" Leena said.

"An overactive imagination is a good thing to have along with the Remote-Control MegaMax," Lulu said. "Or the RCM as I like to call him."

Normally Leena would have walked out right then and there. But her body was still all wound up and humming with unfulfilled lust. Maybe this was fate's way of stepping in and preventing her from doing something with Cole. Maybe she should use the RCM to satisfy her needs.

"Satisfaction guaranteed," Lulu said. "If you're not happy, very happy, just return it within thirty days—"

"I'll take it."

Lulu blinked her black-lined eyes. "You will?"

"Yes." Leena gave Lulu an aggravated look. "Isn't that what you wanted?"

"Yeah but . . . you don't even know how much it is."

"How much is it?"

"Only $19.99."

"Fine." Considerably more than a bag of Cool Ranch Doritos, but more effective hopefully at taking care of her sudden lust-fest for Cole.

"Don't you want to know how it works?" Lulu asked.

"I can read the instructions. There are instructions, right?"

Lulu nodded, still unable to believe she'd made a sale.

"Here." Leena handed her a twenty and took one of the RCM boxes.

"Wait. Don't you want to see the edible chocolate panties?" Sue Ellen asked.

"No thanks."

"How about the vibrating panties?"

"I'll pass. Bye." A minute later, Leena was in her car and driving away, the RCM on the seat beside her. "I got out of there pretty fast, huh?"

Okay, talking to Cole's cat was one thing. Speaking to a remote-control vibrator was something else again.

• • •

Of all the times for Mrs. Schmidt to stop and chat, it had to be today. She'd lived in the Regency Mobile Home Park for as long as Leena could remember. She loved wigs and blush. Today the wig was red to match the twin circles on her tanned and wrinkled cheeks. "Yoo-hoo, Leena! I haven't had to chance to talk to you since you got back home."

She couldn't let Mrs. Schmidt see the MegaMax. Leena panicked and frantically looked around her car for something to cover the box with. Kleenex, too small. A roll of paper towels, grabbed and discarded. She searched the backseat and found a blanket she'd meant to take to the laundry. She quickly tossed it over the box just as Mrs. Schmidt came over to lean inside the open passenger-side window.

"What have you got there?" the older woman asked.

"I, uh . . . a sick animal. I'm taking care of it for Cole. Don't come close. It might bite you."

"What is it?"

"A cat."

"I like cats. Maybe I can help."

"No. It's a dog."

"But you just said it was a cat."

"My mistake." No, her mistake had been thinking she could return to Rock Creek and not have her life filled with embarrassing moments like this.

"Well I like dogs too."

"Stay back." Leena gathered the box closer, cradling it against her, making sure it was entirely covered.

"It says Max."

"That's the dog's name. I really need to get him inside now. We'll have to chat some other time."

"Come over for some of my tuna casserole."

"Yeah, I'll do that." Leena waited for Mrs. Schmidt to back up and head on home, but she showed no sign of moving.

"Want me to open the car door for you and Max?" Mrs. Schmidt asked.

"No, I can do it."

"Nonsense. You've got your hands full there."

Leena clutched the MegaMax closer. Why hadn't she thought to ask for a bag or something before leaving Lulu's? A plain brown paper bag would have been ideal.

"Have you spoken to your mother lately?" Mrs. Schmidt asked as she opened the car door for Leena.

Leena shook her head and kept her attention focused on keeping the box covered.

"Well, the next time you do, be sure to tell her I said hi."

"Will do."

"I heard Mrs. Petrocelli tried to sue you using Cole's cousin Butch. He's not a lawyer, you know. He's attending culinary school."

"Uh-huh." Fifteen more steps and Leena would be at the front door.

"I didn't approve of Mrs.Petrocelli doing that and I told her so. I stuck up for you."

"That was nice of you."

"It's the least I could do. I mean, I've known you since you were a baby. Your sisters too. Things have changed a lot around here since those days."

"Uh-huh." Four steps to safety.

"Want me to open the front door for you? I hope you locked it."

"I did." Leena juggled the box to stick the key in the lock. That's when the blanket slipped.

Mrs. Schmidt stared at the Remote-Control Mega-Max displayed on the box and looked at Leena. "That looks like one sick puppy."

"It's a gift for someone else," Leena said lamely.

"Then you should have gone for the Remote-Control Ultra MegaMax," Mrs. Schmidt said with a wink. "Enjoy."

Four hours later, Leena still hadn't recovered from that episode. She also still hadn't deciphered the instructions, which were more complicated than building the space station. She wasn't about to ask Lulu or Mrs. Schmidt for assistance. Or Sue Ellen either.

Maybe she should have gotten the vibrating panties instead.

She'd gotten the batteries inserted properly, but no matter what buttons she pushed, it just sat there.

She had a robe on, underwear off, and was all ready for the big guy to do his satisfaction-guaranteed satisfying. Instead he was a big disappointment and she was rapidly getting out of the mood. Gee, just like real life.

Maybe the batteries were old. She had more in the kitchen. Taking the vibrator and remote with her, she left the bedroom. She got the batteries and sat on the couch to take the old ones out and replace with new.

A pounding on the front door almost rattled the vibrator out of her hands.

"I know you're in there," Cole said.

"Go away!"

He pounded again and the damn door just popped open, revealing her sitting on the couch. She tossed the vibrator onto the coffee table and quickly covered it with the newspaper lying there. The one with Cole's picture in it.

"I need to talk to you," Cole said.

"This isn't a good time."

"It won't take long. Come on, Leena. Let me in."

"Okay but—"

He was sitting next to her on the couch a second later. She tugged the robe a little closer around her. His hair was still damp from a shower and he smelled really good. She was acutely aware of the fact that she had no underwear on. Which distracted her from the fact that the remote was still on the couch between them.

She grabbed for it. Of course, that's when the Mega-Max decided to work. The newspaper shook and hummed.

Cole's attention moved from her to the coffee table. "What's that?"

"Nothing."

He moved toward the paper.

"If you touch that, I will have to kill you."

Something in her voice made him hesitate and lean back.

"You came here to talk, so talk."

Hard for him to do when the demonic MegaMax now refused to turn off. She frantically pushed more buttons on the remote.

"Give it to me," Cole said. "Maybe I can help."

"No! I don't want anyone to help! I just want to be left alone!"

"Uh, maybe we should talk another time," he said, belatedly realizing she was not in the best of moods.

"Great idea." She practically shoved him out the door, locking and bolting it behind him. Then she lowered the blinds.

"All right, you worthless pile of sex technology, it's just you and me now." Grabbing the still shaking vibrator in one hand and the remote in the other she headed for the bedroom. "Put up or shut up."

The Remote-Control MegaMax responded . . . by dying. Just like Leena's hope of getting any satisfaction that night, or any other night she remained in Rock Creek.

Chapter Ten

. . . .

Leena hadn't had the Monday jitters since she was in middle school. But she had them big-time the next morning. She had yet to decide how to treat Cole. She'd caught a break, sort of, last night when he'd left without discovering the remote-control vibrator on her coffee table. She was sure she would never have heard the end of it if he had found out what was under that newspaper.

But she was still faced with the dilemma of how to handle their make-out session in his kitchen yesterday. Would he refer to it? Should she? Was that why he'd come see her last night? To warn her again that he wasn't the settling-down type?

Should she take the first step and assure him that it was nothing? Act like a woman of the world instead of one who'd had her heart bruised and broken before coming to Rock Creek? Not that she was still pining over Johnny, but she sure wasn't looking for any more romantic entanglements. And Cole was as *entangled* as a guy could get.

The bottom line was that there were certain similarities between Johnny and Cole. Both men were good-looking charmers. Both had commitment issues.

Nope, she definitely was not in the market for romantic entanglements. She just wanted to get her modeling mojo back and get out of town ASAP.

Before she did something foolhardy like having sex with Cole.

Leena arrived at the animal clinic a few minutes early and was greeted by Mindy at the back door. Good. There was safety in numbers. Cole couldn't say anything with Mindy present.

"Have you heard the news?"

Leena's heart stopped. "What news?" Had Mrs. Schmidt told everyone about the MegaMax? Or had Skye talked about finding Cole and Leena making out in his kitchen? Or had both R-rated news flashes hit town?

"Cole was listed as one of the state's sexiest bachelors," Mindy said.

Leena sagged with relief. "Yeah, I heard that."

"You did it, didn't you?"

Did it? With Cole? Yeah, almost but not quite. Had Skye been talking? She was hardly the quiet type. Odds were Skye had talked.

"You're the one who nominated him, right?" Mindy said.

Realizing that Mindy was referring only to Cole's new sexiest-bachelor-in-PA status, Leena let out the breath she'd been holding and simply shrugged. She had no desire to discuss the ad.

Instead she opened the clinic and chatted with the clients about their pets. They all had stories to tell.

"Sarge and Gunny work together." Tina Demato smiled and shook her head at the two terriers lying at her feet. "Gunny is afraid of heights, so he moves a chair over to the kitchen counter. Then Sarge jumps up on the chair and the counter to get any food that I might have left out. I couldn't believe it until I saw it with my own eyes."

"My Doberman Dobie ate my fiancé's engagement ring last year," Tony Kreutz said. "I brought him right in and Cole saved him. Saved the ring too."

Leena preferred the dog stories to the phone calls from women looking to meet Cole. He refused to take any of them, making her write down messages instead. Payback for her putting him in the newspaper.

After the first twenty, she told the women that he'd just eloped and was no longer on the market.

"Then his picture shouldn't be in the paper. That's false advertising," one disgruntled seductress wannabe complained.

Leena was happy to keep busy. When she wasn't answering the phones or welcoming the clients, she "redecorated," hanging up posters on the waiting room wall—a yellow HOT TEMPERATURES CAN BE FATAL TO YOUR DOG on one side and a blue DON'T LEAVE ME IN HERE—IT'S HOT! on the other. She placed an adorable framed print of golden retriever puppies in the middle. She'd found everything just sitting in the storage room, waiting for her to make the place look better.

She couldn't do much about the gray plastic chairs in the waiting room or the standard venetian blinds on the front window. But, thanks to the thrift shop, she'd added a nice valance in shades of yellow and blue that spruced

things up. And she'd moved the local no-kill shelter do-
nation station up to the reception area where clients
checked in and out, which made it more visible and thus
increased the spare change dropped in it.

Yeah, she liked getting things accomplished. It prevented her from dwelling too much on Cole and the mu-
tual seduction scene in his kitchen yesterday. She'd felt
the sexual chemistry brewing between them, but she
was still surprised by how fast things had gotten out of
control—hard and wild and raw. She got all hot and
bothered thinking about it, so she tried not to.

Having completed her "redesign" of the waiting room,
Leena spent the rest of the day avoiding Cole by working
on the accounts payable files. While doing so she couldn't
help noticing how great her latest manicure looked; she
loved the burgundy-toned nail color Mai over at Mai's
Nails had selected for her. She also couldn't help noticing how many outstanding invoices there were. And how
many file folders were marked with his notes—"Pays with
fresh stuff from garden" or "Pays with snowplowing."

How did the man ever expect to get ahead with that
kind of attitude?

She paused to run her fingers over Cole's handwrit-
ing before catching herself. She was getting all sappy.
Next she'd be writing his name hooked with hers and
putting little hearts around it.

Not allowed. She couldn't afford to lose sight of her
main goal—regaining her modeling mojo. She also
couldn't afford to have her heart broken again.

• • •

Sue Ellen stared down at her Blizzard and wondered
where the coach was. He said he'd meet her at four at

the Dairy Queen and here it was a quarter after four and
no sign of him. The coach valued punctuality.

Had she done something wrong? Something to upset
him? They'd gone out to see a movie at the Tivoli over
the weekend and everything had seemed fine. He'd
kissed her at the end of the evening and fondled her
breast just as he always did. No change. Nothing new.

Not that she wanted something new. She was perfectly happy with the coach. She'd totally forgotten
about the vibe she'd felt when Donny had wiped chocolate from her mouth.

Another ten minutes passed before she saw the coach
pull into the Dairy Queen parking lot. "Sorry I'm late,"
he said as he slid into the seat across the table from her.

"That's okay. I hope you don't mind that I got my
Blizzard without you."

"That's fine. They've got too many calories for me.
I've got to start watching my weight."

Sue Ellen instantly lost her appetite. "Me too."

This was where the coach was supposed to jump in
and say that she was perfect just as she was. Instead he
said, "Maybe you should join me in running a few laps
around the track at school."

She shoved her Blizzard away.

"Something wrong?" the coach asked.

Sue Ellen shook her head. She wasn't ready to have
the talk with him just yet, but she realized that talk was
going to come at some point in the next few weeks. The
where-is-this-relationship-going talk. She needed to lose
some weight first.

She also needed to figure out how to use the Remote-
Control MegaMax. Hey, if it was good enough for her
model sister, it was good enough for her. And orgasms

burned up calories, didn't they? Did sex with a vibrator count? Because it didn't look like she was going to have sex with the coach anytime in the near future.

He was a gentleman. That's why he didn't push her into going to bed with him. That or he thought she was too fat to see naked.

She eyed the Blizzard, wanting it so badly that it almost hurt. Her mouth was dry. Her heart was racing. Not because of the coach but because of the smooth ice cream concoction. She was a Blizzard addict. She had to have it.

Her hand reached out. She caught the disappointed look he gave her and instantly returned her hand to her lap, gripping her fingers together.

"Something wrong?" he asked again.

Sue Ellen shook her head.

"What do you think about running laps with me?"

"Okay."

Sue Ellen was having two conversations at once—one with the coach and one with herself. The one with herself was the more interesting of the two.

Why don't you tell him the truth? Tell him you want to run laps as much as you want a root canal. Why can't you stick up for yourself? You're such a doormat. He walks all over you.

He does not, she answered herself. *He's concerned about me. About my health.*

Why doesn't he ever take you out somewhere nice? Why do you hang out at the Dairy Queen?

"Are you ready?" he asked.

"For what?"

"Heading to the track now."

"Right now?"

"Sure. No time like the present, right?"

As Sue Ellen followed him out of the Dairy Queen, she cast one last longing look at her half-finished Blizzard. The present wasn't looking all that great and she was beginning to have doubts about the future as well.

• • •

"I'm glad you decided to join us," Skye said as Leena accompanied her sister to belly-dancing class after work that evening. The cinder-block walls of the Rock Creek Community Center, like the town, looked a little worse for wear.

Leena had decided it was time to face Skye head-on rather than avoiding her and living in fear of what she might say. There was no way Skye could know for sure how intimate Leena and Cole had been when she'd interrupted them yesterday. It's not as if they were rolling around naked on the floor or anything—though that would have happened a few minutes later, probably.

Besides, Leena needed to work off steam after spending the day with her own version of McDreamy. The *work*day. When she should have been focusing on work. Not on how hot Cole was. Not on the curve of his lips or the downward slant of his bedroom eyes. And certainly not on the fly of his faded jeans.

That was a real no-no.

But Leena hadn't been able to help herself. Which was why she was here. To help herself. To regain some control. Back in Chicago she'd visited the ritzy health club Oprah belonged to at least three times a week.

No wonder she'd never been able to afford a bigger apartment. She'd spent so much money on clothes and accessories and the health club that there wasn't much left over.

Since returning to Rock Creek, Leena had fallen into some bad habits: inhaling Cool Ranch Doritos, Hostess Ding Dongs, and Ben and Jerry's Cherry Garcia frozen yogurt. Not all in the same bite, of course. That would be yucky.

As yucky as lusting after the boss? her inner critic demanded in a snotty voice reminiscent of one of the meanest contestants on *America's Next Top Model*.

Lusting was legal. There was no law against lusting. No law against acting on that lust either.

Okay, right, there was no *law* requiring her to say no. But there was a little something known as common sense. Leena needed her paycheck as her ticket out of town.

So she couldn't afford to fall into bad habits. She needed to resume her modeling regime, which meant exercising. Belly dancing burned off four hundred calories, or so Sue Ellen had told her before hauling her in here.

There was only one problem. Well, there were many, but only one pertaining to belly-dancing class.

"I'm really not dressed for this," Leena said, looking down at her tailored black pants and plain white T-shirt.

"I brought something for you. Your T-shirt is fine." Sue Ellen reached into a huge leopard-print bag and pulled out a pair of pink floral leggings. "I've kept them with me in case you ever wanted to join us."

Leena knew she'd look like Laura Ashley wallpaper if she wore those. If only she had her yummy Eileen Fisher workout clothes with her. But she'd left them in the storage unit back in Chicago, figuring there'd be no use for them here in Rock Creek.

I used to have a life.

The thought hit Leena hard.

And she'd get that life back, she vowed. *Fake it till you make it.* That was her motto before and it was still her motto now.

Leena quickly changed in the bathroom and returned to find Skye—looking slim and athletic in a cropped T-shirt and black yoga pants with a coin-covered scarf wrapped around her hips—making some hip moves that Leena doubted she could ever manage in this lifetime or any other.

"Leena, you know several of the people here," Skye said, not pausing in her moves as she went on with the introductions. "You've met Nancy Crumpler, Cole's aunt. And Lulu. And this is my grandmother Violet."

A Betty White clone in a powder blue jogging outfit came forward to shake hands. "My granddaughter Julia went into labor at your place of employment."

"On my first full day at the job." Leena nodded. "Not something I'm likely to forget."

"Yes, well the Wright women do have a certain reputation for walking a little on the wild side. Except for me," Violet added modestly.

"Don't kid yourself," Skye said, finally stopping her hip swivels before turning to face Leena. "Violet is just as infamous as the rest of us. She was almost arrested for frog assault."

"You assaulted a frog?" Leena stared at Violet. She looked like such a sweet white-haired old lady.

"No, she assaulted a bad guy with a frog," Skye said. "Fred the Frog, to be exact."

"I caught him," Sue Ellen bragged.

Leena frowned. "The bad guy?"

"No, silly. The frog. Remember how I used to catch

them from the creek out behind the trailer park—I mean, the mobile home community?"

Leena nodded.

Skye proudly pointed at Violet. "But it was my grandmother here who was the real star of the confrontation."

"Along with Fred the Frog," Sue Ellen said.

"Fred who? Who are you all talking about? My hearing-aid battery died again." This complaint came from an elderly woman wearing purple sweatpants and T-shirt.

"This is Fanny Abernathy," Skye said, raising her voice to continue the introductions. "She lost her hearing using power tools without proper ear protective gear."

"And who are you?" Fanny asked Leena.

Sue Ellen leapt in to answer for her. "This is my famous sister Leena, the plus-size model."

"You don't look plus-size to me," Fanny said, giving Leena the once-over. "I saw a story on *Access Hollywood*, or was it *Entertainment Tonight*? One of those shows. Anyway, they had a three-hundred-pound American model working in Paris. She was plus size."

"Models that are size ten or larger are considered plus size," Leena explained.

"Says who?" Fanny demanded.

"The business. The clients who hire models want a certain look."

"The emaciated look." Fanny shook her head. "I remember when women were women. The classic Hollywood stars like Betty Grable and Ginger Rogers had curves. My favorite was Olivia de Havilland."

"Mine was Loretta Young," Violet said.

"Mine was Katharine Hepburn," Nancy said. "Now there was a classy dame."

"How about that blonde that married Humphrey Bogart? What was her name . . . ?" Fanny frowned, trying to remember.

"Lauren Bacall," Violet said.

Fanny nodded. "She had curves. She was slinky but she had curves. All those movie stars did. Not now though. Now you can see their bones showing through their skin on their rib cages and their backs. It's not natural and it's not healthy. Especially when young girls are looking up to them as role models."

"I read a recent study that showed eighty percent of ten-year-olds worry about their weight," Nancy said. "Society does that. These kids view celebrities who are painfully thin and think that's what they should look like. Skeletons. It's so unhealthy."

"It's not society; it's the media," Skye said. "They are the ones that show those images over and over again, on magazines and TV."

"Personally, I think it's those white foam take-out containers. You know, that terrible squeaking noise they can make?" Sue Ellen shuddered. "I feel ill just thinking about it. Makes me want to hurl."

Yet again Sue Ellen had her own vision of the world around her. A vision no one else seemed to share.

Leena had first realized Sue Ellen was . . . *unique* when an eleven-year-old Sue Ellen had told a four-year-old Leena that Sue Ellen was really the secret love child of Prince Charles of England while Leena was a baby their parents had found in the junkyard and brought home. A few months later, the story was that aliens in their UFO had come to visit Sue Ellen and that they'd wanted to take Leena away, but Sue Ellen had talked them out of it.

For six months after that, Leena had panicked every time she saw lights blinking in the night sky; her mom finally assured her they were only airplanes, not UFOs.

The stories had trailed off once Sue Ellen turned twelve but were replaced by wild New Year's resolutions. At age thirteen Sue Ellen announced she was going to be a teenage millionaire that year. When that didn't come come to pass, the next resolution was that she was going to marry a millionaire when she turned eighteen. Instead Sue Ellen had run away and married Earl a day after her eighteenth birthday.

Leena hadn't seen much of her sister for a few years after that. Once Sue Ellen divorced Earl, she moved back home for Leena's senior year in high school. Leena hadn't made resolutions, hadn't bragged she was going to be a model someday. Rather, she'd quietly done whatever it took to accomplish her goal.

A goal she'd attained and would recapture again.

"Sorry I'm late." The apology came from a young black woman who hurried inside. She had flawless skin and excellent bone structure. And she had curves. Not as many as Leena, but she was no beanstalk. "I had to speak to one of my student's parents and the meeting ran late."

"Tameka is an English teacher at Rock Creek High School," Skye said. "This is Leena, Sue Ellen's sister. She's joining us in class today."

"Wait a second," Tameka said. "You're Leena? You work for Cole?"

"She's just helping him out temporarily. Because she feels guilty for punching him when they were kids," Sue Ellen said.

"Sounds like that TV show *My Name Is Earl*. Where

he goes back and tries to make up for all the bad things he did so he'll get better karma. Is that what you're doing here in Rock Creek?" Fanny asked Leena.

"Ladies." Tameka clapped her hands and used her teacher voice. "If we can get back to me for a moment. Leena, I have some information regarding Cole that you might find interesting,"

"I know, I know. You heard that Cole was listed as one of the state's sexiest bachelors, right?" Sue Ellen eagerly jumped it to say. "Rumor has it that my sister Leena here is the one who nominated him."

All eyes turned to Leena.

"No comment," Leena muttered, feeling more and more like a stuffed floral sausage in the borrowed pink pants. Faking it was much harder without the proper outfit to boost your confidence.

Violet patted Leena's shoulder reassuringly. "If it makes you feel any better, I think Cole is sexy too."

"Sexy or not, the man made a bet," Tameka said.

"A bet?" Leena repeated.

Tameka nodded. "He and Algee made a bet. About us. You"—Tameka pointed to Leena—"and me. And a date."

Leena was confused. "A date?" she repeated. "They made a bet that you and I would go out on a date?"

"I heard a lot of models are gay," Fanny said in a semiwhisper to Violet.

"The two girls would be lesbians," Violet replied.

The sight of two old women talking about Leena's sexual persuasion freaked her out. She needed to nip this gossip-fest in the bud. "I am not a lesbian."

Tameka rolled her eyes. "Neither am I. That's not what I meant. Algee bet that he could convince me to go

out on a date with him before Cole could get Leena to
agree to go out on a date with him."

"Uh-oh." Sue Ellen eyed Leena nervously.

"Are you sure about this, Tameka?"

She nodded. "Algee spilled the beans himself."

"He's a dead man," Leena growled.

Tameka looked alarmed. "Algee?"

"No. Cole. He's a dead man."

Chapter Eleven

. . . .

"What?" Fanny put her hand to her ear. "What did Leena just say about Cole?"

"That he's a dead man," Violet replied.

"But he's Nancy's nephew. You can't kill Nancy's nephew," Fanny told Leena. "That wouldn't be polite"

"I agree," Violet said with a prim nod. "It really would not be at all polite. Tell her, Nancy."

"I've grown rather fond of the boy even if he does stupid things every now and again," Nancy said with a rueful smile. "How did you get Algee to confess to all this, Tameka?"

"I used my teacher voice on him and he crumbled."

"Algee is a tough guy." Skye joined the conversation for the first time. "He's not the kind to crumble easily."

"Okay, so I may have flashed a little cleavage at him too." Tameka threw back her shoulders proudly. "And maybe used one of those hip moves you taught us. The man was putty in my hands after that."

"Leena could do that too," Sue Ellen loyally said. "If she wanted to, she could make Cole melt and he'd be Play-Doh."

Skye just laughed.

Which did not endear her any to Leena "What?" Leena demanded. "You don't think I could make Cole melt?"

"Cole charms women. Not the other way around. Women don't charm him. They don't have to."

Leena wasn't sure, but that sounded like an insult to her seductress abilities somehow. "Does he make a practice of placing bets about convincing women to go out with him?"

"Not that I know of."

"So that makes you special." Sue Ellen beamed at Leena. "Maybe he was paying you a compliment when he placed that bet with Algee."

"He's still a dead man," Leena said.

"Or you could go talk to him about it," Nancy suggested.

"No." Leena stood firm. "I like my plan better."

• • •

"You did what?" Cole stared at Algee in disbelief.

"Tameka made me do it, doc. Made me tell her about the bet."

"What did she do? Tie you in a chair with electrical tape and threaten to neuter you?"

"No, she wiggled her hips at me."

"I hear you." Nathan smacked Algee on the back.

"Tameka is in Skye's belly-dancing class. That's where she learned that move. And believe me, I know how powerful those hip wiggles can be."

"Man rule number two: Never let a woman make you betray your buddies. You protect their back at all costs."

"Affirmative. A Marine would never have divulged that bit of intel," Nathan said. "But Algee here is a squid. A former navy man."

Algee glared at Nathan. "Two seconds ago you were smackin' me on the back and telling me you heard me."

"I did hear you. I just would never break a man rule."

"I never even heard of this man rule junk. What is all that?"

"The laws of nature in a man's universe," Cole said.

Algee frowned. "What, like gravity or something? And I'm not talking about Skye's cat Gravity here."

Nathan nodded. "Yeah, like gravity."

"Is that some kind of Marine thing?" Algee asked suspiciously. "You jarheads are a weird bunch."

"No, it's not a Marine thing. Not that a Marine would ever break a man rule."

"What about Cole? He was never a Marine. He's a vet—as in veterinarian, not veteran."

Cole waved Algee's words away. "The origins of man rules aren't the critical thing here."

Algee asked, "Do you think Tameka will tell Leena about the bet?"

"How should I know?" Cole's voice reflected his aggravation. "They're women. They don't act logically."

"I thought you two were experts on females," Nathan said. "I guess this must be fate's form of payback."

"You've been hanging out with Skye too long," Cole

said. "Fate has nothing to do with this. This is Algee's way of throwing the bet because he knew he couldn't win."

Algee was not amused. "Say what?"

"You heard me."

"He's not himself right now," Nathan told Algee. "He's got a thing for Leena even though he refuses to admit it."

"I'm man enough to admit I've got a thing for Tameka," Algee said.

"Obviously," Cole growled, "or you wouldn't have given me up to her. A man rule cardinal sin."

"Cardinal sin? Don't you go threatening me with that nun aunt of yours." Algee glared at Cole, who glared right back.

"Okay, men, the way I see it, there's only one thing to do here," Nathan said.

"I already know what to do," Cole said. "Damage control. ASAP."

• • •

Leena was out of Ding Dongs, and Sara Lee's siren call was saying, *Buy banana cake now!* So right after belly-dancing class, she headed for the mini-mart. She needed sustenance before killing Cole.

She really needed three packages of cake—one for now, one for later, and one for "just in case."

She'd just tossed the third box of Sara Lee's finest into her shopping cart when she heard the cashier saying, "Hey, Cole, good to see you. Congrats on that sexiest bachelor thing. I was one of the girls who nominated you, you know."

Leena stared down the frozen-food aisle to the

bleached blonde with dark roots and too much eyeliner at the front of the store. How dare she try and take credit for Leena's actions. Or maybe she was one of Cole's previous conquests? Had he at one time bet someone that he could convince the cashier to go out with him too?

"We're all so happy they picked you," the cashier gushed.

All? How many was Bimbo Girl talking about here? Every female in Rock Creek?

Leena unwrapped a Ding Dong and took a big bite.

The crinkling paper gave her away. Cole followed the sound and located her with those too-sexy eyes of his.

Had he tried to be charming and funny she would have slayed him with a single scathing look. But instead he approached her with an expression of serious chagrin and remorse. Smart move on his part.

"I need to speak to you," Cole said.

Leena shook her head. "Forget it. I'm not at work now. You're not my boss after hours."

"I don't want to speak to you as your boss. This isn't work related."

"No?"

"No. Have you, uh, spoken to Tameka today?"

"Tameka?" If the man thought Leena was confessing what she knew and letting him off the hook, he was off his rocker, as her mother would say.

"She teaches English at the high school and she's in Skye's belly-dancing class."

"So?"

"So I hear you joined the class today."

"Is nothing in this town private?" Leena said in exasperation.

"Not much," the cashier called out with a snap of her gum. "Are you going to buy that Ding Dong?"

Leena guiltily stuffed the remainder of the snack into the package. "Yes. And this too." She blindly grabbed something from the display section at the end of the aisle and headed toward the checkout counter.

"Antifreeze?" the cashier said. "You're buying a bottle of antifreeze?"

"Yes." Leena gave her a defiant look. "Do you have a problem with that?"

"Only if you plan on drinking it to wash down the banana cakes and Ding Dongs," the cashier said. "You're the model, aren't you? Is this what models eat in Chicago?"

"Yes." Leena swiped her credit card through the machine. "It is."

"Did you need me to put these in a bag or did you want to eat them right here?"

"A bag will be fine." Leena wanted to place it over the other woman's head.

"Your credit card didn't go through."

"What?"

"Did you want to try another one?"

"I'll pay for it," Cole offered, reaching into his jean pocket for his wallet.

"No," Leena said. "I can buy my own antifreeze and stuff. Here, try this one." Luckily the second credit card went through, but this meant that she'd reached the limit on the other one already. How had that happened? Probably because Leena had been paying so much attention to getting Cole's accounts in order that she'd neglected her own.

"Here, let me carry that." Cole picked up the anti-freeze.

Leena took possession of the important stuff—the bag with her Sara Lee banana cakes and the Ding Dongs—and headed for her car. "You can keep the antifreeze," she told Cole. "Consider it a gift from me to you."

"Is that your way of telling me that you're going to freeze me out?"

"Is there a reason why I should be freezing you out?" she countered. "Have you done something you shouldn't have?"

"Have you?"

"Me?"

"Yes, you. Sending my name in for that ridiculous sexiest guy contest."

"The cashier in there just told you that she was one of the millions of besotted women who nominated you."

Cole raised an eyebrow. "Besotted?"

"That's right. Besotted."

"So, are you besotted?"

"No." She opened the car door and placed her food treasures inside. "Have a nice night."

"Wait a second. I still need to speak to you."

"I don't need to listen."

"So you did speak to Tameka?" His voice was cautious.

Leena rolled her eyes. "It's interesting how you're trying to dance around the subject without admitting that you placed that stupid bet in the off chance that Tameka didn't tell me about it."

"So you know?"

"Leena knows," Nancy said as she strolled past them

on her way into the mini-mart. "She's not a happy camper. I was there when she heard the news so I can testify to that fact."

"Actually I said you were a dead man," Leena told Cole.

He turned to his aunt for help. "Didn't you defend me?"

"I doubt she's really going to kill you," Nancy said.

"That's not what I meant."

"For a guy who's supposed to be such a smooth talker, you sure have trouble finding the right words when you're speaking to me," Leena said.

"Yeah, I wonder why that is," Nancy said.

Cole gave his aunt an impatient look. "You're not helping here."

"I wasn't really trying to help." Nancy eyed the bottle he was still carrying. "What are you doing with anti-freeze? It's May."

"It's Pennsylvania. The weather can change in an instant. That's why we've got those prognosticators like the Punxsutawney groundhog."

"Too bad the groundhog can't help you out with forecasting the outcome of this situation. Well, kids, I need to get some toilet paper. Try not to get into any more trouble, Cole." Nancy waved as she passed them and went on into the convenience store.

"Yes, Cole, try not to get into any more trouble." Leena slid into her car.

Cole opened the passenger door and got in as well, shoving her grocery bag to the floor.

"Don't crush my goodies!" Leena yelled, taking immediate action.

Someone tapped on the driver's window. "Is there a problem here?"

It was the sheriff. Leena froze, her face inches from Cole's crotch as she reached for her junk food on the floor.

"Hey, Cole, is that an amorous woman on your lap?" Nathan asked.

Leena snapped upright, whacking her funny bone on the steering wheel. Her arm tingled clear down to her fingertips.

"Sheriff, are you harassing innocent women again?" Skye joined them, as did several other people from her belly-dancing class.

"No, ma'am," Nathan replied solemnly. "I gave that up when I met you."

"I should hope so." Skye kissed him and then leaned down to look at Leena through the window before giving her the universal signal to lower the window. "What are you doing out here?"

"It appears like they were making out in the car," Nathan said.

"Guess this means Cole won his bet, huh?" Skye said.

"I can't hear," Fanny complained. "What's going on?"

"Cole and Leena are having sex in her car," Lulu said.

"We are not!" Leena said.

"They got caught before they could do the deed," Lulu translated for Fanny.

"That's not true!" Leena shouted.

"So you two *did* do the deed? Right here in front of the mini-mart?" Lulu was impressed. "Wicked awesome."

Leena turned her irritation to Cole. "Look what you've done!"

"Me? What did I do?"

"If you have to ask, you must not have done it very well," Skye noted with a laugh.

"But he's a nominee for sexiest man in the state of Pennsylvania. Doesn't that mean he's supposed to be good at doing it?" Lulu said.

"What's going on here?" Sue Ellen's strident voice carried over the other chatter. "Why are you all standing around my sister's car? Was there an accident?"

"Leena and Cole accidentally did the deed in front of the mini-mart," Lulu said.

"I don't think it was an accident. I think it was deliberate," Skye said.

"We haven't had this much excitement since Zeke did the funky chicken in the nude out here on New Year's Day," Fanny said, rubbing her hands together gleefully. "That was really something."

Sue Ellen nudged Skye aside to get closer to her sister. "Leena, why are you having sex with Cole in public?"

"Remember, she did say he was a dead man, so maybe she was going to kill him by having sex with him. You know, like those spiders who eat their mates." This suggestion came from Fanny.

Several people began speaking at once. Leena put her fingers in her mouth and let out the kind of piercing whistle that could halt cabs on Michigan Avenue. All at once, the babble stopped.

"I heard that!" Fanny said.

"Good. I hope the rest of you heard it too. And hear this. Cole and I did not have sex in my car. Or anywhere else," Leena added, knowing how Lulu thought. "Aren't you going to say anything, Cole?"

"I didn't plan on it, no. You seem to be handling things just fine."

"Oh, so you were just handling his things, and not going all the way," Lulu said.

"I give up," Leena muttered. "You people are all crazed. I'm out of here." She turned on the car, gunned the engine enough to make everyone back away, and then took off. She was half a block away before she realized Cole was still in her car.

She slammed on the brakes. "Get out!"

He shot her a reproachful look. "Is that any way to speak to your boss?"

"You just told me that you didn't want to talk to me as my boss."

"And we still haven't talked, so I'm not going anywhere."

"Then neither am I." She put the car in Park.

"Fine by me."

"Me too."

It wasn't fine by the driver behind them. Sure, *now* there was traffic on Barwell Street. Any other time and the place was dead, even if it was Rock Creek's main street.

"If you keep blocking traffic, Nathan will show up again and eventually the rest of the crowd will as well." Cole didn't seem the least bit perturbed by the possibility, but Leena had had enough for one day. She put the car back in Drive. "Fine. Talk."

"You don't seem to be in a good listening mood."

"Ya think?"

"I wanted to explain about the bet."

"Go ahead. Give it your best shot."

"Agreeing to that bet was probably a mistake."

Probably? *Probably?* Her anger increased. "If that's your best shot, it sucks."

They were interrupted by Sue Ellen driving up beside them in her pink Batmobile. "Do not upset my sister!" Sue Ellen shouted at Cole. "She might hurt you."

"Who do you think she's trying to protect?" Cole asked Leena with one of his killer grins. "You or me?"

"She's in the oncoming traffic lane. Sue Ellen, you're in the wrong lane!" Leena shouted at her sister. "You're going to cause an accident!"

Fifteen minutes later Leena, Cole, and Sue Ellen were all seated in the sheriff's office, facing an aggravated Nathan.

"I thought Cole was your best friend," Sue Ellen said, shaking her head at Nathan. "I can't believe you arrested his girlfriend and the girlfriend's sister of your best friend. Plus my sister is a famous model. You better not leak this to the tabloids."

"I am not Cole's girlfriend," Leena's voice shook with outrage. "And this is all his fault." She jerked a thumb in Cole's direction.

"I was merely an innocent bystander." Cole had taken a straight-backed chair and turned it around so his arms were braced on the top. "You two ladies were the dangerous drivers."

"I'll tell you what's dangerous," Leena said. "Making bets that you can get me to agree to go out on a date with you."

"She's got a point there," Nathan agreed.

Cole quickly defended himself. "The bet was Algee's idea."

Leena waved his words away. "Sure. Try and blame him when he's not here to defend himself."

Cole pulled out his cell phone. "I can give him a call and have him come over."

Leena shook her head. "That won't be necessary."

"Because you believe me?"

"No, because I want this farce over with as quickly as possible," Leena said.

Nathan slapped Cole on the back. "Go ahead and tell her. Algee confessed and you should too."

"Shut up," Cole growled.

"I don't think you're supposed to say *shut up* to the sheriff even if he is your friend," Sue Ellen said.

"Tell who what?" Leena demanded.

When Cole remained stubbornly silent, Nathan answered on his behalf. "He likes you."

Leena frowned. "Who likes me?"

"My cat Tripod," Cole said with a warning speak-and-you-will-regret-it look at Nathan.

"Come on, Sue Ellen, let's leave these two alone for a few minutes to work things out," Nathan said.

Sue Ellen was reluctant, her expression concerned. "What if things turn violent?"

"Cole would never hurt your sister," Nathan reassured her.

"I was referring to Leena," Sue Ellen said.

"They'll be fine. Come on." Nathan guided her out of his office.

Once they were alone, Cole quickly lowered his head to rest on his arms across the back of the chair.

Leena felt guilty at his seemingly dejected body language. He seemed more vulnerable without his cocky attitude. She was incredibly tempted to run her fingers through his hair.

"I'm sorry," she heard herself saying. "I know you've had a long day and so have I. Plus it's no help that people keep thinking I'm going to beat you up." That had to dent a guy's confidence, even someone as sure of himself as Cole. "I probably shouldn't have said you're a dead man."

Leena watched as Cole's shoulders shook.

Oh no! Had she made the guy cry?

Scrambling to her feet, she moved closer to rub his shoulder reassuringly. "It'll be okay."

He shook his bent head.

"Yes, it will. It'll be okay. This incident is just a minor speed bump really."

When Cole lifted his head and dashed away the tears, Leena felt lower than a glob of dirt on a glob of gum stuck on the sole of one of her Naughty Monkey shoes.

Then she heard a sound. Was it a muffled sob?

Wait a second. That was no sob. That was a choked laugh.

Which meant those tears weren't caused by emotional upset at all. The man was laughing at her.

Leena barely restrained herself from socking his shoulder in retaliation. She *hated* people laughing at her. They'd laughed at her when she was a fat kid. Called her names. Made fun of her. Lard-faced Leena. Big Bottom. Fat Pig.

Tears unexpectedly stung her eyes. And they weren't tears of mirth.

"Hey." Cole leapt to his feet and came toward her.

She retreated until her back was up against the wall holding a bulletin board of wanted posters.

"This isn't turning out the way I planned at all," Cole muttered.

"Do *not* laugh at me."

"I wasn't. I'm sorry. I'm sorry. Oh hell . . ." He kissed her. Tender and sweet, hot and healing.

Her anger should have protected her from him, but he slipped past her defenses. As he always did. She melted, as she always did. She responded, as she always did, her lips parting and her tongue greeting his. She wasn't surrendering as much as becoming totally submerged, drowning in the pleasure he created within her.

Leena moaned her approval as Cole slipped his hand beneath her white T-shirt to caress her breast. Her silky bra amplified his touch, making each brush of his thumb across her nipple even more exquisite.

Leena didn't hear the door open, but she sure heard Skye saying, "When I told you guys to get a room, I didn't mean the sheriff's office. Sue Ellen," Skye called over her shoulder, "your sister is making out with the vet again."

Chapter Twelve

. . . .

Leena managed to escape the sheriff's office with some small scrap of dignity left. But even that was torn away when she bumped into Sister Mary right outside.

"I heard you got my nephew arrested," the nun said.

"We weren't arrested. We were—"

"Making out in the sheriff's office," Skye said, joining them. "And I thought *I* was a bad girl. Here. You forgot this." She handed Leena her Coach bag.

"Making out in the sheriff's office?" Sister Mary repeated. "And you chose that location because . . . ?"

"They can't seem to keep their hands off one another," Skye said.

"Because of the bet," Sue Ellen said as she joined them.

Sister Mary frowned at this latest bit of information.

"They can't keep their hands off each other because of a bet?"

Leena couldn't blame the nun for being confused. She was confused too. What had possessed her to let Cole kiss her that way?

She hadn't merely *let* him kiss her, she'd kissed him back. Avidly. With parted lips and merging tongues. Mega French kissing. His hand caressing her breast.

"No, Cole and Algee made a bet . . ." While Sue Ellen tried explaining, Leena felt the top button of her pants pop off. She watched it roll across the cracked sidewalk and fall down the sewer grate.

The fat girl within her cringed.

That was it. The last straw.

Without saying a word, Leena headed for her car parked a few feet away and retrieved the Ding Dongs, aside from her half-eaten one, and the Sara Lee cakes.

"Here." Leena handed the food over to Sister Mary. "For your food bank."

Sue Ellen stared at her sister in amazement. Leena couldn't blame her. She'd been acting irrationally. That ended now.

Sue Ellen owned the irrational title in the family. Leena was the one with dreams. Emma was the smart one.

That's how it had always been. Until Leena's dreams had come crashing down around her head.

Pride was a painful thing. So was feeling like a loser. Failure hurt.

Using food as a crutch wasn't going to help anything even if it did make Leena feel better in the short term. She needed to stay focused on the long term, to remember what her goal was here.

Yeah, right. And what were the chances that a twenty-nine-year-old washed-up plus-size model could make a comeback?

Leena almost snatched the Sara Lee cakes from Sister Mary's hands.

Instead she returned to her car and drove away. She wished she could just keep driving, right out of town, out of the entire state. But the loser state she was in would travel with her.

Losing was a state of mind. One she couldn't seem to rid herself of no matter how hard she tried. *Fake it till you make it* just wasn't working very well.

So here she was, driving her used Sebring with less than a quarter tank of gas in it, with no place to go. Back in Chicago she would have gone shopping. Or would have gotten an essential well-being massage-and-facial combo at her favorite spa. She'd lived the good life, spending her money the instant she got it. Then her career slowed down and she was spending the money *before* she got it. Then she wasn't getting any money in. Or a mere trickle compared to where she'd been at the height of her career.

And okay, she'd never earned the megabucks that supermodels made, but she'd made good money. *Very* good money. Where had it all gone? On clothes and shoes and massages and pedicures?

Yeah, pretty much. And it had gone really fast.

Regrets. Leena had lots of them. She regretted that those days were gone. She regretted not being more careful about her finances. She regretted being forced to come home with her tail between her legs like a vagrant mutt.

But that was only the beginning of the list. She

regretted being the laughingstock of this stupid town. She regretted making out with Cole.

Did she really? Did she really regret him kissing her?

She sure should. She had enough on her plate without falling for a charmer with commitment issues and a short attention span. Cole was the guy who signed her paycheck. A paycheck she desperately needed for now. And she was damn good at the job. Her organizational skills were still something she could be proud of. At least she was still good at something. She'd turned the chaos of his office into an efficient operation.

So why couldn't she do the same with her own life? Why couldn't she organize the chaos?

Maybe because she didn't rule the world.

She couldn't even rule her tiny corner of the world. She couldn't even rule the Regency Mobile Home Park.

She saw Bart sitting out on his deck as she pulled in. When he waved and called out a greeting, for some reason she stopped to talk to him.

Not just rolling down her window and saying "hi" but getting out of the car and sitting down on the empty chair he patted beside him.

"You look like you could use some cheering up," Bart said.

"Your specialty, right?"

"It is what clowns do."

"Did you always want to be a clown?"

Bart nodded and poured her some ice tea from the pitcher on the table. He had a small stack of plastic cups as if he were expecting company.

"Were you waiting for someone?" she said.

"Yes. You."

"Why?" she asked suspiciously.

"Relax. I just wanted to pick your mind a little. But to get back to your question, yes, I always wanted to be a clown. How about you? Did you always want to be a model?"

"Yeah, but I never thought it would be possible unless I miraculously shrank in half. I'm tall but I'm not tiny. Then I heard about plus-size modeling. Even that is a strange title. Plus size. What is that? The average woman in this country is a size fourteen. We're not plus. We're normal. I think the skinny models should be called minus-size models."

"Sounds good to me."

"It's not good. You have no idea how difficult it is for young girls who don't meet those unrealistic standards. They never have a good self-image because their ideals aren't healthy."

"Feast or famine. Neither one is good. Moderation in all things."

"Easier said than done."

"Most things are," Bart said. "Take clowning for example. How many kids wanted to run away and join the circus? Well, maybe not as many these days, but in my time that was the big thing."

"Is that what you did? Run away from home?"

"And my life here. Yes, that's what I did. You too, right?"

Leena nodded.

"Yet here we both are. Back where we began."

"Yeah, but the difference is that you're here by choice."

"So are you."

"No way."

"Think about it. You could have stayed in the Chicago area and gotten a job there. Or gone to a new city. Yet you came back to where you started."

"It seemed the lesser of several evils."

"You returned to your roots to find yourself."

"So now you're a philosopher as well as a clown?"

"It goes with the territory."

"Sister Mary told me you're doing volunteer work with the kids at the local hospital."

"I live to entertain."

"I think it's more than that."

"Does that mean you've forgiven me about the ad?"

"Just don't do it again." She took a sip of her drink. "This is good."

"I hear that you're good with organizational stuff."

"Who told you that?"

"Sister Mary. She said you've really made a difference at the animal clinic."

"Maybe I'm just good working with animals," she joked.

"Me too. Elephants and monkeys mostly. I took clowning classes to learn how to manage. Not just animals but skits, costumes, and makeup."

"Where can you take clown classes?"

"At Clown College in Florida. I'm a graduate."

"Shut up." Leena's eyes widened in surprise. "Really?"

"Really."

"I had no idea."

"Most people don't. Clown College closed in the late nineties. They teach the same kind of courses at various performing arts schools around the country. You know,

now that I think about it, our professions actually have a lot in common. We put on a happy face for others, hiding our own emotions and reflecting what society wants to see."

"Fake it till you make it."

"Right on." Bart gave her a high five.

A moment later, Leena coughed as her sister pulled her pink boat of a car to a hasty stop nearby, kicking up a cloud of dust.

"What are you two doing?" Unlike Leena, Sue Ellen didn't bother getting out of the car.

"Drinking tea and talking," Leena answered.

"Is she threatening you?" Sue Ellen asked Bart. "What?" This as Leena gave her a look. "You weren't happy with him about that ad showing your thighs."

"I've gotten over it," Leena said. "Thanks for the ice tea, Bart."

"Have you gotten over Cole yet?" Sue Ellen asked as Leena walked past her to get to her own car.

Leena pretended not to hear her. But Sue Ellen never took a hint. Sometimes even a hammer over the head didn't make any impression. Such was the case today as Leena's sister followed her inside the mobile home.

"You know what today reminded me?" Sue Ellen asked.

"A million reasons to get out of this town?"

"No. All those people gathered around your car reminded me that we haven't had your welcome-home party yet."

"That's fine by me."

"Well, it's not fine by me."

"I'm not going to be here that much longer."

"What do you mean?" Sue Ellen asked.

"I mean once I have enough money saved, I'll be heading back to Chicago."

"I thought you might be reconsidering that now that you're settling in here in Rock Creek."

"I don't consider being hauled into the sheriff's office as settling in."

"Nathan was just trying to be helpful."

"I don't need that kind of help."

"Well, I'll need your help with the party."

"I don't want you to make a big deal out of it, okay?"

"Okay, sure. Did I ever tell you about the totem party that Skye threw for me? I discovered that my spiritual totem animal is a toy poodle. Skye and Angel seemed to think that was unusual, as if they should talk. I wore a toga. They were surprised by that too."

"You're not wearing a toga to my welcome-home party though, right?"

"Of course not. When should we have the party?"

After the toga talk Leena knew better than to trust her sister when she said she'd keep things low-key. Sue Ellen's idea of low-key never matched anyone else's. Leena's best chance was to limit the amount of time Sue Ellen had to make a big production. "This Friday would be perfect."

"But that doesn't give me much time to get ready."

Exactly. "If you think you can't do it . . ."

"Of course I can." Like Leena, Sue Ellen was a sucker for a challenge. "Is there someone special you want me to invite? Besides Cole, of course."

"Why Cole *of course*?"

"Because you were just making out with him. Which made me figure that you like him."

"Talking about me again, ladies?" Cole said from the other side of the screen door.

"Don't you have someplace else you need to be?" Leena said.

"Yes. *Inside* your house instead of outside of it."

Sue Ellen, the traitor, let him in. Then she made matters worse by saying, "We were just planning Leena's welcome-home party. You're invited, of course. Who else do you think we should add to the guest list?"

"Isn't that a question you should be asking me?" Leena said.

"I did ask you and you didn't answer. So, Cole, who else should we invite?"

"Mindy and her husband."

"Here." Sue Ellen handed Leena the magnetized SNOW MUCH TO DO notepad from the fridge. "Write this down."

And so Leena became the menial note taker to her own party.

"We need a theme," Sue Ellen said.

"I thought *welcome home* was the theme."

"No, that's the reason, not the theme. How about celebrities? You could come to the party as your favorite celebrity. Of course, since you already *are* a celebrity you could come as yourself," Sue Ellen told Leena.

"What are you doing here?" Leena asked Cole.

"I wanted to make sure you were okay after the incident in town."

Which incident? Leena wondered. The one in front of the mini-mart? Or the one in the middle of Barwell Street? Or the one in the sheriff's office? There were so many to choose from. And she wasn't okay about any of them.

She was ready to toss him out when he reached out and gently tucked a loose strand of her hair behind her ear. For once he wasn't trying to seduce her with his touch. Instead she sensed an underlying element of caring in his gesture that made her heart ache.

"I'm okay," she muttered as much for her own benefit as his.

"Hey, Cole, do you think your cousin Butch would be willing to cater the party?" Sue Ellen asked.

"Sure."

It wasn't until much later, when the conversation turned to what to wear, that Cole finally had enough and left. But only after he'd whipped up a surprisingly delicious meal from the leftovers Leena had in her fridge.

"A man who can cook and looks great. You should grab him," Sue Ellen said the minute he was gone.

"He's my boss."

"So get another boss."

"Jobs aren't exactly growing on trees around here."

"Guys like Cole for sure don't grow on trees . . . anywhere."

"I don't want to talk about Cole."

"Fine. What do you want to talk about?"

Leena looked down at her feet and the shoes she'd just kicked off. "Shoe love." Sighing, she wiggled her bare toes. "I used to suffer big-time from shoe love. The thrill of finding the one meant just for me. The excitement of bonding together. The uncomfortable moments forgotten in that initial thrill of infatuation. Then the disappointment of things going wrong, of my expectations not being met. Which was eventually followed by the buzz of finding a new shoe love. Do you want to know how I broke this vicious cycle?"

Sue Ellen nodded.

"Two years ago I broke my foot, thrown off balance by a platform shoe who'd done me wrong. That's when I vowed to forsake shoe love for . . . bag love." Leena held up her Coach bag. "Because bags aren't fickle like shoes. They don't care what size you are. They always fit you. Not like shoes that can squeeze the life out of you. Shoes that can tempt you into thinking they are the perfect fit only to turn on you and torture you. Bag love is much better than shoe love."

Sue Ellen nodded sagely. "Bag love is better. Especially pink-bag love."

"You love anything pink."

"Wait until you see my redecorating plans for my kitchen. You will absolutely die! Think pink and white. Think Good & Plenty."

"You want a kitchen the color of candy?"

"I thought you'd approve."

"Why? Because I'm a candy addict?"

"Not just candy. Cake and cookies too. I can't believe you gave those Sara Lee banana cakes to Sister Mary."

"I know better."

"You'd think so. You'd think you would know better than to give away Sara Lee."

"I mean I know better than to stuff my face and use food as a crutch."

"Russ thinks I'm fat," Sue Ellen abruptly said.

"What?"

"He wants me to run laps around the track with him. I tried before belly-dancing class today, but I couldn't do it."

"He's an idiot."

"No, he's not. He's got a college degree. That's more than you or I have."

"So? That doesn't make him smart."

"Sure it does."

"Trust me, it doesn't. Johnny had a law degree. He was still an idiot."

"Is that the guy who broke your heart back in Chicago?"

"Yeah."

"Was he shoe love or bag love?"

"Johnny was shoe love. Fickle."

"And what is Cole?"

"My biggest nightmare."

"Why?"

"How many times do I have to say this? Because he's my boss."

"And you're afraid that if you have sex with him, he'll fire you?"

"No."

"Maybe he'd give you a raise."

"I am not sleeping with him to get a raise."

"It was just an idea."

"A bad one. It would make things very awkward."

"You can handle awkward. You're a supermodel . . . okay, a regular model. A regular plus-size model. You've got flawless skin, a gorgeous face and smile, and naturally impressive boobs. I'm telling you, awkward is a piece of cake for you. Maybe it wouldn't be awkward. Maybe Cole is the man meant for you. Maybe you'll get married and move into that huge monstrosity of a house of his and I can help you decorate. Or I could find you both a new house. I'll pass my realtor's test soon, I'm sure."

"I am not staying here in Rock Creek forever."

"Of course not. Not forever. You and Cole could retire somewhere warm—"

"No, no, no!"

"You and Cole could retire somewhere cold?"

"There is no Cole and me."

"Uh, yes there is. Remember earlier this evening? In Nathan's office? When you and Cole were kissing?"

"That was a mistake."

"You're not still thinking of killing him, are you?"

"Of course not."

"Well, that's a relief. You wouldn't look good in one of those prison jumpsuits."

"Let's get back to you and Russ. Did he actually say you're fat?"

"No, of course not. He just sort of insinuated it. I probably was being too sensitive. Things are going fine with us."

"I'm glad. That means you can ask him for help. I was talking to Bart about ways to improve Rock Creek, and I suggested that the football team could help out as a community project. You know, do stuff like pull the weeds from the cracked sidewalks and paint the peeling lampposts. You could suggest that the businesses on Barwell Street put out whiskey tubs of flowers on the sidewalks in front of their storefronts. Maybe use the school colors or something to tie it all in to the high school. I said you could talk to Russ about it."

"Me?"

"Yeah, you. Why? Is there some problem with that?"

"No, no problem. Russ and I have no problems. I don't mind that we usually meet at the Dairy Queen. I like the Dairy Queen. And I don't mind that he always fondles my left boob and ignores the right one even when I wear my lucky bra. Honestly, I don't mind any of that."

"O-kay. So you'll talk to him?" Leena said.

"About fondling my right boob?"

"About the team volunteering for community improvement projects."

"Why don't you talk to him?"

"Because he's your guy, not mine. And if I were you, I'd bring up the boob thing too, while you're at it."

"Well, you're not me! And you never will be!"

"Which is fine with me."

"And what about kids, huh? What if I want to have a baby? My eggs are getting older in front of my eyes. Not that I can really see them. The eggs, I mean. They're in my ovaries or someplace like that." Sue Ellen blinked away sudden tears. "What if they all dry up before Russ makes a move? What then?"

"Don't wait for him to make a move. You take charge. You can do it, Sue Ellen. You're great at taking charge."

Sue Ellen's tears disappeared before they fell and her huge smile broke through. "Yes, I am. I am great at taking charge."

"Yes, you are."

"So now I've got a plan."

"Yes, you do."

"Thank you." Sue Ellen gave her a huge hug, cutting off her oxygen flow.

"Can't . . . breathe," Leena wheezed.

"Oh, right." Sue Ellen quickly released her. "Sorry

about that." She did a happy dance around the kitchen. "I've got a plan; I've got a plan."

Watching her, Leena wished she could feel half as confident about her own plan to return to Chicago and her modeling life there.

Chapter Thirteen

• • • • • • • • • • • •

To talk or not to talk? That was the question facing Leena the next morning as she entered the animal clinic.

As luck would have it, Cole was the only one there. No sign of Mindy. Great. That meant that Leena would have to talk. Or give him the antifreeze cold shoulder.

Hard to do considering she'd spoken to him last night when he'd come to her place. And the guy had cooked for her.

No, she refused to be charmed by food. She'd woken up this morning totally irritated with him. She had a right to feel that way. Thoughts of him had kept her up half the night. The rest of the time she'd had X-rated dreams about him satisfying her better than any MegaMax vibrator ever possibly could.

She was surprised to find he'd made the coffee since that was one of her duties. She almost said something before reminding herself she was not speaking to him. Instead she poured herself a cup of coffee and dumped a packet of sugar in it. Just one packet.

She'd eaten a healthy breakfast of bran cereal and skim milk. The frozen blueberries she'd added were guaranteed to give her plenty of antioxidants. Or antisomething. What she really needed was an antidote for Cole.

Why wasn't he saying anything? Did he even notice that she wasn't speaking to him? He was a guy, so he probably was totally obtuse about the entire thing. He was probably thinking about some pit bull he was going to neuter.

She sneaked a peek at him through the cover of her lashes. It had taken her a few weeks as a teenager to perfect that technique. She was now a pro.

Cole was looking at her as if he'd like to kiss her again.

The knowing gleam in his blue eyes told her he remembered their kisses. That he wasn't thinking about any pit bull. That he wanted her. And that he knew she wanted him.

Did he think she was going to throw herself at him just because he gave her "the look"?

The man was entirely too confident. He clearly had no idea that he was dealing with a woman in command here. Probably because her confident self had been dormant since coming back to her hometown.

But fake-it-till-you-make-it Leena could handle a commitment-shy charmer like Cole in her sleep. She got right to the point. "I saved you fifty dollars, you know."

"How do you figure that?"

"You'd have lost the bet you had with Algee and you would have had to pay him the fifty."

"You seem pretty confident that I would have lost."

"Totally confident."

"You doubt my powers of persuasion?"

"You couldn't have persuaded me."

He just smiled.

"You couldn't. Go ahead. Give it your best shot. How did you plan on convincing me that going out on a date with you was a good idea? Especially given the fact that you're my boss and that you'd already given me the warning that you're not the settling-down type."

"I wouldn't have been asking as your boss. I would have asked you as the man you kissed with such . . . enthusiasm."

"Maybe that's the way I kiss all guys. With enthusiasm. Ever think of that?"

She could tell by the aggravated look on Cole's face that he hadn't and now that she'd brought it up, he was not pleased by the possibility.

"Is it the way you kiss every guy?"

"I'm not answering that question."

"Does your mouth tremble every time a guy brushes his fingers over your lips?"

"My mouth does not . . ."

He caressed her bottom lip with his thumb.

Tremble, shiver, tremble.

Traitorous mouth. She'd been able to fake smiles in photo shoots. She could look cool modeling winter coats in the midst of a July heat wave. So why couldn't she hide her response to him?

"I'm ticklish." A lame excuse, but the best she could come up with at the moment. She had no idea she'd be that vulnerable to his touch.

"Ticklish? Really?"

She nodded vehemently, which should have dislodged his thumb. But he just cupped her chin with his big hand. A gentle yet incredibly powerful hand. A work-roughened hand.

"Are you ticklish here too?" He ran his index finger over the bow of her top lip.

Tremble, shiver, shake.

"I guess so." His voice was rough and sexy as he answered for her. He always spoke in a low drawl that wrapped its way around her and pulled her in. Sometimes he added a dash of laughter or, like now, a dose of sensuality. "How about here?" His hand moved so that he could slide a finger around the curve of her ear.

Her resistance was in serious jeopardy here. She really needed to do something about that. Like step away. Laugh it off. Something.

But Leena couldn't seem to rally the strength to do anything but stand there and enjoy the pleasure sifting into her system.

"Or here?" He trailed his fingertips down the curve of her throat. "I can feel your pulse. Your heart is racing. And you're shivering. Are you cold?"

She nodded, doubting her ability to form words.

"Yet your skin feels warm." He brushed his fingers back and forth. "Very soft and very warm." He paused to lift her chin and stare into her eyes. "Still think you'd say no?"

His words served like an alarm, waking her instantly.

So he thought he could play her, did he?

"I don't think I'd say no." She deliberately kept her voice husky and kittenish.

"You don't?" He sounded entirely too pleased with himself.

"No, I don't." She lifted her hands to his chest and shoved him away. "I *know* I'd say no."

Leena was very proud of the way she walked away, adding a bit of catwalk hip swivel to her walk. Score one for fake-it-till-you-make-it Leena.

* * *

Power walking down Barwell Street in Rock Creek did not have the same feeling as power walking down North Michigan Avenue in Chicago. For one thing, the window-shopping couldn't possibly be more different. On the Magnificent Mile she could check out the new arrivals at Chanel. One memorable morning she'd stood in front of Tiffany's eating a danish a la Audrey Hepburn in *Breakfast at Tiffany's* complete with sunglasses and little black dress. Well, not exactly *little*. A classy, elegant size-sixteen black dress. And the Kate Spade vintage-inspired sunglasses she'd worn were awesome. Unfortunately she'd had to sell them on eBay in order to pay off bills.

Rock Creek wasn't a place where you'd wear vintage-inspired sunglasses. Here she looked at empty storefronts with FOR LEASE signs behind dusty windows. She crossed to the other side of the street to head back to the clinic. After eating a healthy salad for lunch, she'd decided she needed some fresh air.

At least Rock Creek had that. The weather was spring perfect with the promise of things to come in the air. Apple blossoms were just beginning to burst on the single tree struggling to survive next to the World War II memorial tank. Even the funeral home looked nice with the red tulips blooming in a surprisingly pretty garden out front.

What did it say about a town when the nicest place was the funeral home? She was pondering that question when someone bumped into her outside the thrift store. "Sorry."

Leena recognized Edie Dabronovitch's daughter, Hannah. The girl was bent over, picking up the contents of her backpack, which had spilled onto the cracked sidewalk. Leena immediately helped her.

"I'm so clumsy," Hannah muttered. "My mom is always telling me."

"You're not clumsy. You couldn't play softball or basketball as well as you do if you were clumsy." Leena looked down at the diet pills that had tumbled out of her backpack. "Are you taking this stuff?"

Hannah just shrugged.

"It's not good."

"You know of a better pill?"

"You don't need pills."

"Yes, I do. I'm fat as a cow. My mother tells me so all the time."

"She's wrong. She called me a fat cow too, yet I was a model."

"She says if you were really a model, then you wouldn't be working at the vet's office."

Score one for Evil Edie. What was Leena doing, giving advice to a kid? She was hardly in a position to be doing that. It wasn't as if she was the model of success here. But the thought of Hannah having such low self-esteem got to her. Because Leena knew what it was like to feel that way.

Granted her mom had never ridiculed her the way Edie did Hannah. But the other kids had.

Leena had been an underdog most of her life—told

she was too bossy, too tall, too fat. But she'd had people, like her mom, who believed in her. Hannah needed that. Everyone did.

"I have my reasons for being here," Leena said. "I can't go into them."

"Are you going to be an actress? A lot of models go into acting. Are you here preparing for a role?"

"I can't say."

Hannah nodded. "I understand. It's okay. Your secret is safe with me."

"Those pills aren't safe. Promise me you won't take any. You are wonderful just the way you are. And anyone who tells you otherwise is just wrong."

"I don't look like my mom. She looks like the models in the magazines."

"Those models are airbrushed and computer enhanced. No one looks that way. Trust me, I've seen the before and after shots. You wouldn't believe what they can do with computer software. Why, they even tried to mess with Katie Couric's picture to make her look skinner. Big mistake."

Sister Mary interrupted them. "Hello, Hannah. Why aren't you in school?"

"It's a teacher conference day."

"I see." Sister Mary turned her eagle eyes on Leena. "Aren't you going to come inside and take a look around?"

Leena took a step back. "I need to get back to work. I was just taking a quick power walk after lunch."

"Yet you had time to talk to Hannah."

"We're gal pals. We've bonded."

"Really?" Hannah stared at Leena in awe.

It felt good to be looked at that way. And it felt good

to let this kid know that there were other points of view besides Evil Edie's. "Yeah, really."

"Sweet." Hannah flashed her a shy smile before turning to leave.

"Remember what I said." Leena didn't want to refer to the pills in front of Sister Mary, but she could tell by Hannah's expression that she understood.

"I will. I promise."

Then Hannah was gone, leaving Leena with Sister Mary. "Come on in and take a look around."

Recognizing an order when she heard one, Leena did, with Sister Mary at her side the entire time. "You've got a ThighMaster for sale here."

"You sound surprised."

"It's just that there's so much stuff here—from couches to Bakelite jewelry. This stuff goes for a lot of money on eBay."

"ThighMasters?"

"No. Bakelite jewelry." Leena slid a red bangle on her wrist. "I've never gotten into the ThighMaster."

"I have," Sister Mary said proudly. "Feel these muscles." She pointed to her thighs.

"No, that's okay," Leena stuttered. "I believe you." What nun would lie about a thing like that? What nun would lie, period?

"I've used the ThighMaster for years. I don't mean to brag, but I've got thighs of steel."

Leena was speechless.

"What? You don't think a nun should have thighs of steel?"

"I, uh . . ." Leena had no idea how to properly answer that question.

"You're not comfortable talking to me about these things?" Sister Mary said.

"No, I'm not."

"So are you still faking it till you make it?"

"Absolutely." Leena's attention returned to the bangle. The price was only two dollars.

"Does that include faking your feelings for Cole?"

"Which feelings for Cole? I have so many."

"Really? Frankly, I expected you to deny having any."

"That would be a little hard to do at this point. You know, when we were kids, Cole always made me feel like he was laughing at me behind my back."

"You still think that way now?"

"Sometimes. He doesn't take much seriously."

"That's what he likes people to think."

"He seems to take great pleasure in teasing me."

"That's not the only thing he seems to take great pleasure in doing to you."

Leena blushed so hard she thought her cheeks were on fire. "We were *not* making out in my car the other day. That was a total lie."

"What about in Nathan's office?"

"When Cole is charming, he's hard to resist. And when he's impossible, sometimes he's even harder to resist, you know? The man drives me crazy. I know he's your nephew, but come on. You've got to see how he could drive a person crazy. But he's my boss. Not that he's used his position in any way to try and get me to . . ."

"Make out with him in Nathan's office?"

"Maybe I should get another job. Are you looking for help here at the thrift shop?" Leena asked as she paid for her bangle.

"No. And Cole depends on you at the clinic. He's always raving about you, about how organized you are and how you've whipped things into shape."

"I need to whip myself into shape," Leena muttered.

"Is that why you gave me the cakes the other day?"

"Yeah. As soon as I got back here, I started falling into bad habits."

"Did you ever consider the possibility that you had to come home to face your fears before you could move on?"

"What fears?"

"You tell me. And don't try telling me you don't have any fears. We all have them. I suspect yours are tied to this town, to your upbringing, to your roots."

"What do you know about my parents?"

The question caught Sister Mary by surprise. "I know they've retired down in Florida."

"Yes, but what about before that? When they were still here?"

"I didn't know your family well, but they seemed a colorful bunch of individuals."

"Right. A polite way of saying they were strange." Leena had talked to her mom on the phone a few times in the past month. Each conversation had been brief. The only comment her mom had made about Leena's return to Rock Creek was a vague comment about it being nice that she and Sue Ellen could spend some time together. Then she'd gone back to talking about her friends in Florida, ending with a halfhearted invitation for Leena to come down and visit them sometime when they weren't quite so busy.

For some dumb reason those awkward calls always made Leena feel as though she wanted to cry. She wasn't sure why. She really needed to return to e-mails as her main means of communication with her parents.

"I'm not like Cole," Leena said. "I'm not in love with Rock Creek."

"You talking about me again, Princess?" he drawled from behind her.

"Yes, I am. I'm trying to get embarrassing information about you from your aunt so that I can use it against you should I need to at some future point."

"No." Cole dramatically placed one hand over his heart. "You wound me deeply."

"I don't want to wound you deeply, just slow you down a little."

"Honey, I can go as slow as you want."

Leena blushed. "Don't talk like that in front of a nun!"

"Not even Catholic, yet she's filled with guilt," Cole told his aunt. "I suspect it's because she wants me but is afraid to admit it. Especially in front of you."

"Then I'll leave you two alone to work it out." Sister Mary gave him a hug before going to help a new customer.

"Why do you do that?" Leena gave him an exasperated look.

"Do what?"

"Never mind. It's useless trying to reason with you."

"Wait a second. Where are you going?"

"Back to work. I have a mean boss."

"I could put in a good word for you."

She gave him an evil glare.

"That didn't come out the way I intended," Cole said. "Never mind. I'll walk back with you. Are you getting excited about your welcome-home party?"

"I'm not sure *excited* is the word."

"Then what is the word?"

"Apprehensive."

"You? You're not afraid of anything."

"Your aunt just told me that we all have fears, whether we admit them or not. Take you for example. You're clearly afraid of commitment."

"What gives you that idea?"

"Your track record. You're a serial monogamist."

"You make it sound like a crime."

"You stay friends with your former girlfriends after you break up because you never really got emotionally involved with them in the first place. Everything was surface. A temporary good time. No broken hearts."

"What's wrong with that?"

"Nothing . . . if you like shallow relationships."

"You prefer broken hearts?"

Remembering the painful humiliation Johnny Sullivan caused her, she wondered if maybe Cole had the right idea after all.

"What's his name?" Cole demanded.

"Huh?"

"The guy who broke your heart. What's his name?"

"None of your business."

"So you don't deny that he did break your heart?"

"We are changing the subject."

"No, we're not. You always do that when things get too personal."

"Do what?"

"Change the subject. Not this time. I want to know who this guy was. Someone in Chicago?"

"Why do you care?"

"Because I care about you. Why do you find that so hard to believe?"

"Because I've heard it before and it was a lie." Fearing she'd already said too much, Leena walked away.

• • •

"You're late," Cole told Nathan. They were in Cole's office, a total contrast to Nathan's obsessively neat workplace. Nathan's desk was orderly. Cole's wasn't. His office was cluttered with boxes, journals, books, pieces of rarely used equipment, and empty paper cups. But he knew where everything was and refused to allow anyone to mess up his system. The jumble drove Leena crazy. Fine by him. She drove him nuts too.

"What is this?" Cole asked as he unwrapped the suspicious-looking package Nathan had handed him.

"Lunch. I told you I'd bring food."

"I thought you meant you'd bring a pizza or a burger or something."

"Consider this *something*. Stop looking at me that way. It's not radioactive waste. It's just a sandwich."

"Why is the bread so funny looking?"

"Because Angel made it."

Cole immediately set the strange-looking sandwich back on his desk. Then he looked at Nathan. "Where's yours?"

"I've got a burger from the Dairy Queen."

"I'm not taking your food." Cole shoved the sandwich toward Nathan. "Hand over the burger and no one gets hurt."

"No way—"

Cole didn't wait for permission. He grabbed the burger and bit into it before Nathan could do a thing.

Nathan gave him a steely-eyed glare. "Stealing a man's burger is illegal."

"So is passing off one of Angel's yellow-squash bread with boiled carrots sandwiches on me."

"She'll be upset if I don't eat it."

Cole shrugged. "Your problem, not mine."

"And if Angel is upset, Skye is upset."

"Again, not my problem." Cole finished off the burger in four more bites.

"Isn't there some animal here at the clinic that would like a yummy sandwich like this?"

"Don't even think about it," Cole growled. "I wouldn't wish that on any creature big or small."

Nathan sighed and tossed the paper-wrapped sandwich in the garbage. "So have you told Leena you're crazy about her yet?"

Cole just gave him a look. "Man rule number forty-one: Never cause a hassle in your buddy's castle."

"You stole that phrase from Algee."

"The meaning is the same."

"I just find it amazing that a man who is supposed to be so charming with women, who always has smooth sailing with the opposite sex, suddenly hits a brick wall with this woman."

"She's not like the others."

"Because she's immune?"

"If she was immune, we wouldn't have been making out in your office."

"You both looked pretty amorous in front of the mini-mart too."

"She was afraid I'd squash her goodies."

Nathan almost snorted the soda he was drinking.

"Not those kind of goodies," Cole said. "I meant food. She'd bought some stuff."

"I heard a rumor that she got you a jug of antifreeze. Is that true?"

"Yeah."

"First time a woman's done that for you I bet."

"No more bets. And yeah, that was a first. I've had a lot of firsts with Leena."

"You're a dead man."

"What?"

Nathan just shook his head. "You don't have a prayer. You're already as good as hog-tied and bound."

"I am not."

"No use protesting, buddy. It's a done deal."

"It is not. Eating Angel's sandwiches has adversely affected your brain function."

"I only had one bite one time and that was months ago. No, I'm not the one with limited brain capability. You are. What are you afraid of? Why don't you want to tell her how you feel about her? She obviously feels the same about you."

"She's going back to Chicago the minute she can."

"And that's a problem? Why? Your relationships don't last all that long to begin with. What's wrong with enjoying the time she is here?"

"When did you become Dear Abby?"

"I'm not sure, but I think she's dead."

"And so will you be if you keep bugging me about this."

"Fine. Don't say I didn't warn you, though." With

those final words, Nathan left Cole alone to wonder what the hell it was about Leena that made her different. He should have figured her out by now.

He'd learned some stuff—like the fact that he loved the way a strand of her hair trailed down her neck when she pinned the rest of it up. Or the fact that she had the best cleavage he'd ever seen and the most voluptuous body. And then there was her husky laugh. He was getting hard just thinking about it. About her laugh. How weird was that?

She was in his dreams every night, teasing him with her smiles and kisses, urging him on with her moans of pleasure.

Was his buddy Nathan right? Was Cole already a goner? Was this what it felt like to go overboard about a woman?

A knock at his office door interrupted his thoughts. "Yo, doc, you got a minute? Leena said I could come on back," Algee said. "And she even smiled at me. I think she's over her mad about the bet."

"Or she's planning some new kind of revenge."

"That's possible." Algee sat in a chair across from Cole. "I just wanted to make sure you and I were good. About the bet, I mean."

"The bet is officially off."

"Yeah, I figured. Too bad in a way, seeing as how I would've won."

"Oh no you don't. You're not drawing me back in. Remember, you're the one who blew it by telling Tameka everything."

"We're dating."

"Bully for you."

"Are you and Leena dating?"

"Not exactly."

"So you're just doin' the deed around town?"

"No, we're not, and even if we were, it's nobody's business."

"I hear you, man." Algee held up his hands in a universal peace gesture. "I just wanted to make sure that you and I were copasetic. I mean after I broke that man rule thing. I didn't want to mess with that."

"Just don't do it again."

• • •

Leena was about to lock up for the day when a boy came to the clinic door just as she was flipping over the OPEN sign to CLOSED. He pounded on the door, his face desperate. "I need to talk to the vet!"

Leena didn't have the heart to turn him away.

Hearing the pounding, Cole came into the reception area as she let the boy in. "What's going on?"

"I need your help to find him!" The boy's face was streaked with tears.

"Calm down." Cole placed a reassuring hand on his shoulder. "Find who?"

"A cold-blooded fugitive."

Chapter Fourteen

. . . .

"**Whoa** there," Cole said. "It sounds like you came to the wrong place. You need the sheriff."

"No. I need you." More tears formed in the boy's eyes. "To find Bob."

"Is Bob your dog?" Leena asked. "Did your dog run away from home? Is he the fugitive?"

"Bob is my tortoise. A red-footed tortoise. He ran away from home."

"Ran?" Leena repeated.

"Okay, crawled. Can you help me find him?" Tears continued to roll down the kid's freckled cheeks.

"Sure." She gave him a reassuring hug. "Sure, we'll help you find him. Cole is a vet. He knows where tortoises go when they run away from home. Right, Cole?"

"I, uh, may have some idea . . ."

"So there's nothing to worry about." She cut Cole off

before he could say anything to dash the kid's hopes. Leena knew all about dashed hopes and she couldn't cope with any more of that today. "Tell him, Cole, that there's nothing to worry about."

Instead Cole said, "Where are your parents?"

"My dad's still at work and my mom is making dinner."

"You're Tommy Taylor, right?" The boy nodded. "So, Tommy, when did Bob go missing?"

"Yesterday."

"Could he have been chasing a female tortoise?" she asked Cole.

"Bob hasn't keep me up-to-date on his dating schedule," Cole said.

"I can pay you." Tommy held up a handful of dollar bills. "I've got a Wal-Mart gift card too, worth ten dollars. I got it for my birthday two days ago, but I'd rather have Bob back."

"Keep your money and gift card," Cole said. "You don't have to pay us to help you. Right, Princess?"

"Right." Why had Cole looked at her that way? Did he think she was so desperate for money that she'd take it off a little kid? "Don't worry, Tommy. We'll find Bob for you."

Since it was a nice sunny May day and Tommy's house wasn't far from the animal clinic, they all walked there, with Tommy telling them all about Bob en route. "He doesn't bite. He eats from my hand sometimes and he's very gentle. He travels fast, for a tortoise I mean, and his favorite hiding places are under bushes or flowers or decks. He's not afraid of the dark. He likes it."

"Where have you looked?" Leena asked.

"Everywhere! We even took some of the boards out of our deck to look under there, but we didn't find Bob."

"Never fear, Cole the super vet is here." Leena was rather proud of the rhyme.

Tommy and Cole just rolled their eyes, indicating they were not similarly impressed.

Cole was good with kids. Leena had noticed it before, many times. She should probably let him handle this search on his own.

As if reading her thoughts, Cole took her hand and told Tommy, "My assistant and I will take it from here. You keep searching inside your house to make sure he didn't hide out somewhere in there."

"You take the yard to the right," Leena said, "and I'll take the one to the left."

Cole didn't budge. "No."

"Okay, then I'll take the one to the right—"

"We stick together."

"Why? It would be much more efficient if we broke up."

"We're a great team together."

"Yeah, right," she scoffed.

"We are. You don't think so?"

"We don't have a lot in common."

"We went to school together."

"You were two years younger. Still are."

"Does that bother you? Because it sure doesn't bother me."

"Shouldn't we be searching for Bob?"

"Right."

He tugged her after him as he headed for the yard next door. She put an end to that by digging in her heels and refusing to move.

Cole turned to face her. "What's wrong?"

"I'm not some dog on a leash you can haul after you."

"Sorry. You want to go first?"

"You said we were a team. We'll walk together."

"Fine by me."

"You can let go of my hand now."

"Do I have to?"

She saw something dark under an azalea bush. "Is that him?"

"No, that's a rock."

Feeling foolish, she freed her hand from his and immediately missed the warmth of his touch.

Which reminded her of something she meant to tell him. "The local newspaper called right before closing. They want you to do a weekly column for them."

"Answering pet questions?"

"Answering relationship questions, dating advice, that sort of thing. Because you're one of the state's sexiest bachelors. Don't worry. I told them you couldn't possibly do such a column."

"Because I'm too busy with my vet practice?"

"No. Because you're clueless about male-female relationships."

"Whereas you're an expert?"

"I never said that." She kept walking, as did Cole. Beside her, not in front of her. "I'm certainly no expert."

"No, you're the high-maintenance model, and I'm the warm and fuzzy and sexy vet."

"I've never been high maintenance."

"Pedicures, manicures, facials . . ."

"That's not high maintenance."

"Then what is?"

"Making demands on others to take care of you. I don't expect anyone else to take care of me. I never have. Even as a kid I—"

"You what?"

"Took care of myself. When other kids made fun of me I didn't expect anyone else to stick up for me."

"What about your parents?"

"My dad told me I had to learn to defend myself, and my mom told me I should get along better with others. They were trying to teach me to be independent."

"I'm sorry about that," Cole said quietly.

"Sorry that I stuck up for myself?"

"Sorry that you didn't have anyone else to do it for you." He tucked a strand of her hair behind her ear, his fingertips trailing against her cheek. "And I'm sorry I made fun of you that one time."

"That's okay." She swallowed the sudden lump in her throat and put a little more space between them. "You learned your lesson. Besides, it made me tougher."

"Right," he scoffed. "You are the poster child of toughness."

"I am."

"That's why you cried with Mrs. Morgan when her twenty-year-old cat died. And why you hugged eight-year-old Jordan when he got a new kitten."

"He got *two* new kittens. Brothers. Seuss and Truman." She ducked to search beneath a huge lilac bush. Nothing, but it sure smelled good.

As a kid, Leena had loved the small lilac bush next to their trailer, but it died when her mom poured half of her dad's bottle of vodka and part of another of tequila into it—refilling both bottles with water.

Unnerved by the memory, Leena quickly straightened.

"Hold on." Cole gently plucked several loose lilac flowers from her hair.

She closed her eyes and gently swayed under the magical influence of his touch. The instant she realized what she was doing, she snapped her eyes open and stepped away. "No tortoise under there. Time to move on." She marched toward the next shrub.

He ambled after her. "We never did discuss the fact that you think I'm PA's sexiest bachelor."

"The paper listed others. A neurosurgeon from Philadelphia, a firefighter from Mifflinburg, a district attorney from Pittsburgh."

"Yeah, but you nominated me, not them. Because you think I'm sexy."

"Because I wanted to aggravate you."

"Which you did. Mission accomplished. And the reason you wanted to aggravate me is because I get to you."

She paused to confront him. "Is this about the bet?"

This time Cole's eye roll indicated how aggravated he was with her question. "Would you just get over the bet? It was a stupid mistake on my part."

"How would you feel if Tameka and I made a bet about you and Algee?"

"Honored, but that's just me."

His rough velvet voice was getting to her, so Leena started walking again. "We're supposed to be looking for Tommy's pet."

"We are. Nothing says we can't talk while we look. You're good with animals. Did you have a pet as a kid?"

"I had a cat. Missy. My dad ran her over and she died. He didn't do it on purpose. But I vowed I'd never have another pet after that."

"You didn't want to feel that kind of pain ever again, huh?"

"Yeah. Which was fine with my parents. They weren't that into pets."

"My family was. We had two dogs and three cats and an iguana and tropical fish. We even had a baby raccoon for a few months. Good thing we had a big house because I was always bringing stray animals home."

"Sounds like you were meant to be a vet."

"Yeah. And you were meant to be a model."

"Yeah." Something she couldn't afford to lose sight of. But it was all too easy to do that when she was so close to Cole. He gave off this it's-gonna-be-okay vibe that was very sexy.

Forty minutes later they'd found a faded flip-flop, an empty large-size bag of M&Ms with peanuts, and a crushed Diet Pepsi can but no sign of Bob.

They moved on to the yard on the other side of Tommy's house. No sign of Bob there either.

"What about that storage shed at the back there?" She pointed to the yard behind Tommy's house. There were no fences between the properties, so they walked over to check it out.

"Do you want me to ask the owner for the key?" Leena asked.

"It's not locked." He opened the door and peered inside. There were no windows, so the interior was pitch dark. "Here, hold the flashlight while I move something . . ."

"You brought a flashlight?"

"Sure. I always have one on my key chain. Come closer. I can't see yet."

She cautiously moved forward. No way was she afraid

of the dark, but after a photo shoot in Mexico a few years ago she had developed a thing for creepy-crawlies. Snakes were okay, but scorpions weren't. She was pretty sure there weren't any scorpions in PA, but she wasn't 100 percent positive.

"Don't move," Cole said.

She froze.

"Aim the flashlight down here."

Since her hand was shaking the beam was wobbly. Maybe a Mexican scorpion had hitched a ride on some gardening stuff and was hiding in here just waiting.

Cole bent and scooped up something off the floor right beside her foot. He was so close that his fingers brushed her bare toes in her Bongo sandals.

Leena didn't faint. She didn't scream, although she had been tempted.

He held up the tortoise in his hand. "Bob, I presume?"

She almost sank to her knees in relief. First, because it wasn't a scorpion, and second, because she hadn't stepped on Bob. She could just imagine the local paper's headlines: "Plus-Size Model Squishes Boy's Beloved Pet." They'd probably add some snarky comment about how if she'd been a size zero, she wouldn't have hurt the tortoise at all.

As she lowered the flashlight, the beam hit the grass-stained knees of her jeans. Luckily they were the pair she'd gotten at Wal-Mart.

"Look at me. I'm a mess." An instant later, Cole kissed her. This time she couldn't afford to melt. She had to protest. Otherwise he'd think she was a complete pushover. "What are you doing? I said to *look* at me, not kiss me."

"What can I say?" He shrugged, his smile endearing. "I'm hopelessly addicted to messy women."

"Then go kiss one of them, not me."

"I don't want to kiss anyone but you."

Leena's heart stopped at his words and the way he said them. The man was holding a tortoise in one hand and still he had the ability to make her knees melt with just a look or a word or a kiss. The combination of all three was enough to knock her off kilter.

"Let's . . ." Leena had to pause to clear her dry throat. "Let's take Bob home."

Home. Leena wondered where *her* own home really was: back in Chicago or here with Cole? The fact that the thought even crossed her mind scared her more than the threat of scorpions.

• • •

"Cole, you're an angel." The woman who'd just complimented him kissed his cheek.

Mrs. Weinstein was in her eighties. He could hear Leena in his head, mocking the fact that women of all ages loved him. Except for Leena. The one woman he couldn't get off his mind.

"Those two special tables you built for my cat Tumtum are working out just perfectly. The arthritis in my knees has gotten so bad that I can't bend down to fill her food dishes or empty her cat box. But because of you, I now have one of those tables in the kitchen so that Tumtum can jump up to eat and the other in the laundry room so she can jump up for her kitty box. She has more energy than I do, and the height of the tables is just right for me. I can't thank you enough."

"I'm just glad I was able to help. Tum-tum here is doing great. Her ears and teeth look good. No problem there."

His problem was Leena and how to deal with her. How to convince her that the two of them needed to get together. That date bet had set him back severely. Not that she'd been flirting with him before that. No, she usually looked at him as if she found him amusing rather than sexy. But every so often, he caught her staring at him as if she wanted him as much as he wanted her.

That was sure how she kissed him. With passion and no regret.

The regret came later, when she was out of his arms.

She'd been so mater-of-fact when she'd talked about how she'd learned at an early age to stick up for herself because no one else would do it for her.

She always seemed so confident and in charge, yet she'd accused him of making fun of her on more than one occasion. It was almost as if she couldn't really believe that he'd be interested in her. Why was that? She was a beautiful, smart, intriguing woman. Any man would be lucky to have her in his life.

Which got him wondering about the ass who'd broken her heart back in Chicago. He wasn't usually a violent man, but Cole wanted to kick the bastard in the balls.

Cole reigned in his thoughts and refocused his attention on his work. His next patient was a huge, twenty-five-pound gray shorthair neutered male cat named Solomon. "How's he liking the new light cat food?" Cole asked his owner, Jeanine, the secretary at the Dunbeck Funeral Home.

"He's eating it." She sounded surprised. "He's lost a pound so far."

"That's good. We don't want the weight reduction to be too sudden. If a cat this size loses too much weight, it can develop hepatic lipidosis, or fatty liver disease, so we have to watch out for that. Also, when owners change cat foods, they sometimes think that if the cat gets hungry enough it'll eat the new food. It won't. Cats can starve themselves into a serious condition. Which is why it's such good news that he likes the new weight-management dry food."

"I feel guilty for feeding him all those treats before."

"Don't. You're both on the right track now. It's not easy, I know. I've got a big cat myself. Midnight. He really looks huge next to his bud Buddy. They're both black cats, but Buddy is wiry and small."

"Those are the Morontos' cats, right?"

Cole nodded.

"I heard you took in the Morontos' cats when the family had to move out of town suddenly. They left them in a large cardboard box in front of your clinic with a note, right?"

"Yeah." He still got a pang when he thought about that note, written in crayon by the youngest of the six Moronto kids: *Pleze take kare of our kats. Daddy is rong. They not bad luk.*

The cats had been too spooked to be adoptable. So Cole had taken them in himself and worked with them. Both still raced under the bed when they heard someone else's voice, but they'd finally bonded with him. And they accepted Tripod and Elf. The dog was outnumbered by cats and was totally bossed around by them. Not that Elf seemed to mind.

Cole's next patient was an orange domestic longhair neutered male named Mouser. "Do you think its normal for my cat to suck his thumb?" Katy Gonzalez, the local postmistress, asked. "He only sucks on the left one."

Cole checked the feline's teeth and left paw. "Doesn't seem to be hurting him any."

"How fast can a cat run?" Katy's nine-year-old son Matt asked. He loved trivia and wanted to be a vet when he grew up.

Cole grinned at the kid. "You trying to stump the vet again?"

Matt just grinned back.

"Domestic shorthairs have been clocked at thirty-one miles per hour," Cole said.

Matt wasn't about to give up yet. "Average cat heart rate per minute?"

"About 155 beats."

"Average temperature?"

"That would be 102.5."

Matt was still asking questions as Cole with Mouser's carrier in hand, accompanied him and his mom to the reception desk to pay the bill.

"The doctor said that it's okay for our cat to suck his thumb," Katy told Leena.

"I told you so," Leena said. "Mouser is probably suffering from separation anxiety from his mom cat. You found him when he was only a few weeks old, right? And you said that he purrs real loud when he sucks his thumb, so it must make him happy."

"Yeah, but he's three years old now."

"Early childhood or kittenhood traumas can affect you the rest of your life." Leena spoke with the authority of someone who had personal experience of early traumas.

"For a model, she knows what she's talking about," someone said from the waiting area. "She told me that my dog Max was lonely and wanted more outdoor play-time, and she was right."

Cole already knew that often during her breaks, Leena went in the back to the clinic area and talked to the recovering dogs and cats. "You're gonna be fine. Don't you worry about a thing." Her voice was always soothing, and he was probably a sleazebag for getting turned on by it.

"Was there something you needed?" she asked Cole as he continued to stand there after the Gonzalez family departed.

He was staring at her so intently that Leena automatically looked down to make sure the buttons on her shirt hadn't come undone. She was wearing one of her favorite J.Jill tops, but she doubted he could tell that.

Cole ran his fingers through his hair, giving him a tousled just-out-of-bed look she found entirely too appealing. "I just . . . I, uh . . ."

Leena was mesmerized by his mouth as he floundered for words.

What was wrong with her? She couldn't look away. His bottom lip was so sexy she was almost overcome by the sudden urge to nibble on it.

Scared she might actually act on her thoughts, she raised her eyes and met his gaze. He looked as though he had some nibbling thoughts of his own going on inside that male brain of his. Nibbling not just on her lips but her entire body.

Leena became hot all over. Was she coming down with something?

Cole fever. That's what she was experiencing. She needed some kind of antidote. Or a vaccine. Fast.

"Ready for our next patient," Mindy said with customary cheerfulness.

Okay, that worked. Interrupted by a coworker. That disrupted the sensual tension. At least it prevented Leena or Cole from acting on it.

Which was a good thing.

• • •

Leena's first hint that Sue Ellen had ignored her request not to make a big deal was the posting on the marquis above the Tivoli Theater Friday afternoon:

WELCOME-HOME PARTY
4 MODEL LEENA RILEY
TONITE!

Sure, Leena knew that her sister planned on holding the event at the theater. But she hadn't realized that the fact would be announced this way. And she didn't like the red carpet that was being rolled out from the front door to the curb.

"What's going on here?"

Sue Ellen looked up. "You're early!"

"I was driving home from work when I saw the sign."

"Wicked awesome, isn't it?" Lulu said as she passed by, heading for the theater. Today she was wearing her GOT BRAINS T-shirt teamed with a red-and-black plaid miniskirt with combat boots and black knee-high stockings.

"I don't know about the awesome, but it sure is

wicked," Leena muttered. "I thought I told you I didn't want a big deal made about this."

Sue Ellen waved her words away, the glittering silver stars on her acrylic nails reflecting madly. "Everyone says that when you're throwing a party for them. They never really mean it,"

"I did. I do."

"Well, it's too late now. At least I didn't have the parade that I wanted. If I'd had another week, I could have pulled it all together, but—"

"No parade. Ever. Seriously. Or I will hurt you," Leena growled.

"Okay, okay. What a party pooper you are."

"It's her party, she can poop if she wants to," Lulu said as she set up a giant poster board in front of the theater.

"What's that?" Leena said.

"It's you. We blew up one of your photos and turned it into—"

"A nightmare." It wasn't just one of her photos. It was the infamous Regency Mobile Home ad photo with her cheesy thighs. Which looked even worse in the grainy version currently on display at even-bigger-than-life size.

"I told you she wouldn't be a happy camper," Lulu informed Sue Ellen.

"She was right," Leena said.

"But this photo sparked a reaction in so many people—"

"No more so than in me," Leena said.

"I mean the women of Rock Creek. The people coming tonight. Bart and Nancy and Skye and Nathan."

All couples, Leena noticed. Nothing like coming stag to your own party.

"And Violet and Owen," Sue Ellen continued.

"Wait until you see the costume that Sue Ellen plans on wearing," Lulu said.

"Costume?"

Sue Ellen nodded. "I told you it was a costume-party theme. I'm coming as Mae West. I've got the wig and the dress and—"

Leena held out her hand in a universal stop motion. "Don't tell me."

"She wants to be surprised," Lulu told Sue Ellen with a grin. "I'll bet Coach will be surprised to see you in your Mae West outfit."

"Russ won't be able to attend this evening." Sue Ellen sounded surprisingly prim. "He had a wrestling match over in Serenity Falls. He might stop by later if he can."

"I thought he was the football coach," Leena said.

"He is, but he coaches other stuff too. Enough small talk. I've got lots to do before the big party tonight." Sue Ellen rushed back into the theater.

"Don't look at me," Lulu said with a shrug. "She's *your* sister."

Leena sighed. "Yes, she is, God help me."

Chapter Fifteen

· · · · · · · · · · · ·

"**You** ready for the big bash tonight?" Nathan asked Cole, who'd run into the mini-mart for some shaving cream. He was all out.

"I am now." Cole tossed the can into his shopping basket. "How about you?"

"I'm not the one hot for the guest of honor."

"No, you're the one hot for the owner of the theater where the party is being held."

"Guilty as charged." Nathan grinned. "So I heard you and Leena were seen making out in George Schoppman's shed. You got a thing against using your own bedroom? Or hers?"

"No way George could have seen anything."

"You forget, he's block captain for the Neighborhood Watch and has those powerful binoculars from his days in the Korean War."

"George should mind his own business. So should you."

"George was minding his own shed. He thought you two might be prowlers."

"We were looking for a runaway tortoise."

"So I heard. Tommy wanted me to file a missing tortoise report, but I told him we couldn't do that and sent him over to you instead."

"How kind of you."

"Yeah, that's me. A real kind guy."

"Right. So are you and Skye coming to this party tonight?"

"Yeah. It's at her theater, remember?"

"Right." Cole felt like an idiot for asking such a dumb question, but his thoughts were on Leena and the kiss they'd shared in that stupid shed. "You sound thrilled about the festivities."

"I'm not the party guy you are."

"You've had your moments."

"Yeah, and I'm going to have more with Skye."

"You're such a cute couple," Cole mocked.

"Just like you and Leena." Nathan gave him a look. "What, no instant denial that you two aren't a couple?"

Cole shrugged. "I'm saving my energy."

"Got big plans for later in the night, do you?"

"When did you get so nosy?"

"I'm in law enforcement. It's my job to be nosy."

"Not about my sex life. Man rule."

"There is no such man rule. There is one for not talking at the urinal but nothing about discussing sex in the mini-mart."

"We need to add it then. Or how about man rule nineteen: The dumber the man, the louder he talks."

"Is that why you're yelling?"

"Very funny. You know, I'm beginning to regret not giving you more trouble back when you were angsting over Skye"

"Guys don't *angst* over women. Man rule nine."

"Right."

"Hey, how's that younger brother of yours doing? You heard from him lately?"

"He took the breakup of his engagement pretty hard. Finding his fiancé in another guy's bed on New Year's Eve is about as bad as it gets. He's off to see the world now. No settling down for him."

"For you either."

Cole's voice hardened. "Are you saying I'm setting a bad example for my brother?"

"Hey, lighten up, would you? I wasn't inferring that at all."

"Because I don't see you and Skye setting a date."

"I'd ask her," Nathan said quietly, "but she has a thing against marriage. She's not exactly into tradition."

"While you are Mr. Tradition."

"Makes for an interesting life."

"Or a lot of conflict." Cole remembered all too well how his buddy Nathan had totally fallen apart when his first wife Annie had been killed in a car accident. Still waters run deep, wasn't that the saying? It sure applied to Nathan. Not to Cole. He sailed through life. That was the image he projected and he preferred things that way.

"Like you and Leena aren't always arguing. Talk about conflict. You two are the poster children for conflict. Yelling at each other and then making out in my office."

"Bad choice."

"Leena is a bad choice? I think she's good for you. She shakes you up."

"I'm sure there's a crime somewhere you could go solve," Cole growled.

"You two are such a cute couple." Nathan threw Cole's mocking words back at him before walking out.

It was only when he reached the cashier that Cole realized Nathan had tossed a box of condoms into his basket along with the shaving cream and six-pack of Bud.

• • •

"Shouldn't you be getting ready for your big bash?" Bart asked Leena as she pulled into Regency Park. He was sitting out on his deck.

She stopped to join him. "Did my sister tell you to make sure I didn't skip town before the party?"

Bart just grinned at her.

Leena shook her head. "You're a devious clown, you know that?"

"Just be glad I'm not coming in costume tonight, despite Sue Ellen's best efforts to persuade me."

"What else do you know?"

"My lips are sealed."

"She and Cole aren't planning any surprises, are they?"

"Sue Ellen and surprises go hand in hand. But I don't know anything about Cole's involvement. The only news I've heard about Cole is that the two of you were very involved in Nathan's office a week or so ago."

"Does nothing escape notice in this town?"

"Not much, no."

Leena turned her attention elsewhere. "What's that music you've got playing in the background?"

"Yo-Yo Ma. He's a classical cellist. This piece is by Bach. His cello suite. I'm a huge fan."

"Of Bach?"

"Of Yo-Yo Ma. My clown name, YoYo the Clown, is my way of honoring him."

"A clown who likes classical music, huh?"

Bart shared her smile. "Strange, I know."

"Not strange. Impressive."

"If you really want to be impressed, then I should tell you that the art of clowning dates back thousands and thousands of years to the time of the pharaohs."

"Makeup dates back that far too. Kohl eyeliner was very big in those days," Leena said with a grin.

He lifted his glass of ice tea in salute. "To clowns and models. We're kindred spirits."

Bart was right. Of all the people in town, he was the one she seemed to be able to relate to the best. This despite the fact that he liked being laughed at and she hated it. "I meant to tell you that Sister Mary is very impressed with the work you do at the children's ward in the hospital. But she wasn't impressed with my idea of beautifying Rock Creek," Leena said.

"She has different priorities. That doesn't mean you're wrong."

"It didn't feel that way."

"Maybe your ideas about Rock Creek and staying here will change now that you're involved with Cole."

"I'm not involved with him. I work for the man."

"Believe me, I'm the last guy to give you any relationship advice. I've been divorced twice."

"Well, you'd be the only person not trying to give me advice about Cole. The entire town acts as if they have the right to butt into my private affairs. Not that Cole and I are having an affair," she quickly added. "But even if we were, it wouldn't be anyone's business but our own."

"In an ideal world, that would be the case, yes. But this is Rock Creek."

Leena sighed. "Yes, it is."

"Well, I don't want to keep you. I know you want to get ready for tonight."

"No matter what I do, there's no way I can possibly get ready for tonight. You just can't get ready or be prepared for one of my sister's celebrations."

"You can't take off." Bart gave her a worried look.

"No, I can't. Unfortunately." Leena straightened her shoulders. "No problem. I should be able to do this. I did a photo shoot once where I had to kiss a toad, so you'd think this would be a piece of cake compared to that."

"You'd think."

"Well, it's not."

"Hey, look at it this way: It's better than being shot out of a cannon."

Leena gave him a worried look. "My sister's not planning on doing that tonight, is she?"

"No. No cannon."

"Thank heaven for small favors. Thanks for the pep talk, Bart."

"I didn't do anything."

"You made me feel better, which is a major accomplishment considering the mood I was in." She hugged him. "Thanks."

Once inside her trailer, Leena had a hard time deciding what to wear. She wanted something that would give her confidence and make her feel she looked good. She'd been wearing jeans to work all week. Not the most feminine attire.

She went through the dresses she'd brought with her. Too fancy, too revealing, too short.

What about her hair? That question distracted her from the dress issue. Should she wear it up or down? Curl it? Maybe she should just chop it off and put on a fedora?

Leena flopped onto her bed and closed her eyes. She tried to visualize a suitable outfit and look. Instead she saw Cole right before he'd kissed her the other day.

He wasn't supposed to be invading her mental images this way. But he did it all the time. A constant barrage day and night. She daydreamed about his blue eyes and how many emotions he could convey with just one look. She hungered for the sound of his voice, which rolled over her like rough velvet. Or something.

His voice wasn't the only thing she hungered for. Kissing him hadn't made her longing go away. No, it had only made things worse. The longing to get him naked in bed was so strong she wondered how much longer she'd be able to fight it.

Maybe she was going about this all wrong. Maybe having sex with Cole would get him out of her system. It could happen.

In the end it was easier finding something to wear than it was deciding where her relationship with Cole should go.

Two hours later, Leena parked her Sebring a block from the theater and checked her makeup in the visor mirror. The classic red lipstick drew attention to her mouth while the smoky, slightly shimmery powder and dark mascara added depth to her eyes. She'd swept her hair into a simple updo and was wearing her little black dress of *Breakfast at Tiffany's* fame. She spritzed a little Happy perfume on the back of her neck. The movement of the few tendrils of hair she'd left loose would throw the scent around in a discreet yet intriguing way—a beauty tip she'd learned early in her modeling career. Her killer black heels not only looked great but were actually comfortable as well.

"Pssst!" Leena looked around to see who was trying to get her attention and found Hannah hanging out in the shadows to the side of the Tivoli Theater. When Leena walked closer, Hannah yanked her into the shadows with her. "I need to tell you that I'm so sorry."

"Sorry about what? You didn't take any of those pills, did you?"

"No, no, I promised I wouldn't. But I also promised I wouldn't tell your secret and I did. I didn't mean to. My mom was saying nasty things about you and I was just trying to defend you. I didn't mean to tell her that you're researching a role as an actress. It just came out. I'm so sorry."

"That's okay." Leena patted her shoulder.

"My mom said it was a lie, but I said you wouldn't lie to me."

Okay, that made Leena feel like cow dung. "If you recall, I never actually *said* I was here researching a role."

"Well, of course you wouldn't actually say it because it's supposed to be a secret. But now everyone knows about it."

Leena almost told her the truth. That she was down on her luck. But she just didn't have the heart to do it. Not with Hannah gazing at her with such admiration.

"Don't you worry about it, Hannah. I'll just deny the story. I appreciate you giving me the heads-up, though."

"I hope I didn't ruin your welcome-home party."

"No, not at all. Like I said, stop worrying about it. Everything will be okay."

"You really think so?"

"Yes, I do." Leena had to. Or she'd run screaming down Barwell Street. "So stop worrying."

"Okay." Hannah smiled gratefully before disappearing into the shadows.

Leena almost called her back to invite her into the party before realizing that Edie wouldn't let her daughter attend.

"What are you doing out here?" Sue Ellen demanded from the middle of the red carpet spread in front of the Tivoli. "It's time for your grand entrance."

"Am I being shot out of a cannon?"

"No." Sue Ellen's expression turned worried. "Is that what you wanted?"

"No way. Quiet and understated, remember?"

"That's why I decided not to wear my Mae West costume after all. Lulu talked me out of it."

Leena made a mental note to thank her.

"Now get in here. You're missing your own party."

Leena stared at the mob in the lobby. "Who are all these people?"

"Guests."

"I only recognize maybe"—Leena counted—"a dozen. Who are the other forty or fifty?"

"Prospective clients."

"What?"

"For when I get my realtor's license. I figured I might

as well promote my professional career while having the party." Only now did Leena realize that Sue Ellen's outfit was conservative for her. While it was hot pink, the suit had a flattering line. Her acrylic nails were a matching color with silvery dollar signs on them.

"Be sure and have some crab puffs," her sister continued. "Butch did the catering." A second later Sue Ellen flitted off.

"Wow, this is a big party," Mindy said from beside Leena.

"I don't know most of these people."

"When you live in a small town everybody knows everybody else."

"I haven't lived here for a decade."

"Right." Mindy nodded nervously.

"Sorry. I didn't mean to bite your head off. I'm just a little nervous."

"No way. You? Nervous? Not possible."

"Totally possible. You look great."

"I don't, but it's nice of you to say so."

"Okay, that's got to stop right now."

"What did I do wrong?"

Leena tugged her friend into a quieter corner. "You keep insulting a good friend of mine and I want you to quit it."

"I'm so sorry." Mindy hung her head. "I try to never insult anyone."

"The friend I'm talking about is *you*. You keep putting yourself down and I want you to stop doing that." Leena lifted Mindy's chin. "You are a smart and beautiful woman."

"I'm not beautiful."

"You accept a compliment with a thank-you. You are worthy and lovable and have so much to offer. You have the best smile, excellent cleavage, gorgeous skin, and you always see the good in people. Everyone but yourself."

"I'm not like you."

"And you're not supposed to be. Trust me, I'm no role model."

"Yes, you are. You're a successful model about to embark on a new exciting career in film."

"All lies. Except the model part."

"What?"

"There is no movie. That was total speculation and . . . never mind about that. We were talking about you. I want you to come with me to belly-dancing class."

"I couldn't." Mindy's face turned apple red. "I'd be too embarrassed."

"Just come with me once. If you really hate it, you don't have to do it again. Come on. Just once. As a welcome-home gift for me."

Mindy held out her hands in surrender. "Okay, okay."

"There you are. I thought you'd kidnapped my beautiful wife," T-Bone said. Like Butch, T-Bone had been on the state championship wrestling team and had the no-neck build of a wrestler. The adoring look he gave Mindy made it clear that he loved her as much now as he did back in high school.

"I'm not beaut—" Mindy stopped when Leena gave her "the look." "Uh, thank you?"

Leena nodded her approval. "That's a much better way to accept a compliment."

244 · Cathie Linz

"Mindy never believes me when I compliment her," T-Bone said.

"She's going to do better about that in the future. Right, Mindy?"

"I'll try."

"You go, girl." Leena gave her an encouraging hug. "Carry yourself as if you're proud of what you have. Head held high, shoulders back. You'd be surprised how well that works."

"Leena, what are you doing in the corner?" Sue Ellen demanded. "You're supposed to be mingling." She dragged Leena across the lobby. So much for head held high. Hey, it was always easier giving advice to others than taking it yourself. "Now talk to people."

A woman approached her. "Leena, long time no see. Do you know who I am?"

Leena didn't have a clue.

"I'm Connie Clayton. We went to school together. You didn't recognize me, did you?"

"I, uh . . ."

"That's what four kids will do to you. And Clairol. I used to be a brunette with long curly hair and now I'm a short-haired redhead." Connie laughed and preened a bit. "So Leena, tell us more about this movie you're going to be in."

"I can't." She just couldn't say it was all a mistake. Not to anyone other than Mindy. Certainly not to Connie Clayton, leader of one of the cool-girl cliques in high school. A clique that had never included Leena. "So you have four kids now?"

Connie nodded. "They drive me nuts. There's no place for them to play here. There was talk a while back of opening a playground in that vacant lot just north of town, but nothing ever came of it."

"There are nonprofit organizations that help out with setting up playgrounds for communities that need them," Leena said. "You could check on Google and see what you find."

"I don't have time to do that. Not with four kids." Connie drifted away.

"Some things never change, huh? Connie never wanted to take the initiative. Hi, I'm Vanessa Jacobs. I was in English class with you." The woman smiled.

"I remember you. You took great notes."

"Still do. I've got a blog and website for women entrepreneurs. Angel is a member. Her Angel Designs is really hot right now."

"Skye's mom runs Angel Designs?" Why had no one mentioned this before? Their fuzzy scarves and shawls were all the rage.

"So you've heard of it?"

"Who hasn't?"

"Our site is all about empowering women. I'd love for you to be a guest blogger and talk about learning to love your body."

Sue Ellen had clearly been eavesdropping nearby. "Is she talking about the Remote-Control MegaMax—"

Leena cut her sister off. "No, she's not. Excuse us a moment, will you?"

Vanessa nodded as Leena dragged Sue Ellen away to the ladies' room.

"What's wrong?" Sue Ellen demanded. "I'm not the one talking about loving your body."

"Loving as accepting. Not loving as sex and orgasms

with vibrators." A toilet flush in one of the two stalls sent Leena into a blind panic.

"Chill out," Skye said as she opened the stall door and joined them at the sink. "It's only me."

Leena sagged in relief.

"I already knew you both bought one of Lulu's RCM vibrators," Skye said.

Leena looked at Sue Ellen. "You didn't tell me you got one too."

Sue Ellen shrugged. "I couldn't get it to work."

"Me either," Leena admitted.

Skye shook her head while washing her hands. "Amateurs."

Leena ignored the comment. "Do you two know Vanessa Jacobs?"

"Sure," Skye said. "She runs a great website."

"She asked me to be a guest blogger and talk about empowerment for women. Accepting yourself and your body. That kind of thing."

"Tell them that big hair makes you look smaller," Sue Ellen said.

"Did you accept her offer?" Skye asked.

"I was about to when Sue Ellen here interrupted us."

"Sue Ellen, don't you have a cake to prepare?"

Leena stared at her sister in surprise. "You baked?"

"No. Butch made it. But I have to light the candles."

They ran into Butch outside the restrooms. "There you are," he said. "I've been looking for you. The cake is ready to go." He pointed to a large sheet cake on a wheeled cart a few feet away. "Here." He handed Sue Ellen an elongated candle lighter. "You do the honors."

"It's banana cake," Sue Ellen told Leena.

"Why all the candles? It's not my birthday."

"I put ten on here because that's how long you've been gone." Sue Ellen reached out to steady one of the candles. Instead she ended up igniting her long acrylic nail.

Leena grabbed her sister's hand and blew her nail out before it scorched her. "That was a close call."

Sue Ellen sniffed back tears.

"Did you get burned?" Leena asked in concern, taking hold of Sue Ellen's hand again to look. There was no sign of injury, other than to the fake nail.

"They don't match anymore," she wailed.

"We are *not* burning your other nine nails," Leena said.

"I wanted tonight to be perfect."

"It will be." Leena patted her sister's shoulder. "Go on into the bathroom and run some cold water on it. We'll wait for you. Hurry up." Leena blew out the few candles Sue Ellen had successfully lit. "You get a do-over. Only this time *I'll* light the candles."

The cake made its entrance without further mishap. A few minutes later, Leena accepted Vanessa's blogging invitation and worked out the details with her. She also talked with her about the undeveloped playground.

Catching sight of Tameka, Leena excused herself.

"Do you know Hannah Dabronovitch?" she asked Tameka.

"Yes. She's a student in one of my classes. Why?"

"She's having some body image issues, and I thought maybe you could help her. I tried, but I don't know how successful I was."

"I can help out. There are some passages in a book called *The Body Project* that might help. I'll also touch base with her softball coach. She might have some ideas too."

"Hey, I don't mean to interrupt," Julia said, looking radiant in a simple floral dress. "But I just wanted to thank you for your help, Leena, when I barged into the animal clinic and my water broke."

"I didn't do anything."

"You called for the ambulance. I'm sorry I was so crazed that day. My husband Luke will tell you that I'm not usually like that."

"You were under a lot of stress."

"Yeah, well, so were you. Your first day on the job and all. Anyway, I just wanted to say thanks."

"Where's your baby?"

"With Angel. She couldn't get Tyler to come to the party. He hates crowds, so they decided they'd rather babysit our darling. It's the first time I've left her," Julia admitted. "It's only for an hour and they're right upstairs in Skye's apartment over the theater, but I miss her."

"Miss who?" Luke asked as he joined them, sliding his arm around his wife's waist.

"Our amazing baby girl."

"We could always go check on her," Luke said.

Julia nodded. "What a great idea." A quick smile and she was gone along with her husband.

"How the mighty have fallen," Cole whispered in Leena's ear. "Luke used to be a tough guy and look at him now."

She shivered. His warm breath tickled a tendril of her hair. He'd done it again, sneaking up on her and stealing her composure.

"We'll talk later," Tameka said, leaving them alone. Alone with the sixty other people crowding the elaborately elegant lobby.

"Come on." Cole gently steered Leena through the throng to the doors leading into the theater.

"Have you ever made out in the back of a dark theater?" he said with a wicked gleam in his eyes.

He was wearing jeans, but tonight he'd teamed them with a crisp white shirt, the sleeves rolled up to reveal his muscular forearms. But it wasn't just his great looks that got to her. He had the kind of magnetic sex appeal that would capture any woman's attention. He also had a talent for making her feel as if she were the only person in the entire universe that mattered. Powerful stuff.

She looked at him and just knew. "Tonight's the night."

"Yeah, it is." He smiled with just a hint of a sexy dimple. "A special night."

"A *very* special night."

"Yeah?"

She licked her lips. "Oh yeah."

"I can hardly wait."

"Me either."

He gave her a look. One of those smoky, erotic I-want-you-naked-now looks. "Are we talking about what I think we're talking about?"

"Making out in the back of the theater? No, something even better."

"Really?" He trailed his fingers down her cheek.

"Yes, really."

"If I'm dreaming, don't wake me up. You've already caused me plenty of sleepless nights."

"Same here."

"So we're going to make up for that tonight?"

Leena nodded and nervously ran her tongue over her bottom lip. "That's the plan."

Cole slowly brushed his thumb over the curve of her mouth. "You always have a plan."

"I try to."

"One of the many things I like about you. How soon can we leave this party?"

"Right now."

"Then let's do it."

In that moment *doing it* all night with Cole seemed like the most brilliant idea she'd come up with in her entire life, more important than all the commonsense reasons why caution would be a safer path.

Leena was tired of playing it safe. Just this once, she wanted to give in to the needs storming through her body.

"Where to?" Cole asked.

"My place."

Chapter Sixteen

. . . .

Leena watched the headlights of Cole's Ford truck in her rearview mirror and prayed she didn't get cold feet. The drive wasn't long, but it gave her enough time to be logical if she wanted to be. She didn't.

They'd made their escape through an exit in the theater near the stage. Sue Ellen wouldn't be pleased. Leena had left without eating one of Butch's crab puffs. Without kissing up to any of her sister's prospective realtor clients.

Kissing naturally led her thoughts back to Cole. He was right behind her, and he jumped out of his truck the instant they arrived at her mobile home. He had his lips on hers before she got both feet out of her Sebring, tugging her into his arms and running his hands up and down her back.

"Inside," she whispered or gasped, she wasn't sure which. She couldn't think straight.

He took the keys from her hand and unlocked the front door while stringing kisses across her face.

This continued all the way down the hallway to her bedroom.

He nuzzled against her neck as he freed her hair, sending it tumbling down. "Mmm, you smell good."

"Happy," she murmured.

"Yeah, me too."

"No. My perfume. It's called Happy."

"I like it. And I like this." He braced his hands on either side of her face, threading his fingers through her hair to rest behind her ears. His thumbs rested near the corner of her mouth. "I like kissing you and touching you."

He barely brushed his lips over hers while he slid his hand to her breast, down to her waist and around to the small of her back and then her bottom.

The last time she'd made love with a guy he'd ended up calling her thunder thighs the next day. The sudden awareness of that fact sent a chill through her as panic replaced passion. Cole instantly sensed the change in her.

"It's okay." He used that incredible voice of his, the one that made her believe whatever he said. Believing was a powerful thing.

Great sex was more than just physical. It involved the body *and* the mind. Not that Leena was an expert in the great-sex department. Mediocre-to-okay had been her limited experience. She could count the number of men she'd been intimate with on one hand.

But none of them got to her the way Cole did.

"It's okay." He kissed the tip of her nose. "We'll go

slow. I don't want to rush this. I want you to enjoy every single second. And if you don't, then just tell me."

Yeah, right. Like that was going to happen. She adored everything he was doing to her. She might be scared, but she still wanted more. She told him so in the way she kissed him, her lips parted, her tongue slickly tangling with his. He tasted like the icing on her cake. Heaven, sheer heaven.

She ran her palm along his jaw. He'd shaved recently and his skin was smooth and warm. He looked great when he had that sexy stubble thing going on, but when it came to practical matters she wasn't a fan of stubble burn.

Lowering her hand, she fumbled with the buttons on his shirt. His body radiated heat through the thin cotton. She shoved the material off his shoulders and stood back to admire him.

That meant breaking off the kiss for a moment, but it was worth it. She no longer had to fight the urge to touch him. Now she could indulge to her heart's content. Crisp hair spread out from the center of his chest, arrowing down over his muscled abs to disappear into the waistband of his jeans. He wasn't overly hairy. He was just right. She trailed her fingernail down the dark swirl to the button on his jeans. Leaning forward, she licked his tanned shoulder, then the coppery circle of his nipple.

She could feel him swell beneath her fingers as she lowered his zipper.

She liked focusing on him. It prevented her from worrying about her own body and what he might think of it. She wanted to come to him as an all-powerful Goddess of

Love, but the reality was that confidence was still something she faked sometimes. Like now. He sure helped matters by being so irresistible.

What woman could turn away? Which got her thinking about the other women who'd seen him naked and whom he'd seen naked. All of them probably skinnier than she was.

She took a step back. He followed her, backstepping her toward her bed. She stopped when she felt the mattress at the back of her knees. Instead of shoving her onto the bed, he started kissing her again, building her pleasure. She didn't even notice that he'd undone her dress until it fell down around her waist and she felt the cool air against her skin.

At least this time she was wearing her favorite underwear set. No pink polka dots tonight. Her bra and panties were matching mocha silk. Fabulous. Surely a confidence booster. Definitely a breast booster. Her cleavage was awesome.

Cole clearly agreed. He stared down at her with awe and appreciation. He wasn't even touching her there yet and already her nipples were pebbled.

When he lowered his head, she wondered if he planned on ripping off her bra with his teeth. But he had a better plan. He licked her skin, right where the silk met flesh, along that lacy edge. His actions drove her closer to the brink. As promised, he took his time, and didn't miss one inch. Only when that territory had been completely explored did he move on.

Surely now he meant to remove her bra. She braced herself. The silk might not provide much protection, but it stood between her and nudity.

But Cole didn't reach for the front fastener of her

lingerie. Instead he shifted his attention to her nipples, brushing them through the material. The ensuing friction was incredibly arousing.

She arched her back, thrusting her breasts against him. He responded by taking her into his mouth and tonguing her nipples through the silk and then blowing on the damp material.

Leena had never experienced this kind of pleasure before. And she was still mostly clothed. But that wouldn't last forever. When he eventually did reach for the fastener of her bra, she reached behind her for the bedside table lamp and turned it off.

The room was plunged into darkness.

"I can't see what I'm doing," Cole said.

Leena pressed his hands against her breasts. "Feel your way."

He did, removing her bra and seducing her with his mouth and devilish tongue. Torturing her with such pleasure that she almost came.

His hand moved up her thigh beneath the hem of her silken underwear, caressing the swollen nub hidden there until she did come. Hard and fast. Flying to the moon and back, again and again.

She dropped her head to his shoulder, embarrassed by how quickly she'd reached an orgasm. He refused to let her retreat. He slid her dress down her body and shoved his jeans out of the way, toeing his shoes off before peeling all his remaining clothing onto the floor. And all the while he was telling her how she turned him on, how ready she was for him, and what that did to him.

Since she was now totally naked she wasn't really paying attention to his exact words. She quickly slid beneath her five-hundred-thread-count top sheet. He slid right after her, leaning over her. She tugged him down to her, running her hands over his body. They fit together so well.

Ducking his head, he once again took her breast into his mouth, his teeth nibbling around the edge of her nipple. She was totally breathless when he moved on. He'd disappeared under the sheet. Where was he going? And what was he going to do when he got there?

She soon found out. The pleasure was so intense she had to grab hold of something. She dug her heels into the mattress. He dipped his tongue into her.

She moaned and flew apart.

He popped out from under the sheets to reach down, grab a condom from the pocket of his jeans, and roll it on.

The sheet was shoved aside as he slid into her with one sure thrust, filling her completely. She was still vibrating from her last orgasm as he rocked against her, each move taking him deeper until the inner walls of her vagina convulsed around him.

He stiffened in her arms as he reached his own climax then collapsed against her.

Some time later, when they could actually form words, she spoke first. "I had sex with you *before* our first date. What does that make me?"

"Smart?"

"Not the first word that comes to mind about me."

"It should be." He brushed his knuckles over her cheek. "You're smart, empathetic, funny, creative, and sexy, sexy, sexy."

"In the dark."

"Your choice, not mine. I say we do it again, this time with the light on."

"Wait." She grabbed hold of his arm as he reached for the lamp. "I'm not ready."

"I can fix that." He cupped her bare breast in his big hand.

"*I* need to fix it."

"Uh, okay, if that's your thing."

"I don't mean . . ." She shoved him aside and sat up in bed, hunching forward to hug her bent knees. This position left her back bare. "I'm not talking about sexual arousal."

He trailed his fingers down her spine with gentle reassurance. "Talk to me. What's wrong?"

"I fake it till I make it."

He paused mid caress to take hold of her shoulder and turn her to face him. "You're telling me you just faked your orgasm?"

"No. I'm talking about confidence and self-esteem. I fake a lot of that."

"Is this because of the man who hurt you back in Chicago?"

"Let's just say he wasn't a confidence booster and leave it at that."

She heard the slide of his body against the sheets as he got out of bed. He was leaving. She couldn't really blame him. Who wanted to hear her whining? She should never have opened up to him emotionally the way she had.

Leena was so engrossed in her own thoughts that it took her a moment or two to realize Cole wasn't grabbing his clothes and making a run for it. Instead he lit the pair of thick vanilla candles she had on her table.

"My sister almost set herself on fire tonight."

"Yeah?" The flickering light rippled over his body as he rejoined her in bed. "I'm not interested in your sister. I'm only interested in you."

"What are you doing?" This as he slowly but surely tugged the sheet away from her. She tightened her grip.

"If you have to ask, then I must be doing something wrong." His voice was husky. "Let me clarify things." He kissed her. Unlike last time when he was slow and seductive, this time he was hot and hungry.

His caressing hands roamed all over her body as his words and actions told her how beautiful he found her. Every curve, every dip, every inch was treated to his undivided attention and raw appreciation. He nibbled, licked, kissed, sucked, erotically bit her from the curve of her ear down to the soles of her feet and every erogenous zone in between.

He made her believe she was a goddess. And he made her come more than once. Rolling on another condom, he surged into her, growling her name as he did so.

She could see him in the candlelight. His face was etched with passion and his blue eyes burned as he stared down at her, watching her as she moved from one plateau of almost unbearable bliss to the next. Everything else was stripped away. All fear, all questions. Nothing mattered but this. Only this. Only him. Only her.

Her climax totally consumed her. When she finally came back to earth, it was in time to hear his shout of satisfaction as he came.

As she cuddled against him afterward, she couldn't remember ever feeling happier.

Cole turned her face up to his, gently tucked her

tousled hair behind her ear, and announced, "Next time I'm not only turning you on, I'm turning the light on."

Twirling her index finger in his chest chair, Leena gave him a naughty look. "How about next time *I* turn *you* and the light on?"

His smile was wickedly appreciative. "Deal!"

• • •

"I'm so glad you were able to drop by," Sue Ellen told Russ. She was determined to think of him as Russ. Maybe they hadn't been able to move forward because of her thoughts of him as the coach.

He looked around the empty Tivioli lobby. "It looks like the party is over and everyone has left."

"That doesn't matter. I'm still here. Come on, let's go."

"What about locking up?"

"Skye, we're leaving now," Sue Ellen called out. Her friend was probably making out with Nathan in the theater office where the two of them had retreated.

Sue Ellen should be making out with Russ. "We need to go someplace private. My car." She dragged him outside and down the street to where her pink Batmobile was parked.

"What's going on?" he asked suspiciously.

"Nothing," she said as she shoved him into the passenger seat. Only problem was that he wasn't shoveable. "Okay, you can drive." She dangled her pink Beanie Baby key chain in front of him.

Russ failed to see the huge honor she'd been willing to bestow upon him. "I don't want to drive. I just want to know why you're acting so strange."

"We need to talk. And not at the Dairy Queen."

"They're closed.' "

"All the more reason to talk in my car." When he still didn't move, she added, "It's about the team."

That got him. Russ finally got into the car. She quickly hopped in and peeled out of town. Russ clutched the dashboard with white-knuckled fingers.

"You'll want to put on your seat belt," she said. "It's the law."

"So is driving the speed limit."

Sue Ellen squinted into the darkness. She'd forgotten to turn on her headlights. She quickly fixed that. Okay, now she could see much better. She wasn't going far. She turned her pink Batmobile into a pull-off along the two-lane highway leading out of town and cut the engine.

"Now will you tell me what this is about?"

Staring at him in the semidarkness, she lacked the courage to begin *the talk*. He didn't seem ready to talk about their relationship yet. She had to warm him up first. And nothing did that faster than talking about the team. "What do you think about the team doing a community service project?"

"Which team? The wrestling team or the football team?"

"All your teams. Put together. They could do a cleanup of Barwell Street. Pull weeds, pick up garbage, sweep, that sort of thing." If he hated the idea, she was going to say it was her sister's and she was just passing it along. If he liked the idea, Sue Ellen was claiming it as her own. Leena wouldn't mind. And too bad if she did mind. She'd left early tonight.

"My guys aren't garbage sweepers," Russ said.

"Of course they're not. Bad idea." She decided to try

a little reverse psychology on him. "Just because the team over at Serenity Falls has done this doesn't mean we have to."

"Hold on a second. Anything Serenity Falls can do, we can do better."

"Well, that's what I told my sister, but she didn't seem convinced."

"Then we'll just have to show her, won't we?"

"Yes, we will."

Russ hugged her.

Sue Ellen kissed him. *No fireworks.*

He kissed her back. *Still no fireworks. A nice feeling but nothing special.* She tried not to panic.

She knew guys hated being asked where things were going, where a relationship was headed. Most of the time, it was the kiss of death as far of they were concerned; they were out the door faster than the Road Runner on that cartoon. Maybe she could get the info without actually asking that exact question.

"Are you happy?" she murmured against his lips.

"Mmm. We won our wrestling matches tonight."

She shifted away from him. "I mean about *us*. Are you happy about us?"

"Sure. Why not?"

What kind of answer was that? Not one she was very happy with. "Why not? How about *why*?"

"Why what?"

"Why are you happy about us?"

"What is this, an essay question?"

"You're a teacher. You're smart. You should do great on essay questions."

"Not on this kind of sappy stuff."

"Sappy stuff?"

"Yeah. PA isn't a touchy-feely kind of state. You should know that."

"So that means that no male living in this state has to verbalize his feelings?"

"I told you I was happy about us. What more do you want?"

"More than you can give apparently."

"Aw, come on. Be a good sport."

"A good sport?" She was spitting mad now. "I've been a good sport for weeks now."

"Yeah, you have. A real good sport. You're a team player. Part of my team. I can count on you to carry the ball when needed. You're my go-to gal."

That sounded better. "I am?"

"Of course you are."

He kissed her again. Still no fireworks. He squeezed her one breast. The left one, as always. Nice. Not spectacular but okay.

"We okay, my go-to girl?"

"Yeah, we're okay." Sue Ellen wondered if she was being greedy by asking for more than okay. She should be happy with what she had and not want more. Maybe she didn't deserve more. She wasn't settling; she was accepting. There was a difference, right?

Russ might not be the most romantic guy on the planet, but he was dependable. Reliable. You could set your watch by him. He always kissed her the same way. Always squeezed only her left breast. Plus he was the coach. Respected around town. Reliable and respectable were good things, especially to a girl who'd grown up to be called Our Lady of the Outlandish.

Okay, then Sue Ellen was doing pretty good here. Nothing to worry about. Nothing more she wanted. She wasn't making do. Convincing herself of that should be easy. It was her new goal.

• • •

Leena woke the next morning to find that Cole was gone. He'd left a note: *I didn't want to wake you. See you later.*

Could the man be less romantic? Where were the flowery declarations that she was the most awesome woman he'd ever encountered. That he didn't think she had thunder thighs. That he loved her just was she was.

Hold on. Love wasn't in her plan. But then neither was having mind-blowing, life-altering sex with her boss. That was definitely not in her BlackJack's plan of action to regain her modeling mojo.

He'd sure helped her regain her female mojo, though. He might not have written anything romantic in his note, but he'd said plenty last night the second time they'd made love. Or had it been the third?

She smiled and stretched, then caught sight of the time on her bedside clock. She had to move it or she'd be late for work.

She made it on time, just barely. She'd had to gather her hair into a no-fuss ponytail and swipe on lip gloss, eyeshadow, and a touch of mascara while she drove to work. Yeah, she'd heard the news reports about how that kind of multitasking was dangerous to do, but Rock Creek didn't have a rush hour. Didn't have much traffic either. Still, she felt guilty enough to promise herself she wouldn't do it again.

Mindy greeted her when Leena walked in. They talked about the party for a moment or two. No sign of Cole yet. Seeing her looking around, Mindy said, "He's in his office."

"Oh. Okay. That's fine." Leena felt herself blushing like an idiot.

"Are you okay?"

"Fine. I'd better get to work."

For a Saturday, it wasn't busy. Later, when Mindy offered to cover the desk while Leena took her morning break, she accepted and headed toward the staff room. Cole was there. She already knew he didn't have any patients waiting and his next appointment was half an hour away.

They reached for the coffeepot at the same time, their fingers meeting on the handle. Their fingers intertwined, their eyes met, and the next thing she knew he was kissing her.

He pulled back. "I'm sorry. That was inappropriate."

"Yes, it was," she said primly before switching to her vamp voice. "Do it again."

Seconds later they were in his office with the door locked. He had her backed up against said door and was kissing her senseless. Tugging her closer, he lifted her right leg so her pelvis was cradled against his arousal. The soft cotton swirls of her skirt allowed him easy access to her panties.

"Not here," she said.

She could feel the disappointment coursing through his body as he freed her leg and let it slide back down to the floor.

"Over there." She nudged him toward a nearby armless chair and finished undoing his jeans.

He helped her, getting his and her clothing out of the way. She kept her skirt but got rid of her underwear. He barely got a condom on before tugging her down onto his erection. She was already slick with wanting him. He filled her, taking total possession of her body. She arched her back and tightened her grip on his shoulders. Her orgasm came fast and furious. Her inner muscles milked him, and wave after wave of seismic pleasure consumed her. She bowed forward, resting her head on his shoulder as he buried his face in her hair and reached his own orgasm.

Her skirt still covered them both, hiding their intimacy from view and somehow making it even racier. She lifted her head to grin at him with satisfaction. "You do inappropriate very well."

He grinned back at her. "So do you."

Leena was still grinning when she returned to the reception desk.

"Looks like the break did you good," Mindy noted.

Cole did her good, and Leena couldn't be happier about it. For now . . .

· · ·

Sue Ellen was waiting for Leena when she got home later that afternoon. She was practically dancing with excitement.

"I put together a website for you. A little work on the side. And I printed up business cards on my computer. Here, look."

Sue Ellen proudly handed one over.

LEENA RILEY
Pet Detective and Pet Therapist

"Why would you do this?"

"You said you wanted more money. And since you found that missing turtle—"

"Tortoise." Leena had found it only because she'd almost stepped on it. "I wish you hadn't done this."

"What are you so crabby about?" Sue Ellen followed her inside and stared at Leena intently as she dropped onto the couch. "Oh no. You didn't . . ." Sue Ellen zoomed right over to the couch, sat down, and went almost nose-to-nose with her. "You did! You slept with Cole!"

Since there had been very little sleeping going on last night and certainly none during her break at work today, Leena said, "I did not sleep with him."

"Yes, you did. Don't even bother lying to me. You slept with your boss. And that's why you're crabby. Unless the sex was no good? That could also be why you're crabby."

"The sex was great." The words were out before Leena could stop them.

"I figured it had to be. I mean, look at the guy. He's Cole. People and pets adore him."

"So everyone constantly tells me."

"You don't adore him?"

"Why should I?" The possibility that she might scared her spitless.

"Because you had great sex with him."

"True, but it's more complicated than that. He's my boss." Leena slumped onto the couch. "I don't know what to do. I can't think straight around him. I need a new boss."

"Hello?" Sue Ellen waved the business card she'd created. "That's why I did the pet detective–therapist thing for you."

"I need a *paying* job."

"Some of these pet detectives make good money. I saw a special on Animal Planet about it. And pet therapists aren't cheap either. You can help people become as emotionally available to others as they are to their pet. Help them erase behaviors that might trigger jealousy because their pet has taken up too much space in their heart."

"I need a job that pays me well right now, not at some imaginary point in the future."

"Well, that would be at the animal clinic. There's nothing else available that comes close."

"Then I'm doomed."

"Doomed to have great sex with Cole. Yeah, it's a tough life but someone has to live it."

Leena grabbed her sister's shoulders. "If you tell a living soul about this, I will tell everyone about your boob job. Including Russ."

"Relax. I can keep a secret." Leena gave her a look. "Well, not always, but this time I will."

Leena prayed that was true.

• • •

Two weeks later, Leena was listening to Sheryl Crow on her BlackJack as she power walked down Barwell Street. Things were good. She'd lost the weight she'd gained since coming back to Rock Creek. But more important, she was starting to feel good again about her body. Even her thighs. She was faking it less and making it more. Making it with Cole.

Not that this was all about him. It was all about *her*.

Okay, and him too. She avoided thinking of him as her boss. She also avoided thinking of him as someone she was falling for big-time. For once she wasn't planning ahead, but was basking in the moment. Every sexually fulfilling, orgasmic moment. Yum.

She hummed along with "Soak Up the Sun" as she passed the recently added whiskey barrels on Barwell Street planted with colorful red, white, and purple petunias. The flowers were courtesy of Greenley's Garden Center and the work courtesy of Rock Creek High School wrestling team. Maybe there was hope for the world after all if a business in Serenity Falls was willing to help out Rock Creek. Maybe there was even hope for her and Cole.

The thought made Leena pause in front of Sisters of the Poor Charity Thrift Shop.

"See something you like?" Sister Mary asked.

The nun, like her nephew, had a way of sneaking up on her. Leena had learned to just accept it.

"You really need someone to make a nice window display for you. I think you could do a lot more business if you changed a few things."

Sister Mary drew her inside. "Show me."

Leena stopped near the door. "Right here. This mannequin. You're not putting her to the best use. The clothes she's wearing aren't very flattering. Vintage clothes are in, but you're not taking advantage of that. Look." She exchanged the polyester pants and flannel shirt with jeans and a ruffled shirt. Then she added a chunky bohemian-style necklace. "There. That's better."

As if to prove her point, a woman stopped by and pointed to the outfit. "I love that top and that necklace." Leena removed it from the mannequin and handed it to the prospective buyer. She replaced it with another top-scarf-necklace combo.

"And if you set other similar items on a table here, then you could increase sales. And then there's your jewelry section. That vintage costume jewelry is going for top dollar on eBay. You really should have an account set up there so people can bid on your items. Here." Leena took a picture of a rhinestone broach with her BlackJack and then went online with it. Half an hour later, she'd set up an account for the thrift shop and people were already starting to bid on the jewelry item.

"Twenty dollars?" Sister Mary gasped.

"I'd keep these vintage pieces separate to sell online." Leena handed a small boxful she'd selected from the stock to Sister Mary. "I can stop by after work and take more photos with my phone."

"Thank you. We aren't normally open on Sundays, but do you think you could stop by maybe in the afternoon to do up a display for the front window?"

"Sure. We could do something patriotic for Fourth of July coming up."

"That would be great."

And so Leena found herself on Sunday afternoon standing behind the plate glass window fronting the thrift store. Her sister had insisted on helping her. "After all, I'm the one with the interior-decorating degree."

And the velvet Elvises. Even so, Leena didn't have the heart to turn her away. Sue Ellen had been bummed out the past few weeks. Ever since Leena's welcome-home party. Leena had asked if Sue Ellen had fought with Russ, but she hadn't really ever answered her. Which was Leena's family's chosen means of communication: CTS—change the subject.

So far, the display area held a red high-back wooden chair and a blue table. A pile of denim and red-checked gingham pillows were in the corner while a poster of the Statue of Liberty provided the backdrop. The female mannequin wore jeans and a red T-shirt with a jaunty navy scarf.

"What's going on out there?" Sue Ellen pointed to Skye and Nathan, who were across the street and pointing up. "You don't think it's a meteorite, do you? I saw some show on cable that said the earth is vulnerable to meteorite attacks."

Leena pressed her nose against the newly cleaned glass and peered up at the sky. "No meteorite. It looks like . . . a plane. Writing something in the sky."

"Great marketing idea. I should do that when I get my realtor's license. What's the message say?"

"Marry me, Skye."

"Oh my God! Nathan has proposed to Skye!" Sue Ellen started shrieking before racing outside.

Leena followed at a much slower rate, taking the time to lock the thrift shop door behind her. She didn't want anyone walking in and stealing anything. Not that crime was a big deal in Rock Creek, but even so, she didn't want to take any chances.

"Congratulations!" Sue Ellen had Skye in the midst of a python-strong grip before quickly releasing her. "I'm so happy for you both. Nathan, what a romantic way to propose."

"It wasn't me," he quickly told Skye. "I didn't hire any skywriter. I'd never do that to you."

"What are we looking at?" Cole asked as he joined them. He had a takeout cardboard box from Angelo's Pizza in his hands. Leena's mouth watered at the smell. Her mouth also watered at the sight of him in his customary jeans and navy T-shirt.

"Nathan just asked Skye to marry him by hiring a plane to write the proposal in the sky."

"I didn't do it. It wasn't me." Nathan sounded a little desperate.

"Well, it sure as hell wasn't me." The look Cole shot Leena told her she was the only woman in his thoughts these days.

Skye looked at them all with pissed-off frustration. "It was *me*, you idiots!"

Chapter Seventeen

. . . .

"I don't understand," Sue Ellen spoke for them all. "Why would you propose to yourself?"

"I was signing my name at the end. There were fewer letters in my name than in Nathan's. Oh hell, just forget it! Forget I said anything. Or wrote anything. Or had the skywriter write anything."

"Is this some kind of joke?" Nathan said.

Seeing the look on Skye's face, Cole said, "Wrong way to react to a marriage proposal, bud."

"Do not even speak to me." Skye's voice was icy. "Come on, Sue Ellen."

Nathan took off after them, leaving Leena and Cole alone.

"Well, that was fun," he drawled with a grin.

"I feel bad for Skye," Leena noted. "Talk about

wearing your heart on your sleeve. She just wrote it clear across the sky."

"Yeah, but she did it without giving Nathan a clue. He told me that he wanted to propose to her but that she didn't want anything to do with marriage."

"She probably wanted to surprise him."

"She succeeded."

"Yeah, well, she also succeeded in taking my help with her." Looking down, Leena wished she'd worn something a little more flattering than jeans and a plain light blue T-shirt. She hadn't expected to run into Cole but had planned on seeing him later, wearing something more attractive. "Sue Ellen was helping me do the window display at the thrift shop."

"It's closed on Sundays."

"I know. Your aunt gave me an extra set of keys." She held them up.

"I can help you. I've even got food." He waved the pizza box in front of her.

"Yeah, I noticed. I could use the help." She couldn't use the calories from the pizza, but as long as she stuck to one slice she should be okay. She actually found it easier to resist pizza than to resist Cole.

They walked across the street and were soon at work behind the plate-glass window of the Sisters of the Poor Charity Thrift Shop.

"Hey, how do you think I look in this?" He put on a fedora hat that would make Justin Timberlake jealous. Justin might be bringing sexy back, but Cole made sexy irresistible.

Without waiting for an answer from her, Cole swapped the fedora for a straw cowboy hat. "Or is this better?"

He gave her a classic Clint Eastwood narrow-eyed look.

"You had me at 'hey,'" Leena said with a grin.

"I wish."

She stuffed a piece of pizza in his mouth.

He tugged her against him and smeared tomato sauce from his lips to her cheek.

"Are you two at it again?" Sister Mary asked.

They jumped apart guiltily.

"Why didn't you tell me she was here?" Cole said.

"I just arrived," Sister Mary said. "Looks like I got here in the nick of time."

Cole grabbed his pizza box and tried to make a quick exit. "I'll leave you two alone."

"No, you won't." Leena went right after him, grabbing hold of the back of his T-shirt as he reached the door. "You are not leaving me here alone to face an angry nun."

"You're not Catholic," he said. "It shouldn't be a problem for you."

Leena hung on tight. "Well, it is."

"I'm not angry," Sister Mary said. "Now get back here, Cole, and bring that pizza with you. And yes before you ask, Leena, nuns do eat pizza."

"Yes, Cole, get back here." Leena tugged on his T-shirt.

Cole tossed her a wicked grin over his shoulder. "The woman can't keep her hands off me."

Out of view of his aunt, Leena slid her other hand around his waist and down the placket of his jeans to cup him intimately. A second later she used the same hand to catch the pizza box he'd just dropped.

Recovering quickly, Cole tipped the box, trapping her hand between the cardboard and his body. "You've got tomato sauce on your face."

She released him and the pizza to wipe her face.

"You can't seem to keep your hands off her either," Sister Mary said. "You two need a chaperone. And I need some pizza. So get over here and let's eat, and then get this window display finished."

As she and Cole worked together, Leena realized that for the first time she felt part of something larger than herself. She felt part of a community. She felt part of Cole's community, and it was both thrilling and terrifying.

• • •

The following Sunday found Leena in the pink Batmobile with her sister. She looked at the pink and black sign for the Sugar Shack and then looked at Sue Ellen. "Why are we here?"

"I told you." Sue Ellen opened the door to her pink Batmobile. "Research."

Leena was not eager to leave the safety of the car. "Why do you need me? Why not bring Lulu or Skye?"

"I wanted to get your opinion first."

That alone was a milestone. Sue Ellen never wanted Leena's opinion about anything. She reluctantly opened the passenger door and got out. This wasn't the way Leena had planned on spending her Sunday afternoon. "I don't have long. I have to be at Cole's house in a few hours. What?" This when her sister rolled her eyes. "I'm helping him with his house."

"Removing his tool belt, more likely. You don't think the entire town knows what's going on? His truck is parked in front of your mobile home all night. Or your car is at his house."

"I park it in the back."

The possibility that everyone in Rock Creek knew Leena was banging her boss was mortifying.

Seeing her stricken expression, Sue Ellen gave her a comforting hug—more teddy bear–like and less python-like. "Don't worry about it. Actually the town is more interested in Skye and Nathan's engagement and their wedding plans. That's why we're here today."

"Because Skye wants to get married in a strip club?"

"No, because I'm in charge of her bachelorette party."

"I thought her sister would be doing that."

"Julia is no fun. She'd probably have sherbet punch and Pop-Tarts at the library. Besides, she's got a little baby to take care of. I can handle this much better than she could."

"Did you bring me here to check out male strippers?"

"Not this time."

"Then why are we here?"

"You'll see." She opened the door to the club.

Once inside, Leena had to pause to let her eyes adjust from the bright sunshine outside to the comparative darkness.

"Hi." An athletic-looking woman in black short-shorts and a halter top bounced over to greet them. She looked like a Dallas Cowboys cheerleader, a petite and pretty size six who'd probably never chowed down on a family-size bag of Cool Ranch Doritos in her entire life. Leena sure hoped not. Because if Ms. Halter Top were one of those women who could eat anything and not gain a pound, then Leena would have to hate her. She wouldn't be able to help herself. Petty perhaps, but hey, she never claimed to be perfect. "I'm Gigi. You must be Sue Ellen."

"That's right."

"Well, like I told you on the phone, the bachelorette party package here includes a pole-dancing lesson for all the attendees."

"You said you could demonstrate what a lesson would be like."

"Sure. Come on up." She indicated they should follow her onto the stage, where two poles were installed.

Leena wondered if they cleaned them after each show. She was wearing pants, but her sister had on a short denim skirt with pink go-go-style boots from the sixties.

Leena was sure that Donna Karan never intended for the sleeveless navy knit top and matching pants Leena was wearing to be worn for pole dancing. She could tell by the look on Gigi's face that she agreed Leena's attire didn't cut it.

"If you'll just sign this release form, we'll get started."

Sue Ellen signed without reading it. Not Leena. She checked every word before putting the paper down. "I'm not signing this."

"Then you can't perform."

"Fine, I'll just watch you two."

"Come on, Leena," her sister said. "Have some fun."

"I'm all for fun that doesn't involve personal injuries."

Seeing the stubborn look on her face, Sue Ellen gave up and instead concentrated on Gigi's instructions.

"We'll start out with something simple. Some lean-out stretches. Pole dancing really builds upper arm strength. And builds confidence."

The playlist started out with a little Clash and some

Guns N' Roses and Black Eyed Peas. Gigi said, "It's all about unleashing your inner hottie."

"I can't seem to get into it," Sue Ellen said. "Maybe if you played the music I brought. Taylor Hicks. 'The Runaround.' Track number one."

The minute she heard the song, Sue Ellen starting jiving, performing the hip circle, something she'd perfected from her belly-dancing classes. She added the swing walk Gigi had shown her earlier along with several slow bends and hair flips. She was clearly having such a good time that Leena started having second thoughts, wishing she'd joined her.

Crack. Whomp. Sue Ellen went down like a ton of bricks.

Leena rushed over to her. "Are you okay? What happened?" Remembering how Sue Ellen had cried over her singed nail, she said, "Are you hurt?"

"Yep," Sue Ellen croaked.

"Where?"

"My knee. I hit it on the pole."

"I'll get some ice," Gigi said.

When that didn't help with the pain or the swelling, Leena suggested calling 911.

"No way!" Sue Ellen said. "I can't let Russ know about this. I can't have an ambulance pick me up from a strip club. No offense, Gigi."

"None taken. But this Russ, whoever he is, is going to know if you have the bachelorette party you're planning here. Word gets around."

"His name is Russ Spears. He's the coach—"

"At the local high school." Gigi nodded. "Yeah, I know him. He comes in here occasionally."

"He does?"

Gigi put her hand to her heavily glossed mouth. "Maybe I shouldn't have said anything."

"Hello?" Leena waved. "If we can get back to my sister's injury here. You have to get medical attention for this.

"Remember, you did sign a release form," Gigi said.

Sue Ellen grabbed hold of Leena's arm. "You can drive me to the emergency room."

"Can you walk to the car?"

"Sure." She needed both Leena and Gigi's help to stand up and limp to the car, which luckily was parked right beside the door.

While Leena drove her sister in the pink Batmobile to the local hospital's emergency room, Sue Ellen spent her time calling Russ on her pink Razr phone.

"I keep getting his voice mail. He'll come as soon as he gets the message. You'll see. He'll be there for me."

"I'm your sister. I'm here for you."

"You don't want to be here. Russ does. You'll see."

What Leena saw was Donny, standing outside the entrance to the emergency room. He wasn't wearing his Smiley's Septic uniform but was dressed in khaki pants and a green polo shirt.

"What are you doing here?" Leena asked.

"The bartender at the Sugar Shack is a buddy. He knows Sue Ellen is a friend of mine, so he called me to tell me what happened."

A hospital orderly quickly joined them with a wheelchair. "Be careful with her," Donny ordered him, fussing like a mother hen.

"Russ is coming," Sue Ellen told them all as she grimaced with pain.

"I'll stay until he gets here," Donny said.

The waiting room was full. A triage nurse took their information and then told them to wait.

Three hours later they left with Sue Ellen's knee in a bandage, a pair of crutches, and a prescription for painkillers.

"I can't believe they don't let you use a cell phone in there." The minute they were outside, Sue Ellen frantically checked her phone for messages. "I'm sure Russ has been trying to reach me."

Leena could tell by the way her sister's face fell that Russ was a no-show. No response.

Sue Ellen snapped her pink Razr shut.

"Why don't you go get her prescription filled while I take her home," Donny suggested.

"In your truck?"

"No, I can drive Sue Ellen's car if that's okay with her. You can drive my truck," he told Leena.

And so five minutes later Leena pulled in front of Wal-Mart in a Smiley's Septic Service truck. Certainly a new experience for her. The truck hadn't been as difficult to drive as she'd expected. Then again, after managing the pink Batmobile, Leena figured she could handle any vehicle.

Her plan was to run into the store and get the prescription filled and quickly slip out again before anyone caught her. But Cole's appearance put a stop to that plan. She should have expected him. He had a track record of showing up when she least expected it.

"You doing a little septic work on the side?" Cole asked as she walked away from the truck.

"It has been a shitty day."

He cupped her face with his big hand. "What happened?"

"My sister hurt her knee while learning how to pole dance at the Sugar Shack."

"What?"

"You heard me the first time."

"Yeah, but I figured you were kidding me."

"I wish. Donny drove her home. I'm here to fill a prescription for her. He lent me his truck."

"That was nice of him."

"He's crazy in love with my sister."

Cole didn't seem to have an answer to that statement. Instead he said, "Do I want to know what you were doing pole dancing at a strip club? Trying to earn extra money?"

"*We* weren't pole dancing. Only my sister was. Sue Ellen was checking out a bachelorette party package they offered. For Skye. You look disappointed that I haven't taken up a second career as an exotic dancer."

"I'm sure you'd be great at it."

"Yeah, right."

His response was to kiss her, right there in the Wal-Mart parking lot. "Want me to convince you?" he murmured against her lips.

"Convince me of what?" she murmured right back.

"How good you'd be. Good at being bad."

"I already know how good I am at being bad."

"Do you? It didn't sound like it a minute ago. Maybe I should see about getting a pole installed in my house. You could practice your moves on me."

"That's generous of you. But I've got to get my sister her pain pills."

"Right." He reluctantly released her. "You're right."

"Of course I am." She gave him a jaunty grin. "I'm always right."

"Me too. Something else we have in common." He took hold of her hand and threaded his fingers through hers. "We might as well hang out together while you wait for Sue Ellen's prescription to be filled."

"Don't tell anyone how Sue Ellen was injured," she told him. "She doesn't want Russ to know the details."

"Okay, but people tend to find things out in this town."

"Like the fact that we're together?"

"Does that bother you?"

"I don't like being the center of gossip."

"Skye and Nathan are the center of gossip right now. He accepted her proposal, you know. And she accepted his apology. Finally."

"Thanks for the latest update. I'm going to have to take a rain check on our plans for this afternoon, I'm sorry to say. I have to stay with my sister." Seeing her sister collapse onstage that way had shaken Leena. Sure Sue Ellen went from one a crisis du jour to the next, but this was different.

"I understand."

Leena wished she understood the tangled jumble of emotions she was feeling. About Cole. About her sister. About her own future. Nothing was tidy and organized the way she wanted, and she didn't like that one bit.

• • •

"Brownies aren't dinner," Leena told her sister. "You need to eat something healthier with those pain pills."

"Did you know that bossy behavior is the result of unresolved anger, sadness, or anxiety from childhood? I read that in a magazine at the hospital in the waiting room."

"I noticed you were ignoring Donny. I thought it was very sweet of him to stay and help you."

"He was sweet. Helped me get inside and everything."

"He seems like a really nice guy."

"Yeah. But getting back to your bossiness . . ."

"You're just as bossy as I am."

"So we both have unresolved issues from our childhood. We're both stubborn too. You think we got that from Dad's stint in the Marine Corps when he was young?"

"Huh?"

"I've heard Marines are stubborn."

"So are Irishmen."

"You do know that with a name like Flannigan, Cole is Irish too."

"Yeah, but he's not like Dad."

"No one is like Dad. Remember how he always told us that we should expect the worst because then we'd never be disappointed?"

"Yeah."

"I don't like that philosophy," Sue Ellen announced. "I think I'm going to change it. If you expect the worst, then that's all you're going to get. I want more. I deserve more. Dad was wrong."

"Do you remember when he used to get drunk?"

Maybe the pain pills had lowered Sue Ellen's defenses because for once she didn't change the subject. In fact, she was in conversation-domination mode.

"Sure I do. I hit my knee, not my head. My memory is just fine."

"You never talk about those days."

"Because they stunk."

Leena had to laugh at her sister's bluntness. "Yeah, they did."

"Why bring them up now?"

"Because since returning to Rock Creek, I've been thinking a lot about that time. Sister Mary said that maybe I had to come home to face my fears before I could move on, that you can't really move forward until you've made peace with your past."

"Have you made peace with it? You were just a kid."

"I was nine, almost ten when Dad finally stopped drinking."

"He's been sober for almost twenty years now."

"I know. Maybe that's why I feel so guilty about being upset about it still. It's such a cliché, you know? The alcoholic father screaming while the little kid hides in the corner with her baby sister." It helped just to talk about it. Stashing the memories away in a closet and locking them in there only made things worse, not better. Harder to deal with, not easier. "I was so scared. I guess that's why I'm bossy now, because I like being in control."

"I didn't realize you remembered so much."

"You were gone a lot."

"Yeah, I had to get out and stay with friends. I'd had sixteen years of it by then. You only had nine. You know why Dad quit, don't you?"

Leena shook her head. "Did Mom threaten to leave him or something?"

"She did that several times and he'd promise to quit, but that didn't work. He quit because he almost got you killed. He was driving drunk and swerved into oncoming traffic. Barely missed having a head-on collision with you and Emma in the car. He came home and never drank again."

"They never talk about it. Not Dad or Mom."

"They started life over that day."

"How do I do that? I've tried reinventing myself, but there's a part of me that stays the same. They're the reason I am the way I am."

"And what's wrong with the way you are? Other than your bossiness, I mean."

"I'm not the successful model you think I am. My agent fired me."

To Leena's surprise, Sue Ellen took the news nonchalantly. "Yeah, I figured something like that had to have happened."

"You did? But you wanted to have a parade for me and everything."

"Yeah, well, you're my sister. I was prepared to back you in whatever you said."

Leena felt the threat of tears sting her eyes. Sue Ellen's loyalty was absolute. She was only now realizing how valuable that was. "So you think I'm crazy to be worrying about stuff that happened all those years ago?"

"What good does worrying do? You can't change the past. It's over. All you can do is enjoy the present and look forward to the future."

The words made a huge impression on Leena; it was like one of those a-ha moments they talked about in *O* magazine. "When did you get so smart?"

"It wasn't my idea. I think Angel taught me that. She's real big on building self-esteem and stuff."

"The road to self-esteem is a long one—filled with detours and dead ends."

"And construction zones, potholes, and roadkill," Sue Ellen added. "Dead possums and squirrels—"

"Yeah, that's enough. Thanks for the nice visuals there."

Sue Ellen grinned.

Leena grinned back and offered her bent pinkie.

Sue Ellen met her halfway, her pinkie bent as well.

They linked pinkies and repeated in unison the vow Sue Ellen had made up so many years ago. "Believe it or not, we're sisters—no snot."

• • •

Sue Ellen shooed her sister out the next morning, assuring her she'd be fine with Donny's help. He'd insisted on staying with her while Leena went to work today.

"What about you?" Sue Ellen asked him. "You have to go to work too."

"I didn't have anything important on the agenda for today. My employees have got it covered."

"Are you sure? I could call Skye or Lulu . . ."

"I'm positive. Now what can I get you? More ice for your knee?"

"That would be great, thanks."

He'd just retrieved an ice pack from the freezer when her cell phone rang. She checked caller ID. It was Russ. Finally. He'd better have a damn good excuse for not calling her earlier.

"Hey," he said cheerfully. "We were fishing. The guys and me. Anyway I figured you had plenty of people there to take care of you."

"People?" she repeated in disbelief.

"Yeah, your sister and friends."

Sue Ellen needed to clarify what Russ was saying here, because it sure sounded as though he didn't give a damn that she was injured. "So you were fishing with your buddies and didn't get any of my dozen voice-mail messages?"

"I got them."

"When? Just now?"

"No, when you sent them. Like I said, I figured you had people to help out."

"So you couldn't even be bothered to call me back?"

"I'm calling now," he said impatiently, as if she were the one being unreasonable. It was a technique he'd used on her before, and it had worked. But not this time.

"Yeah, you're calling me now. Almost twenty-four hours after I was hurt so badly I had to go to the ER. Well, buddy, it's too little, too late."

"You have to understand, I was busy."

No, Sue Ellen suddenly realized with 20/20 clarity. *I don't have to understand. I don't have to accept. I don't have to settle.* "We are *so* over."

"What do you mean?"

"You heard me. This relationship, if you can even call it that, is over. Through. Finito."

"You're just upset right now. You'll shake it off."

"The only thing I'm shaking off is *you*! Don't call again." She hung up on him.

"Are you okay?" Donny asked in concern. "Want me to go beat him up for you?"

"I'm well rid of him. I deserve better."

"You sure do."

She looked at Donny as if seeing him for the first time. In a way, she was. "Come here and kiss me."

He blinked. "Huh?"

"You heard me right. Get over here and kiss me. Unless you don't want to?" Sue Ellen asked uncertainly.

Maybe Donny was having second thoughts about her. Maybe she'd misconstrued that chocolate-brownie moment they'd shared weeks ago. Maybe he'd moved on and found someone else.

"Oh, I want to. I've wanted to for a very long time." He was beside her an instant later and gently leaned forward to touch his lips to hers. Fireworks. He gave her fireworks. Big-time Technicolor fireworks.

Sue Ellen started crying.

Donny panicked. "What is it? What's wrong? Did I hurt you? Is it Russ?"

"No, it's you," Sue Ellen whispered in awe. "It's always been you. I just didn't know it until now. Or maybe I knew but I fought it." She cupped his cheek. "It's you. Not Russ. You."

· · ·

Leena had been a zombie at work all day because she hadn't gotten more than an hour's sleep last night. She and her sister had talked for hours. And no CTS— changing the subject.

Leena just needed a quick nap and she'd be fine. She'd checked in with Sue Ellen several times and been told that Donnie was taking excellent care of her and no, she didn't need anything. He gave her fireworks and a woman didn't need more than that.

Leena would figure out her sister's cryptic remark later. For now she walked in her front door and headed straight for her bed. Before she got there, her BlackJack rang. A quick look at the screen told her it was her agent from Chicago. She took the call.

"Leena, it's Irene. Listen, I've got great news! A

client wants you for his new ad campaign for a new line of jeans for plus-size women. You have got to get back here ASAP. In the next forty-eight hours."

"But you fired me."

"Minor detail. Just get back here."

Leena heard the dial tone in her ear.

She was too exhausted to deal with anything. She just needed to lie down for a second and then she'd figure everything out. She took off her clothes and crawled into bed.

She woke up to find Cole kissing her. "Hey, Sleeping Beauty. I knocked but you didn't answer. I was getting worried."

She'd kicked off the sheets in her sleep. He viewed her nearly naked body with wicked appreciation.

"I didn't get much sleep last night," she admitted.

"Let me kiss your temple and make you feel better." He parted her legs.

"That's not where my temple is."

"Trust me, I'm a doctor."

"Of veterinary medicine."

"I know what I'm doing. This is your temple." He brushed his fingers against her face. "And this is your temple." He used his other hand to brush his fingers over her clitoris. "Up here is where you get headaches . . . and down here is where you get other aches."

"Mmm." She was melting.

"Temples like this should be respected and worshipped." He lowered his head to do just that.

The ensuing sharp pleasure was divine. Downright blissful.

While she lay there, steeped in sensual satisfaction, he quickly removed his clothes and joined her in bed.

She assisted him in putting on a condom and then guided him to her.

He filled her so gloriously. With each powerful thrust, she came closer and closer to reaching that apex of orgasm again. The pressure built until her very universe expanded and contracted as she came.

She clenched her nails into his back as wave after wave consumed her. He heard him shout her name as he climaxed.

Afterward, hot and sweaty, they showered together in her tiny bathroom. She pinned him to the wall, intending to have her wicked way with him, but he turned the tables on her and seduced her instead, his slippery fingers working their magic. She returned the favor to his utter delight.

Later, as they finished off some leftover cold chicken, Leena confessed that her agent had called. "She wants me to come back to Chicago right away."

Leena was undecided about what her next step should be.

But before she could say that, Cole stated his opinion. "You should go."

At her look of surprise, he added, "I always knew you'd be leaving. We knew this was temporary."

"That's all you have to say?" What had she expected? Passionate declarations of his love for her? Husky requests that she not leave him? Romantic vows that she was his soul mate? Clearly that wasn't what he was feeling.

His expression was impassive as he looked at her. Gone was the fire of an hour ago. "Do you need the money to get there? I can help you with that." He peeled off some cash and tossed it on top of her coffee table.

Leena stared at the money and felt her heart shatter. Cole was paying her off. As if she was a whore he'd had sex with. The town golden boy dumping her, the poor trailer-park trash. The fat loser.

Her shame was complete and ran bone deep. Pain and humiliation lasered a hole clear through to her very soul. She couldn't speak. Couldn't breathe. She sat there frozen. How had things gone so wrong so fast?

"Have a good trip." He was gone before she could throw him out.

Chapter Eighteen

· · · · · · · · · · ·

Cole was no idiot. He knew he'd messed up big-time last night. But Leena's announcement about her agent wanting her to return to Chicago immediately had completely blindsided him. Even so, he shouldn't have blown her off the way he had.

After years of perfecting his nothing-bothers-me persona, he'd been in danger of losing it last night. That's why he'd gotten out of there so fast. Because he was in over his head with her. His problem, not hers. He wasn't about to stand in the way of her big dreams.

She'd told him from day one how she hated Rock Creek and how she had no interest in anyone who wanted to stay here. She'd made that perfectly clear.

For once, his charm had deserted him and he'd shut down. Because despite all his best efforts, Leena had slipped into his heart. She hadn't asked him to fall for her. She hadn't tried to seduce him with her smart mouth and big heart. No, the blame was all his. He's the one who'd fallen in love with her.

Cole had tried to do the right thing and give her access to her dreams by giving her the money she needed to accomplish her goals. Leena always had a plan, and he realized her plan hadn't included returning to Chicago this soon, which meant she might not have the funds to do that.

But he'd handled it all wrong. Instead of giving her encouragement and support, he'd thrown the money at her and walked out. Because he'd panicked. He had no experience with this love crap.

This was why he'd kept things light and carefree in all his previous romantic relationships. Because he'd always known that if he fell, he'd fall too hard.

Cole was in a bad mood even before he walked into his office the next morning to find the money he'd given Leena on his desk. No note, nothing.

"Where's Leena?" he asked Mindy.

"She's gone. She called me at daybreak and said she was leaving. She got Mrs. Petrocelli to fill in for her at the reception desk. Mrs. Petrocelli's broken leg is healed now, and she has some experience since she used to work at a dentist's office as the receptionist."

"She's gone?"

"Leena? Yes. She's driving back to Chicago. She sounded really upset. Like she'd been crying."

Cole's stomach clenched. "When did she leave?"

"She dropped something in your office about an hour ago. Hey, where are you going?"

"To get her."

• • •

"Traitor." Leena kicked the tire on her Sebring. Not hard, or she'd have a broken toe to add to her troubles. Just a token kick. She'd only gotten an hour outside of town and the stupid vehicle had stalled on her. She'd forgotten to recharge her cell phone so that was useless. She'd eventually hitched a lift with a Doritos delivery truck. The irony there was not lost on her.

And here she was—back at the Rock Creek Gas4Less Mini-Mart.

Now what was she supposed to do? She'd arranged for a tow truck to go get her car, but she couldn't wait around here for that to happen. And she couldn't ask her sister for a ride to the nearest airport because Sue Ellen's knee was still too bad off for her to drive. Lulu didn't own a car as far as Leena knew. And Skye was engaged to Cole's best friend, so that nixed asking her for help.

Leena had to come up with a new plan pronto. She had to focus all her attention on that. Otherwise she'd start crying again. No way that was happening. Big girls don't cry. They hauled up their big-girl panties and sucked it up. They moved on. She'd wasted enough tears on Pet Boy Cole Flannigan.

He'd done her a favor by shaking her out of her romance-induced stupor. She deserved better. So she'd covered her hurt with a thick blanket of anger. She was woman, hear her roar.

She still needed a plan. How to get out of this damn town . . .

A school bus pulled in to get gas. Sister Mary got off and pumped it herself. "Leena." She waved.

Leena looked away. No way she wanted to speak to Cole's aunt.

Sister Mary didn't take the hint and came over, delegating the gas-pumping job to the bus driver. "Anything wrong?"

"My car broke."

"I'm sorry to hear that."

"I was heading back to Chicago. It's important I get there." Leena needed to get out of town before Cole threw any more money at her.

"Well, you're welcome to hitch a ride with us. We're taking a field trip to Pittsburgh. You could catch a flight from there to Chicago. I hope everything is okay?"

"Yeah, just fine. Are you leaving now?"

"Yes. We have a few empty seats—"

Leena grabbed her suitcase and climbed onto the bus.

"Okay, then." Sister Mary followed at a slower rate. "What about your car?"

"I'll make arrangements for it and the rest of my stuff later, don't worry."

"I am worried. You seem terribly upset about something. Does that nephew of mine have something to do with your sudden desire to get out of town?"

Leena avoided answering by saying, "My agent called me with a wonderful job offer."

"Is that what you want? To go back to modeling?"

"I was only here for the summer, to get enough money to go back to Chicago."

"The summer isn't over yet."

"It turns out I can leave earlier than expected."

"If that's what you want, then I'm happy for you."

"Why wouldn't it be what I want?"

"You tell me."

"Oh no!" Leena saw Cole out the bus window. "Don't tell him I'm here," she pleaded with Sister Mary. "Get rid of him. Please," she begged before practically shoving the nun back out of the bus.

Leena crouched down in the aisle, out of sight.

"You'll get hemorrhoids doing that," an elderly woman with bright orange hair said.

Leena ignored her and tried to focus on the conversation outside the bus.

"Have you seen Leena?" he asked his aunt. "I thought I saw her as I drove by."

"What's going on, Cole?"

"I don't have time to talk about it . . ."

His voice was getting closer to the bus's door.

Leena scrambled into a seat near the back. She hunkered down and tried to be invisible. Impossible to do at her height and size. Especially given the fact that the other passengers on the bus were all senior citizens. *Short* senior citizens.

He found her easily and got right to the point. "Don't leave."

She shook her head. Her throat had clamped shut. Seeing him made the pain come rolling back.

"If you don't get off this bus, I'll have to pick you up and carry you off," he said.

Just the thought of him struggling to carry her like a two-ton weight made her grit her teeth as rebel tears formed in her eyes. She refused to let them fall. She really should have gotten some sleep last night. Then she would have kicked his sexy butt right off this damn yellow bus!

Her vision was slightly blurred, but she was pretty sure Cole now looked totally panicked. A recalcitrant tear rolled down her cheek before she angrily scrubbed it away. She turned to face the window, expecting Cole to leave. Instead he dropped into the empty seat beside her. "Okay, then I'll just go with you."

"Go . . ." Hiccup. "Away." Great. When Leena cried, or was on the verge of doing so, she got huge, honking hiccups. Backward ones.

Furious with herself and him, she wiped away another tear.

"Do you love me?" He tenderly cupped her chin in his hand.

She shook her head.

"Are you sure?"

She glared at him. The anger was coming back. "Beat it, Pet Boy," she growled. Or tried to between hiccups.

"If you'd just get off the bus, we could talk—"

"I do not want to talk to you. Ever. Not even if we were the last two people on the planet."

"Not even then, huh?"

"Sure, laugh while you can. You're gonna miss me when I'm gone."

"I miss you already. I messed up."

"Ya think? I'm not some slut you throw money at after having sex."

He looked shocked. "That was never my intention."

"Then what was your intention?"

"To be supportive."

"Hah! You failed, big-time."

"Yeah, I get that now."

"Too late."

"It's not too late."

"I want you off this bus!" she shouted at him. "Right now!"

"If you'd just calm down a minute—"

"I am not calming down! I'm not doing anything you say. You're not my boss anymore. You can't tell me what to do!"

"I never could."

"You've got that right. So go away!"

"What's going on here?" Nathan demanded as he boarded the bus. "I was in the mini-mart when I got a call that there was some kind of altercation out here." Spotting them, Nathan rolled his eyes. "Not you two again. What's your problem this time?"

"I love this woman and she refuses to listen to me," Cole said.

"You don't know the first thing about love," Leena retorted.

"Then teach me."

She shook her head. She wasn't buying his declaration of love for one second. "Do not use that voice on me."

"What voice?"

"You know what voice, Pet Boy. That everything-is-gonna-be-okay soothing voice. It's not going to work on me. Not this time."

"Then I'll just come with you to Chicago."

"Yeah, right. You've got a vet practice here. You can't leave."

"Dammit, Leena, if you'd just listen to me . . ."

She was really tempted to stick her fingers in her ears and sing la-la-la, but that would be childish. Rewarding but still childish.

The old woman with the orange hair tugged on Nathan's uniform. "He called her a slut."

"No," Leena corrected her. "He just treated me like one."

"I did not!" Cole looked around at the audience, mostly female, all seniors who were glaring at him. "Leena, we have to talk. Can't we go someplace a little more private?"

"No."

Cole tilted her up chin, forcing her to look at him. "When you told me you were leaving for Chicago to take a modeling job, I felt as though you'd yanked my heart out and stomped on it."

"Welcome to the club. When you tossed money at me and told me to have a good trip, I felt the same way."

"I had to get out of there so you wouldn't see how upset I was. I didn't want to stand in the way of your dream. You've told me from the beginning that you didn't plan on staying in Rock Creek. The fact that I'd fallen in love with you was my problem, not yours."

Leena stared at him uncertainly. Was he telling the truth . . . or trying to charm her? He sure looked like he was telling the truth. There was a grim determination about him that she'd never seen before. "You love me?"

He nodded and tucked a strand of her hair behind her ear. "That's what I've been trying to tell you."

"You hurt me."

"I know." He trailed his fingers down her cheek regretfully. "I'm so sorry. Can you forgive me?"

"Life is short. Kiss her, for crying out loud," the lady with the orange hair ordered Cole.

He did, his lips consuming hers. Leena tugged him closer. "I love you too," she whispered against his mouth. "I'm not sure I want to go to Chicago right now."

"If you don't go, you'll always wonder what you were missing. I want you to be as sure of this as I am. When you come back to Rock Creek, it has to be because you want to, not because you had to." One last kiss, one final stroke of her hair, and then he was gone.

Leena blinked back the tears. He was right. She knew he was right. That didn't mean she had to like it. She missed him already.

• • •

"You don't look very thrilled," Irene told Leena twenty-four hours later. "Didn't you hear what I said? This client picked your photo out of all the other models he could have had."

"I heard you. I'm just not sure how I feel about it."

Irene stared at her in disbelief, her eyes wide behind her expensive Chanel glasses, her short, platinum white hair sporting the latest trendy haircut. She was aiming for Meryl Streep's look in *The Devil Wears Prada*. "What did they do to you in that Podunk town? Brainwash you or something?"

"I fell in love."

"Well, fall out of love," Irene said sharply. "This is your career we're talking about here. Snap out of it."

"I don't know if I can do this."

"Of course you can. You're a pro. Don't let some stupid guy distract you."

"It's not about him. Well, it is a little, but mostly it's about me. I've changed." Leena looked out the window of her agent's office. While not on Michigan Avenue, it was near enough that if she leaned a little to the left she could see the traffic on the Magnificent Mile and even a bit of the Chicago River. Closing her eyes, she pictured the rolling green hills around Rock Creek and that poor apple tree struggling to survive next to the World War II tank in the center of town. Michigan Avenue had gorgeous landscaping with thousands of flowers compared to the few that Rock Creek had.

And yet . . .

"I have to figure out if modeling is shoe love or bag love," she muttered to herself.

She already knew that Cole was bag love. He couldn't have shattered her heart as badly as he had if he'd been only shoe love. He was the real thing. But there were still so many obstacles in their path. She needed some time to think about this.

So Leena sucked it up and for the next three weeks worked at trying to recapture her dream. Her former roommates hadn't found a replacement for her, so she was able to move back in temporarily. They were off on a South American shoot for the month, so Leena had the place to herself.

She was busy from dawn until late at night. She'd been able to speak to Cole only a few times. She missed him terribly. No surprise there. The shocker was that she also missed her sister's pythonlike hug. She missed Skye and Lulu with their outrageous comments. She missed Bart and his words of wisdom. She missed Mindy and her big heart.

Irene didn't have a heart. Instead she had a plaque on her desk that read WICKED BITCH OF THE MIDWEST.

"Haven't you ever been in love?" Leena asked her.

"You bet. I'm in love with my job. If you don't have the balls for this job, then you should get out right now."

"I don't have balls," Leena said. "I'm a woman. I have curves." She pointed to her T-shirt, which had a picture of the Statue of Liberty and the lines GIVE ME YOUR CURVES,

YOUR WRINKLES, YOUR NATURAL BEAUTY YEARNING TO
BE FREE.

"Is this about your weight? All the client said was
that your butt looked big in the photo yesterday. We can
change that on the computer."

Right. And yet again make women think they should
look smaller than they were. Diminished instead of em-
powered. "Speaking of computers, did I tell you that
I've been blogging? It's been a real eye-opener," Leena
said. "There are hundred of thousands of women out
there with body-image issues."

"I'm only trying to deal with one of them right now.
You."

Since Leena had returned to Chicago, the self–trash
talk inside her head had returned with a vegeance. Was it
really smart for her to stay in a business that focused 110
percent on image and not substance? She felt like a
stranger in her own life. She didn't want to be judged by
her butt size. She wanted to be judged by the quality of her
character, not the shade of her lipstick. Okay, the reality
was that she'd probably always care about both. Still . . .

"It's not about your dress size. It's about your health
and happiness," she said, finally.

"My health and happiness depends on you getting
this job."

"Maybe, but mine doesn't," Leena said. "I'm sorry,
Irene." She briefly hugged her stunned agent. "I can't go
back. I need to go forward with the next chapter of my
life."

• • •

"The county cadaver bloodhound looks happier than
you do," Nathan told Cole as they sat sipping their

beers at Nick's Tavern. "What happened to man rule number nine: No angsting over a woman? Angsting over sports teams winning is okay. Not angsting over women."

"This from a man who doesn't know when a woman is proposing to him in letters twenty feet high in the sky right over his head."

"I said yes as soon as I figured out what she meant."

"I'm not angsting over women. Just one. Leena."

"I can't believe you told her you loved her in front of a busload of white-haired old ladies."

"One of them had orange hair. Anyway, I was desperate."

"No kidding. Yet you let her take off for Chicago."

"It wasn't a matter of letting her. Leena does what she wants. I want her to *want* to be with me."

"Instead of some glamorous job in Chicago? That's asking a lot."

"You really have a way of making a guy feel worse."

"Aw, come on." Nathan punched his shoulder. "She'll be back. After all, you're one of PA's sexiest bachelors. How can she resist you?"

"Yeah, right."

"You two mind if I join you?" Bart asked.

"Pull up a chair," Nathan said.

"Cole, have you heard from Leena lately?"

"Not for a couple of days," Cole admitted before defending her. "She's really busy with this new ad campaign they're starting."

"Next time you talk to her please tell her that the information she gave me about the nonprofit group that helps build community playgrounds is paying off," Bart said, his enthusiasm clear. "They were so impressed with the package she put together that they approved us."

"Us?"

"Rock Creek. They've already got us scheduled for early October. It only takes the group one day, with help from local volunteers, to build everything. So that vacant lot on the north side of town will be a community playground by fall. Leena sure knows how to get things done. You've probably heard Vanessa bragging all over town how many hits her website has gotten since Leena became the guest blogger."

"This is all news to me," Cole said.

"I knew all about it," Algee said as he pulled up a chair to join them. Unlike Bart, he didn't ask for permission first. "Tameka filled me in. Not that I'm into bragging. My new motto is, 'Stay humble or you'll stumble.'"

"Yeah, mine too," Luke said, hauling over another rickety chair. "What are you guys doing in this dive when you could be over at Maguire's eating great food with your beer?"

Cole shrugged. "I believe in supporting local businesses."

"How about supporting your friends?" Luke said. "You believe in that?"

"Yeah."

"Then look at these great baby pictures." Luke pulled a batch out of his wallet. "Have you ever seen such a beautiful kid?"

Algee grinned. "Not that you're bragging or anything, right?"

Luke nodded. "I'm just stating facts here. Hey, when you talk to Leena next time, Cole, tell her that Julia said she's doing a program at the library like she suggested."

"On what?" Nathan asked. "Applying makeup?"

"On achieving self-esteem," Skye said as she joined them, her hands on her hips. "How typical of you testosterone-driven males to jump to the wrong conclusion."

"I'm so sorry." Nathan tugged her onto his lap and nuzzled her neck. "Let me make it up to you."

Watching them made Cole miss Leena even more.

• • •

Leena pulled her blue Sebring into the parking lot. Donny had driven it up to Chicago with a pal of his so she'd have wheels. Not that she'd really needed them in the city, but they were a requirement for her new plan to succeed. Her palms were damp with nerves. She flipped down the vanity mirror to check her appearance. This gig could be the most important of her entire life. She couldn't blow it.

Color her shallow, but she'd needed two days to plan what she was going to wear today. She'd do better, be less superficial for her next life-changing milestone, but for today she'd need the boost.

The irony, which her life was so full of these days, was that this morning she threw all those wardrobe plans out the window and instead put on her Wal-Mart jeans and LOVE YOUR BODY T-shirt. Beneath it all, however, she wore a very impressive lingerie set in a gorgeous shade of peach. For good luck she wore the

Bakelite bangle she'd gotten at the thrift shop all those weeks ago.

Okay, this was it. Her big moment. Leena walked into the Rock Creek Animal Clinic to find utter pandemonium. The Great Dane with anxiety issues was cowering and whimpering in one corner of the waiting room while a mutt howled in another. A parrot kept repeating, "Shit, this is just shit!" from inside its cage, and two Siamese cats hissed and growled at each other from neighboring cat carriers.

She grinned. She could manage chaos. She couldn't manage a life without Cole.

"What's going on here?"

"Leena, you're back!" Mindy hurried to her side and gave her a quick hug.

"Mindy, you look great."

Instead of denying it as she once would have, Mindy said, "Thanks, I feel great. I've joined Skye's belly-dancing class. Sorry about the mayhem. Mrs. Petrocelli quit two days ago."

Leena gave her attention-getting whistle and started issuing orders. "Great Dane in empty exam room one. Dueling Siamese, retreat to opposite corners, please."

Everyone scrambled to obey and the place soon quieted down. "Where's Cole?"

"In exam room two."

"Is he with a client?"

"Not exactly."

Leena didn't wait to hear more. When she opened the door to the exam room, she found Cole cornered by Evil Edie. "Everyone knows you take pity on strays," she was saying. "That's what you did with Leena. I get that."

"You better get your hands off my man," Leena growled. "And I am not a stray."

Edie backed up so fast she almost fell on her fanny.

"Don't let me keep you."

Edie raced out.

Leena focused her attention on Cole. His hair was shaggier than when she'd left and he had that sexy stubble thing going on. "I brought you something."

"Who's this?" He took a cat carrier from her outstretched hand and set it on the stainless steel exam table.

"Her Prozac is wearing off." *Mine too.* Not that Leena had taken any, but that herbal tea she'd had with breakfast that was supposed to soothe and relax hadn't done a thing. Of course, she had followed that with two cans of Diet Pepsi and a Red Bull drink. She was going to stick to green tea from now on, she really was. Or skim milk. That was real healthy, right? What were they talking about? Oh yeah, the cat.

"Her name is Petra and I brought her from Chicago with me. She was a stray I'd been feeding by the Dumpster. I asked a neighbor to feed her when I came here in April. Anyway, I couldn't just leave her there, so I brought her with me this time."

"You couldn't find a vet you liked in Chicago?"

"Not one I could love, no."

"You just love me for my veterinary talents?"

"I love you because you're bag love."

"Huh?"

"There's shoe love and there's bag love. Shoe love wears off because your feet get too big, but bag love stays with you no matter what. Never mind. You're a guy so you wouldn't understand. The important thing is that you're it. When I left, you said if I came back it had to be because I wanted to, not because I had to. Well, here I am."

She moved toward him and almost fell over a suitcase. "What's this?"

"I was taking a few days off and coming to Chicago after work today. To remind you of what you're missing."

"Remind me right now."

He tugged her into his arms.

She placed her fingers on his lips, stalling his kiss. "And I'm not a stray."

"I never thought you were." He nibbled on her fingertips. "You're infuriating, bossy, smart, sexy as hell, and full of surprises."

"You've got that right," she murmured against his mouth.

Everything was right. The way he kissed her, the way she kissed him back. After three weeks apart it was no surprise that things got quickly out of hand. His hand was beneath her T-shirt while hers was undoing his jeans.

"Wait." She pulled back, breathless. "We can't do this here. Not in front of Petra. She's still traumatized."

"So am I," Cole muttered.

"I'll meet you in your bedroom in two hours when the clinic closes."

He stole a quick but intense kiss before she left. "The front door is unlocked."

Leena was waiting for him on his bed. She was on her tummy, her bent legs languidly moving to and fro as she typed on a laptop. Looking up, she saw him and smiled. "You're early. I was just finishing my blog entry." She quickly set aside the computer. "I made Petra comfortable in your spare bathroom. Set up a kitty box and food for her in there. You do know that Elf feels left out as the only dog, right? And that Midnight and Buddy are okay as long as you honor their space and don't butt into it. And Tripod just wants her tummy rubbed."

"What about you? What do you want?"

"You." Grinning, she took hold of his T-shirt and tugged him closer.

"You've got me. I love you."

"I love you too."

Absence not only made the heart grow fonder, it also made the body desperate for satisfaction. He pulled her T-shirt off and tossed it in one corner of the room while she did the same with his. The remainder of their clothing was discarded with similar speed. He paused a second to admire her lingerie before removing it.

His mouth was hot and wet as he adored her nipple, seducing her with his tongue touches that moved from her breasts to her tummy and below. She went up in flames. The second he had the condom rolled on, she guided him to her, whispering how good he felt inside her. He rocked against her, creating an erotic friction that swiftly brought her to climax. He followed moments later.

When coherent thought finally returned, she found herself cuddled in his arms.

Cole had the power to make her believe in their love. And Leena had the power to believe in herself. . . just the way she was.

Broke and skinny might beat broke and chunky in some people's eyes, but no longer in hers. At ease with her healthy curves, Leena now knew that being in love and loving in return was the very best of all worlds.